THE
ENGLISH
WAY OF DOING THINGS

THE ENGLISH
WAY OF DOING THINGS

William Donaldson

Futura

A Futura Book

Copoyright © 1984 William Donaldson

First published in Great Britain by
George Weidenfeld & Nicolson Limited

First Futura edition 1985

ISBN 0 7088 2650 4

Reproduced, printed and bound in Great Britain by
Hazell Watson & Viney Limited,
Member of the BPCC Group,
Aylesbury, Bucks

Futura Publications
A Division of
Macdonald & Co (Publishers) Ltd
Maxwell House
74 Worship Street
London EC2A 2EN
A BPCC plc Company

It is through an ideal of authority that the conservative experiences the political world.

What satisfies people is not freedom, but congenial government. Government is the primary need of every man subject to the discipline of social intercourse.

ROGER SCRUTON

Wednesday. 2.00 p.m. The Ivy Restaurant.

'If I might read the script, perhaps?'

Toby Danvers, presenter of some fifty theatrical entertainments in his time, four of them profitable more or less, could scarcely believe his ears. Once, a components manufacturer from Swindon, whose life's savings were riding uneasily in a musical, had asked for first-night seats, but Danvers had put that down to the loutishness of middle-management. Never before had a punter asked if he might read the script.

'Read the *script*, my old turkey? And what purpose would that serve? Are you suddenly literate?'

Bred to take a joke against himself (which this might be – Danvers had always had a taste for the obviously uncalled-for), Scott-Dobbs assumed the strained half-smile of an unhorsed Windsor. 'Rather an unnecessary remark, old chap. No need to be offensive. Hardly the way to get a fellow to invest.'

Nor was it, Danvers had to admit. But raising capital – parting a juggins from his money over lunch and using it to fund his dreams – had always seemed to him the crudest aspect of his calling. Even with the energy of youth, he'd found it demeaning, obliging him, as it had, to lunch for hour after bruising hour with the profit-conscious and the adequately insured. Now, in middle age, he should really engage a spring-heeled optimist with pens and pocket-calculator to do it for him: a man to whose lips the banal language of profit and loss, of balances carried forward, of costs, both above and below the line, came unironically, a Financial Director (Angels and Tradesmen) to tug and smother, budget and goose, leaving him free to focus his special talents where they could least be spared – on the artistic side of things.

He looked into Scott-Dobbs's uncomprehending face and tried to forgive it for causing him so much pain. Some might have found the expression brutal, but Danvers, out of the same top drawer, knew it was merely careless. In youth it would have been a face that gate-crashed parties and rowed with nightclub doormen, not one that bullied systematically. The honest eyes, baffled now rather than indignant, were mercilessly well-intentioned. The puzzled frown and goofy grin were those of a paternalist under fire. Danvers had seen that face, hurt and at bay, struggling to remain firm-jawed at the wet end of the Tory Conference platform, as Christian ladies from the floor brayed lustfully for the noose and rubber bullet. Scott-Dobbs was a decent man, no doubt of that. A man who took his holidays in Scotland and was keenly saddened by the great disasters: the sinking of the *Sheffield*, the modernization of the Prayer Book and the deaths of ancient film stars. Not a man to savour gross behaviour off the ball, lie for a friend on oath or credit hearsay allegations against the Met. He's looking at me, Danvers thought, as though I've lost touch with my spiritual centre; as though I'm the sort of man who wilfully ducked the Wedding of the Century on television. And yet until now he'd been civility itself. For an hour already he'd endured Scott-Dobbs's bland, middlebrow objections to his project, nodding automatically, like a toy dog in a car's rear window, in rhythm with his booming, paltry views on this and that, battling against the enervating boredom that threatened to shrivel his impresario's will. And now the confounded fellow wanted to read the script! Should he go down with all guns firing, rake Scott-Dobbs from bow to stern with one pre-emptive volley of abuse and then stride from the restaurant trumpeting generalized rage and pain like a mad woman on a bus? No. Warmly alluring though the prospect of utter catastrophe was to someone of Danvers's precariously balanced ego, he must, whatever the consolations of self-pity and defeat, beef himself up for one last attempt at separating this sausage from his money. He owed it to the live theatre, he owed it to Dawn, God bless her, and, most pressingly, he owed it to himself to hit Scott-Dobbs for a couple

2

of units in *Satan's Daughter* before the lunch was done. This, he told himself, was his last chance at a theatrical come-back. It would be his Ardennes offensive. His Battle of the Bulge. His final assault on the commanding heights. Danvers, in so far as he could distinguish at all between reality and fiction, tended to see life in these dramatic terms.

'No insult intended, my dear fellow,' he said. 'Fancied you were questioning my judgement, do you see? My nose for a hit.'

'By no means. I merely. . . .'

Danvers, a chubby arm thrust suddenly upwards like a policeman's halting the traffic, waved him down.

'Take the following. You come to me with some investment advice. Inside knowledge, behind the hand stuff, gleaned from a dubious colleague in the City. . . .'

'But I'm not in the. . . .'

'Pray allow me to complete the analogy. Some bucket-shop characters, associates of yours, are flying a kite, let's say. Clever money, after hours, getting in and out, leaving the uninformed to catch a cold. . . .'

'I say look here. I must pro. . . .'

'You tip me off. "Toby, old horse," you say, "you could make a killing here. Create a nest-egg. Educate your children privately." Tax-deductible endowment swindle, index-linked, no doubt. You'd know the sordid details. Don't have children, thank God, but you're not to know that. Thought that counts.'

'But you do, surely?' Scott-Dobbs wore a puzzled frown.

'Do what?'

'Have children. One at least.'

It was Danvers's turn to wear the puzzled frown. Then the truth came back to him. 'So I have! Well well well.' He leaned forward and prodded Scott-Dobbs just below the watch-chain. 'But I prevailed against him!' he cried smugly. 'The father must subdue the son, don't you agree? Usurp his future, else one's in for an envious old age. Still, that's neither here nor there. Where was I? Ah, yes. You've come to me with this investment dodge. Would I question your judgement? Ask to see books, brochures, prospectuses? Certainly not. Nod's as good as a wink. Horses for courses.'

Scott-Dobbs managed at last to enter his objection.

'But I'm not in the City.'

'Not in the City? How jaw-dropping! Had you as an asset-stripper in my files.'

What a confounded nuisance if he was lunching the wrong punter. And what would that be – a mistake or an accident? No point in asking Scott-Dobbs, if indeed it *was* Scott-Dobbs. Once he'd have known himself. Now, with the brain-cells packing it in at the rate of a million a minute, he'd have to check the matter out in Austin's *A Plea For Excuses* when he got home. If he still had it. Someone who'd changed addresses, in haste and often after dark, as frequently as he had in the last few years, could never be certain which of his accumulated odds and ends had made the journey with him. Only the week before, anxious to fire a couple of warning rounds up the back of his neighbour's poodle, whose habit it was to yap dementedly while he was trying to sleep in the afternoon, he'd been unable to locate his grandfather's twelve-bore in its usual place beside the bed. Then he remembered that he'd popped it some years previously to finance an agreeably undemanding comedy with one set and a cast of four. Those had been the days, when you could mount a fiction for the price of a shotgun. Ah – he suddenly had it. Lunching the *wrong* punter would be a *mistake*. By Austin's ruling it would only be an *accident* if he'd intended to lunch a *non*-punter. And why would he do that? Still, mustn't wander. Who *was* he lunching then? Certainly, when the date had been made, he'd been far from sure who the fellow was. Despatched by Dawn to carry out a routine household task – the purchase of douche-gel came to mind – he'd used this unexpected windfall to finance a nostalgic tour of the West End. Treading cautiously up Shaftesbury Avenue – reliving past glories and dreaming of the day when his triumphant revival of *Satan's Daughter* would, to the consternation of his enemies, have his name in lights again – he'd sighted this chap with the cut of a past investor. Normally he'd have ducked such a potentially acrimonious confrontation, but high on a courage born of fantasy and indignation (he'd been comparing the menopausal comedies on offer – all starring that policeman's wife from *To The Manor Born*, or so it seemed to him – unfavourably with his own past efforts in the field) he'd jumped the fellow in Cambridge Circus and held him in conversation. To disengage himself, Scott-Dobbs – or a Scott-Dobbs look-alike – had said: 'We must have lunch some time,' in the way you do when it's the last thing you intend. 'Thank you very much,' Danvers had said. 'What about Tuesday? Got something on the drawing-board might be of interest to you.' 'Oh dear,' Scott-Dobbs had said, 'I'm afraid that on Tuesday I. . . .' 'Make it Wednesday, then,' Danvers had said. 'Ivy, one o'clock. If anything crops up, ring my secretary.' And off he'd shot with the startling speed off the mark of the constitutionally plump, leaving Scott-Dobbs, a socially conscientious man, little alternative but to keep the date.

Danvers decided to tackle him head-on.

'Scott-Dobbs, is it?'

'Of course! Good heavens! We've known each other on and off for thirty years! We were at Shrewsbury together. Not to mention University.'

Scott-Dobbs had once again assumed the apprehensive half-smile of a man who fears he may be the butt of a party-game, the mug with a donkey's tail pinned to his back or a piece of paper with the larky injunction 'kick me'. Danvers had always had a peculiar sense of humour, descending, particularly after a drink, to horse-play and silly buggers. Once, at Oxford, he'd suddenly seized a policeman in a wrestling-hold with a cry of: 'This is a citizen's arrest! Spread yourself!' The startled bobby, imagining himself to be in the grip of a madman, had cried, 'Spread yourself too!' and had retaliated with an arm-lock of his own. The two of them, grunting angrily, had grappled up and down the High, first one and then the other seeming to have the upper hand, crying, 'You're nicked!' until they'd been prised apart like copulating dogs by re-inforcements from the local station. That incident alone had convinced the youthful Scott-Dobbs that Danvers might not make a go of things.

'Odd,' said Danvers. 'What's your line, then? Definitely had you filed as an asset-stripper.'

'In fact I'm a lawyer. For my sins.'

'Same difference,' said Danvers, who placed lawyers, in the general scheme of things, in that wafer-thin half-gap between handbag-snatchers and Young Conservatives. He'd no sooner said this, however, than he regretted it. If he was to steer some of this chap's capital in his direction he'd be well advised to stop insulting him. 'No!' he cried, holding up a hand as though to forestall a protest. 'Quite uncalled for. Definitely going too far.'

'Don't apologize,' said Scott-Dobbs smugly. 'We're quite accustomed to remarks of that ilk, I assure you.'

Perhaps you aren't so accustomed to a punch up the nose, thought Danvers. It wouldn't be the first time that he'd sent a useful business contact reaching for his brains at the end of an unexpected upper-cut. Once, acting against his granny in the matter of a family trust, the proceeds of which, he'd judged, would be better employed financing his current schemes than her old age, he had, in conference, boxed her aged solicitor on the nose, quite terminating that old gentleman's interest in the case.

'Well done. What are you? Solicitor? Barrister?'

'I'm a barrister in fact.'

'Splendid! Prosecute, do you? Sent a few losers to the pokey, have you?' Once again a plump hand went up in self-reproach, rather as a soccer player acknowledges a professional foul, hoping with this show of contrition to take some of the steam out of his crippled victim's sense of grievance. 'No! Out of order! I take that back. Someone's got to do society's dirty work, that's what I always say. Dustmen, sewage workers, policemen, prison warders, treasury counsel – where would we be without them? Easy to criticize.'

'In fact I specialize in. . . .'

But Danvers had more to say. 'A moment, please. Mention of sewage-workers brings to mind a remark by McTaggart. Didn't he, *pace* Roger Scruton and other believers in the

6

existence of the state, say: "Compared to the worship of the state, worship of a sewage-pipe, which possesses considerable value as means, would be rational and dignified"? A small digression, but a happy one, if I'm not mistaken. I see you as a sewage-pipe, Scott-Dobbs, part of the drainage system by which society's wrong-doers – its excreta, do you see? – are flushed away. I take my hat off to you. Some more *Sancerre*, do you think?'

'Oh. Er – of course. By all means. Waiter!'

With another bottle on its way, Scott-Dobbs was at last able to put the record straight.

'I was going to say that I specialize in divorce and probate, that sort of thing.'

'You bowl me over!' Danvers recoiled with exaggerated admiration, causing his chair to tip backwards so that it caught the departing *sommelier* in the backside, lifting him a few quick steps forward as though suddenly butted by a goat. 'Watch out, my good man!' cried Danvers crossly. 'You nearly had me off my chair.' The *sommelier*, accustomed to eccentric theatricals the worse for wear (a knowing ancient with a face like a decomposing cheese, he'd served here long enough to remember the night Binkie had slid weeping under the table after an imagined slight from a chorus-boy), apologized with the suave insincerity of one whose livelihood's in tips.

'Hardly his fault,' hissed the mortified Scott-Dobbs. 'You barged right into him.'

'Nonsense! Now. Back to business, don't you think? Let me explain why your reading of the script of *Satan's Daughter* would serve no purpose. Take *Hair*. Remember that?'

'Indeed.'

'One of my shows.'

'Really?'

'Well no. To be boringly literal, in fact it wasn't.'

'Oh.'

'But the Dutch production was. Did it in a tent in Amster– You were in that, surely?'

'No I wasn't.'

7

Just as well, thought Danvers. A notable *débâcle*, that one. Glum Dutch tradesmen with *aides-mémoires* but little understanding of an English gentleman's notion of extended credit had come to take the set away minutes before the curtain was due to rise on the opening night. Loud backstage cries of 'I'll have you in escrow, you Dutch pig!' and 'You'll be hearing from Lord Goodman in the morning!' had mingled confusingly with the message of peace and goodwill being proclaimed onstage.

'A pity. You'd have doubled your money. Trebled it, in fact. Well, that was a concept show. No point in reading the script. Doubt if there was one. The mix was everything. It's the same with *Satan's Daughter*, do you see? What we call total theatre. The common man – yourself, say – would be utterly at a loss if confronted with the disparate elements that blend magically, in the hands of an experienced impresario, to become an unforgettable theatrical event. Woods and trees. Wholes and parts. Not your fault. You have to be of the theatre.'

Danvers, satisfied with his careful exposition, sat back and sipped his *Sancerre*. It was really excellent. On the assumption that he could swing the bill Scott-Dobbs's way, he ought, perhaps, to order a couple of bottles just before leaving, to be smuggled out under his coat. He toyed with this notion for a while, and then discarded it. He'd done exceptionally well so far, refusing to be provoked by Scott-Dobbs's buffoonish views, and, as a result, now had him leaning in his direction after a sticky start, the contents of his wallet a mere finger-tip away. It would be a mistake to create the wrong impression now by seeming to lack wherewithall. There was nothing, in his experience, that so discouraged those with funds as the realization that they were in the company of those without. He'd forego the *Sancerre*, but on the way home stop off at The German Food Centre in Knightsbridge, where he'd recently managed to unearth a deep seam of credit. He'd marched in on a whim one day and barked out orders with such ferocity that the staff of well-drilled Prussians had allowed him, on supplying them with his name and address, to struggle out some

8

twenty minutes later laden down with bottles, if not of *Sancerre*, at least of a very decent Hock, together with cigars, wild strawberries out of season and other Bavarian delicacies. He'd repeated the exercise half a dozen times since then and, though written requests for something on account were becoming less courteous in tone, no one had yet turned up in person at his door demanding payment.

'Correct me if I'm wrong, of course,' said Scott-Dobbs, 'but I was under the impression that you'd not been of the theatre for the past five years. Might you not be out of touch?'

Should he laugh or cry – or strike with the speed of a mongoose across the table-cloth and take Scott-Dobbs by the throat? Had an impresario, enraged past endurance by a turkey's inability to spot artistic merit, ever throttled one here at the Ivy, increasing the pressure on his windpipe until his little feet, expensively shod, drummed a death-tattoo upon the carpet? In the old days, no doubt, when plays had been mounted by men of passion, such things had happened. But where was Cocky now? Where were Firth Shepherd and old Tom Arnold? Where was Henry Sherek, who by the end had become so heroically fat on theatrical lunches that the disposal men had been unable to slot him through the bedroom door but had been compelled instead to crane his body from an upstairs window to the waiting hearse? Where, come to that, was old Jack Hylton, who usually had lipstick on his fly? They had been giants, but today's impresarios, grey men with minds like underfelt, were hardly to be distinguished from the marketing men with digital watches now munching their way through *escalope de veau* to left and right. Only the couple at the next table, a whinnying Henry, with the bulging eyes and receding jawline of a haddock, and an accompanying, heavy-featured Caroline, raised the tone at all. (Danvers had already marked down Fish-face as a potential investor, an assessment that had caused him once or twice to wink conspiratorially in his direction, so far without acknowledgement.) And where were the grand old theatrical tarts of yesteryear? Where were Sybil and Edith? Sonnie and Jessie? Binkie and Bottom? Once they'd

9

have gathered here to swap anecdotes before the show, but in these alternative days of workshop theatre and left-wing food the star of a West End show was as likely as not to arrive for a matinée at the jog, having lunched, if at all, on half a carrot. Yet he'd had some moments here, winged some pigeons in his day, once shot down an extortioner called Snipe to the tune of ten thousand pounds, brought to the restaurant in a shoe-box. Snipe's investment, earmarked for a show that had unexpectedly paid off, had been used, for reasons that had seemed sound at the time, to shore up a less successful venture, but before Snipe had been able to effect a reckoning he had himself been jugged, happily for Danvers, on a charge of causing an affray. He'd torn the arm clean off a defaulting colleague, his subsequent defence (energetically seconded by the defaulter, who wanted, if possible, to hang on to his other arm) being that the clumsy fellow had caught it in the fridge door. The judge had believed neither of them, and Snipe had drawn seven years. He'd be out soon, thought Danvers, and coming after his kneecaps with a gun: a prospect that now produced a sharp intestinal chill in the region of his lower-bowel. He lifted himself fractionally off his chair and back-fired stupefyingly, causing Fish-face and Caroline to jump like hares and stare accusingly at one another.

'Excuse me,' said Danvers.

'I say!' said Scott-Dobbs.

Danvers turned to Fish-face. 'I do apologize. Toby Danvers Productions. My card.'

'What *do* you think you're doing?' hissed Scott-Dobbs, gobbling with confusion.

'Something came to mind. A past investor.' Danvers turned again to Fish-face and Caroline, judging that he ought, perhaps, to include them in his explanation. 'Quite extraordinary,' he said. 'Always has that effect.' He smiled reassuringly. 'Got something in the pipeline might be of interest to you. *Satan's Daughter*. A revival. Minimum units of a thousand pounds.' He winked and made the circular 'spot-on' sign with fingers and thumbs, leaving Fish-face gawping.

'*Who* has that effect on you?' said Scott-Dobbs. 'And confine your remarks to *me*, for heaven's sake.'

'Fellow called Snipe. Damn.' Danvers had broken wind again, even more loudly than before, causing Fish-face and Caroline to drop their knives and forks and push their plates away. 'There you are!' he cried, turning once more in their direction. 'What did I say? Happened again, you see. If you're interested, ring my secretary. Number's on the card. Delfont's in.' He smiled encouragingly and turned back to Scott-Dobbs. 'Better change the subject,' he said. There'd be plenty of time to worry about Snipe later. He'd square him with the profits from *Satan's Daughter*. And Fish-face was a useful contact. 'What were you saying earlier?'

'I said you haven't been of the theatre for the past five years. Disappeared. Rumours flying about. Moira Lister with an overnight bag stranded at Liverpool Station without her fare to London. Made quite a BF of yourself from all accounts.'

A BF, was he? Well, he found the term quite endearing, as it happened, summoning up, as it did, memories of prep-school scrapes and exasperated, half-mad masters, too dicky mentally to participate in World War II. Where he'd first boarded, aged eight or so, it had been the habit of a little boy called Pettifer to position his slippers last thing at night in such a way that he could jump straight into them in the morning and thus be first to the washroom. One night Danvers had glued them to the floor, so that when Pettifer had jumped into them in the morning his upper-trunk had moved as usual hard towards the washroom but his little legs had been held fast in his immovable slippers, causing him to pivot through ninety degrees, like a comedian theatrically shod, concussing himself as he hit the floor. Danvers had barked with laughter, but the headmaster had called him a BF, and he didn't think he'd been called one since. He was grateful to Scott-Dobbs for conjuring up this safe world in which it had been possible to ignore the rules without dire consequences. They didn't call you a BF now, they buried you. It made him, for the moment, regard Scott-Dobbs in a confusingly warm light, and he decided to make one last attempt to reason with him.

'Merely regrouping,' he explained, brushing the rumours aside as casually as he might remove cigar ash from his threadbare velvet jacket, as worn and scuffed in places as Court Three at the end of Wimbledon fortnight. 'Mustering my resources, do you see? Securing my means of exit while reccying my next advance. Naval man myself, but infantry metaphors spring to mind on such occasions. Took a long hard look at myself and at the theatre. Didn't like everything I saw. Fancied I spotted some kind of puritan backlash involving geriatric musicals and dirty-minded comedies as often as not featuring Peter Bowels. Unfortunate name that, I've always thought. Still, that's neither here nor there. Upshot was I decided to bide my time. Get the logistics right before the big push. The decisive victory. So – if you weren't in *Hair*, what the hell were you in? Got you filed as a mug.'

'*Toby Danvers's Big Night Out.*'

Here was a ball-breaker. His courageous attempt to revive burlesque and another colossal flop. His mistake had been to put the seals on first. Les Girls, on next, had skated straight into the stalls. The comedian, Mrs Shufflewick, rat-pissed, had refused to leave the stage during Princess Soraya's snake act, carrying out a disrespectful running commentary from the wings. 'Don't put your snakes on the stage, Mrs Worthington,' Mrs Shufflewick had said as the Princess had prepared to distribute her pythons here and there, causing her to have a temperament and run weeping to her dressing-room. Demetrius the Gladiator and Cheryl, contortionists from Frimley, had been doing well until a particularly unusual convolution of the lower limbs had made it clear to those in the more expensive seats that Cheryl had forgotten to put her knickers on. Demetrius the Gladiator, on his own, had blown up hot-water bottles until one had exploded in his face, ricocheting him off the back wall into a three-week coma. Equity had closed the show, ruling it a hazard to the *artistes* as much as to the public.

'Ah yes,' said Danvers. 'A brave experiment. Nearly brought

it off. Well, as I was saying – I bided my time. Waited for precisely the right moment, theatrically speaking, to revive *Satan's Daughter*. This I judge to be it.'

Scott-Dobbs looked puzzled. 'I don't quite see why, I must admit. The original production was a bit of a flop, wasn't it? A bit shambolic?'

'A bit *shambolic*? A bit sham. . . .'

Hell, he was tired. His limbs ached with fatigue and his eyelids pressed down like manhole covers. Should he have a little nap, canting gently forward until his head rested on the table-cloth, there to enjoy forty winks while Scott-Dobbs droned on in his insultingly literal-minded way? No, he must battle it out, jack himself up for one last assault. Dawn would have a new pair of boots, this fool permitting, and a holiday too. She deserved a break, poor angel, saddled as she'd been for the last two years with a man who hadn't danced since 1958. Funded by Scott-Dobbs, and with Arthur Eperon to mark his card, he'd have her in France via the Dover ferry and down Route 2 to the Dordogne in a hired Fiesta. 'Ah, here's an agreeable inn, my dear. I see it has two stars for its Pig's Ball *en croute* and a stomach-pump mounted in the *lavabo* in memory of Godfrey Smith.' No, sod all that, they'd be straight down the *autopiste* to the south, staying *en route* at motorway hotels where they have mugs in plastic bags by the bedside for you to put your teeth in overnight, fetching up at a tower block by the sea with its own *piscine* and disco. Dawn, splendid in a new bikini, would pull rotters who'd packed their dancing shoes and he'd sit suited in the shade, casting *Satan's Daughter* and, through a peep-hole deftly cut in his airmail edition of the *Telegraph*, snap, with his Rollei Automatic, huge topless Swedish girls, oiling one another's tanned, ballooning buttocks. It would be, above all, a stylish holiday, the very best that Scott-Dobbs's money could provide. He owed Dawn that much at the very least.

Scott-Dobbs's insistent tones dragged him from his reverie.

'Yes. A bit of a flop, wasn't it?'

Danvers prised open his leaden eyelids and took a deep breath.

'A bit of a flop? You could say that, I suppose. But a flop only in the sense that – what? – that Pinter's *The Birthday Party* was a flop when first produced. You saw it?'

'*The Birthday Party*?'

'No. *Satan's Daughter*.'

'I'm afraid not.'

'Nor did I.' Danvers had never seen one of his own shows in performance. They had all been so richly, so faultlessly produced in his own mind that he'd never cared to see them vulgarized on stage by vain, power-mad directors and puddle-headed mimes. 'But I can tell you this. The public, the critics even, are ready for it now.' Danvers, his voice rising with indignation at the memory of the uncomprehending insults heaped upon *Satan's Daughter* when first produced, suddenly struck downwards with his fist so hard that the table jumped a little, obliging Scott-Dobbs to clutch his plate and glass as though on a small ship caught in a storm.

'I say, do watch out. You almost had the table over. And for God's sake keep your voice down. Everyone's listening.'

The crack of Danvers's fist on the table-top had indeed called the room to order as effectively as three raps from a toast-master's hammer, but, fuelled by mounting rage – at the critics, at the general public, at Scott-Dobbs for having such a stupid face and for defiantly refusing, as Danvers now saw it, to finance a much deserved holiday for Dawn – he thundered on through the respectful silence.

'People need to be shaken up,' he roared, 'disabused of their smug assumptions, woken from their suburban wet dream. . . .'

'I say. . . .'

'That is the function of the theatre. To jolt, to disturb, to *indict* the audience.'

'Actually, I go to the theatre to be enter. . . .'

'Even the most self-satisfied and ignorant,' shouted Danvers, 'estate agents, brokers, sellers of goods, commodity men, stock-control enthusiasts with buff envelopes commuting between London and Virginia Water. . . .'

'For God's sake shut up!'

Only a busy scraping of cutlery and the occasional em-barrassed cough broke the awe-struck silence that continued to grip the room.

'Green-belt voyeurs,' bellowed Danvers, 'paranoid *Daily Mail* readers, their hideous girdled wives, force-fed on a diet of Lee-Potter, prejudice and fear, waddling on mottled legs like Strasbourg geese behind their privet hedges . . . how is Marion, by the way?'

'Who?'

'Your wife. Marion.'

'Jennifer actually.'

'That's right. How is she?'

Danvers, his fury spent, had now dropped his voice to a socially more acceptable level. Scott-Dobbs was grateful for this at least.

'She's very well, thank you.'

'Striking woman, as I recall. Small. Dark-complexioned. Face like a ferret.'

'She's quite tall actually. And blonde. Here, I think I have a photograph.'

Scott-Dobbs, much relieved by this diversion and prepared, therefore, to overlook any insults to his wife, produced a Boots five-by-three from his wallet and passed it across the table. It showed a formidably glum-faced woman, scarved and gum-booted like the Queen in a drizzle at Balmoral, surrounded by little heaps of slaughtered wild-life.

'Good shot, is she?'

'No no. She sometimes comes out for the exercise and a little beating. O/C refreshments too. She brings the soup.'

Small wonder, thought Danvers, that Scott-Dobbs's face sometimes had a rather melancholy aspect to it. Anyone would look a trifle sad after years of dogged coupling once a month with Jennifer, occasional beater and O/C soup, gum-booted among those little corpses. A flutter in the theatre was just what the poor chap needed. An arrangement with the ingénue, perhaps? 'Ah, Miss Goodbody. A word in my office, if you please. I was wondering if you'd like to try for better billing? You would? Sensible girl! There's this punter, do you see, needs cheering up. Need I say more?' No, not a chance. Jennifer would have had his balls off long ago, probably with her soup tureen.

'And what about you?' said Scott-Dobbs. 'Do you – er – live with anyone?'

'I currently share chambers with an actress. She danced in *Oliver*, I gather, but then who didn't?'

'So you live in a flat?'

'Indeed.'

'Where do you put your rubbish?'

'In a bin. Where do you put yours?'

'Oh – I don't know, really. I imagine it's easier with a house. Jennifer deals with that side of things.'

'Of course. Another bottle of *Sancerre*, do you think?'

2.10 p.m. Victoria Station.

Ronnie Snipe, hard and circular, like a billiard ball in a tight suit, rolled purposefully towards the taxi-rank at Victoria Station. He'd been released that morning from Ford Open Prison in Sussex, where he'd served the last eighteen months of his seven-year sentence – cut to a handy four and a half for good behaviour. He wanted to buy some clothes, he wanted a decent meal and he wanted, most immediately, to discover how his little firm had been doing in his absence. It owed him, by his calculation, at least twenty grand in accumulated dividends, so a word with its deputy managing director was his first concern.

'Chelsea Police Station, Lucan Place,' he said to the driver at the head of the rank. Snipe had disregarded the queue of patient commuters, and, a low chorus of subdued muttering apart, none had cared to argue the odds with this hard little man, bulging with menace under his cheap suit.

'Been on leave, then, guv?' asked the cabbie, as they drove off into Victoria Street. Snipe's face had an open-prison tan. 'Weather must have been kind for you.'

Snipe, in no mood for taxi-drivers' relentless chatter, banged the glass partition shut by way of an answer. He had things on his mind. His man in 'B' Division, D/C Kevin Smiley, hadn't been in touch with him for the last six months, and he hoped for both their sakes that Smiley hadn't become leery in his absence, reckoning to pull a fast one with his twenty grand or otherwise cause aggro. He had enough on Smiley to put him away for twice the stretch he'd just done, but he hoped it wouldn't come to that. Smiley was a flash sod, but he'd been more than useful to him over the years. Snipe chuckled to himself – a sound like a knife being sharpened – at the thought of the comfort-loving Smiley doing eight. He'd done his four and a half on his prick, but Smiley was a jammy bastard and he'd be a basket-case within a week.

He had other matters to settle too. Like discovering the current whereabouts and financial standing of that well-born patter-man who'd tucked him up for a cool ten grand just before he'd been nicked for doing Scotch Jack. Last time he'd try and launder money with smooth-talking theatricals. 'In one end, Mr Snipe, somewhat tainted, no doubt – not for me to know the details – and out the other as clean as a whistle with preferential profit-participation, *and* the ingénue down on your helmet in no time I wouldn't wonder.' Toby fucking Danvers. Finding him shouldn't be difficult. Smiley could help with that. Obviously a type to change his address from time to time for health reasons, but equally the sort you'd expect to figure on the police computer. Must have previous, that one. Snipe couldn't believe he'd been spun by a fat amateur with no form. He looked forward to recovering that ten grand with interest, and if it had to be extracted by deep surgery, all the better. Snipe chuckled to himself again.

2.25 p.m. Nell Gwynn House, Chelsea.

'Those of you at home who don't want to know what our next

contestant does for a living, close your eyes now.'

Dawn, naked at her dressing-table, smiled – just – at her own small joke, but it seriously startled her friend Dolores, who was stretched on the bed, balancing on her knees an LP called *Highlights From Rigoletto – Various Artistes*, on to which she was crumbling a substance with the tightly focused attention of those who defuse bombs for a living. She sat up anxiously, her eyes scanning the room in a fearful arc, as though searching for hidden cameras.

'Here,' she said. 'What's going on? We're not on one of those fucking game-shows, are we?' With one leg over the side of the bed now, and the other ready to follow it should some manically babbling host with hand-held mike suddenly spring into the room, she pleaded for reassurance. 'What contestant? What's going down here?'

'Dawn Codrington,' said Dawn. 'Thirty-six. Unmarried. Might need a bottom-lift before long.'

'Oh, her.' Dolores relaxed a little, but she kept one foot on the floor for decency's sake and her eyes continued to roll watchfully in her head until a sudden perception caused them to slow to a halt, like two ping-pong balls decelerating on a gaming-wheel. 'Hey. Dawn Codrington? That's you. What's going on?'

'*Course* it's me. Honestly. You black chicks. You're out to lunch the lot of you.' Dawn had done time in Los Angeles towards the end of 1979.

'Right.'

Dawn continued to gaze critically at her reflection. 'Can people tell, do you think?'

'Tell what?' Dolores, satisfied now that they weren't on camera, was propped once more against the pillow, carefully building a joint the size of a German sausage.

'*You* know.'

They probably could, thought Dawn. Why, after all, would someone of thirty-six strive so angrily to look thirty-five unless there was money involved? And who but a business-girl would put herself about in the early afternoon slapped up as though for participation in a floor-show? She sighed at the sadness of it all.

'Oh yeah,' said Dolores, the penny dropping. 'Well – in your case maybe. I mean, you're striking, right? Sort of flamboyant. Know what I mean?'

Dawn, wheeling on her dressing-table stool, stared at Dolores in amazement.

'Whereas you like to dress inconspicuous, right?'

'Right.'

Dolores was a Vietnam veteran in a ra-ra skirt today, the USAF master-sergeant's combat tunic riding rather stylishly, in fact, over the knicker-revealing mini in traffic-light red that gripped her strapping thighs like a ribbon round a chocolate cake.

'You're off the wall,' said Dawn. 'You know that? Anyway, I expect they can.'

'Can what?'

'*Tell*.' Why was she friends with this pot-head? You couldn't hold a simple conversation with her, never mind discuss philosophy and art and the meaning of life and that. Not friends *with*, friends *at*, Toby had once said, and while she hadn't been precisely sure what he'd meant, she'd found the observation, like so many of Toby's, most significant. He had a way with words, did her Toby. 'You're doing too much of that stuff, you know. Your brain's dropped out. It does after a while. Well-known medical fact. Then your skull collapses. Eventually you swallow your own head.'

'Right.'

'Anyway. Take last Thursday. Fat Antoinette rings up and asks me to a straight party, doesn't she? Emphasizes there'll be no gays or professional people there, right? So I've got to be very ladylike and that.'

'Fat Antoinette's not ladylike.'

'She's got GCE, has Fat Antoinette.'

Dolores looked at her scornfully. 'You don't have to have GCE to fuck, you know.'

'You're missing the point of my anecdote, aren't you? It wasn't *that* sort of party. Anyway, I hadn't been there ten minutes before this bald little man grabs my tits in the kitchen and asks me to Positano for the weekend. I mean, you don't grab someone's tits in the kitchen and ask them to Positano unless you think they're at it, do you?'

'Not Positano, no. Definitely not Positano.'

'Here. What do you know about Positano?'

'Went there with Upper-Class Andrew once, didn't I?' said Dolores. 'Indulged in foreplay in the morning, did Upper-Class Andrew.'

'In the *morning*?'

'Right. Woke up to find him rummaging away. "What the hell's this?" I said. "Foreplay," he said. "Well fucking cut it out," I said. Foreplay in the morning! Here. Want a pull?'

'No thanks,' said Dawn. 'I'm working, aren't I? And don't set fire to the bed with that thing. Cost me two thousand pounds, did that bed. It's computerized, isn't it? I've got the receipt somewhere.' Conspicuously well though she'd been doing for many years, Dawn still couldn't believe that others would think her many possessions honestly come by, or worse, that they would be able correctly to estimate their value. So she kept receipts, as proof of her worth as much as of the goods that they legitimized. ' 'Scuse me Eddie.'

Steady Eddie, as sweet-natured as he was beautiful, inched obligingly sideways to allow Dawn more room at her dressing-table, but over her shoulder he continued to study his reflection in the mirror with no very obvious signs of displeasure. Dawn had been changing to go out when he and Dolores had turned up unexpectedly, so she had taken them into the bedroom, where they were now chatting in a disconnected way. Dawn, at least, was chatting, floating small conversational topics and then chasing them gamely herself, like the hostess of a talk-show whose guests have been stupefied by nerves or too much prior hospitality. Dolores, who had never suspected a causal connection between her startling looks and the fact that men in dark-glasses followed her down the street, had recently convinced herself that she was under surveillance and could, in consequence, concentrate on little other than her immediate arrest and deportation; and Steady Eddie rarely spoke, since all his available energy went into dramatizing an appearance that was quite as remarkable as hers. He'd discovered early that it wasn't necessary, in the circles in which he moved, to *be* interesting; as long as you looked interesting someone would usually pick up the bill. Dolores now enjoyed this privilege and would continue to do so until she decided that it was time – taking depreciation into account – to trade him in. (She had herself acquired him, in part exchange for Steve the Stud, from Pretty Marie, who had in her turn got him, in a straight swap for Basil the Black Actor, from Moscow Road Pat via Dopey Linda, *Sun* Page 3 Carol, Motor Show Polly, German Helga, Skinny Angela, Stella Who Stutters, Black Danielle, Blonde Sue and Swiss Elizabeth.) Now, as Dawn rejected a remarkable range of clothes and accessories as not being quite suitable for her coming rendezvous, trying them on and then discarding them, Eddie picked them up and, competing with her for space in front of the dressing-table mirror, modelled them himself. At the moment Dawn was wearing nothing at all, but Eddie could have attended the Woman of the Year Lunch without arousing comment.

'Here,' said Dolores, who for some time had been staring with fierce concentration at all the activity across the room, trying to figure out what it might portend. 'You going out, then?'

'Me? Going out? Whatever gave you that idea? No, I always change for *Afternoon Plus*.'

'Oh.'

'Mark of respect for the *artistes*,' continued Dawn. *Artistes* was one of the words she'd caught from Toby. 'If Mavis Nicholson can go to the trouble of making herself look nice before entering my living-room uninvited, I reckon the least I can do is reverberate.'

'Mavis Nicholson coming over, then?'

'Not today, no. 'Scuse me, Eddie. *Course* I'm going out, you

21

big black dollop. I'm off to hit a guy's prick with a ruler over in Dolphin Square.'

'Hm,' said Dolores, pulling a face. 'Glad someone's hustling. Did you hear the news? Pretty Marie only got busted, didn't she?'

'Golly. Was that on the *News*?'

'Yeah. *No*. And she reckoned she was organized. Know what I mean? Been bunging half "B" Division for years.'

'Been bunging the wrong half probably,' said Dawn. 'That's the trouble nowadays. Half the police are straight. You don't know where you are. I blame McDuff. Big Glasgow pudding.'

'Right,' said Dolores, pulling so deeply on her joint that her eyes dipped and rolled in her head like peeled eggs caught in an air-pocket. 'There's some high-flyer putting himself about you can't pay off.'

'One good apple. Can cause a lot of harm, can one good apple.' Dawn, rather better organized than Pretty Marie, bunging the right half of the local force and with a list of clients that might have been the index to Anthony Sampson's *New Anatomy Of Britain*, could afford to take a more relaxed attitude than Dolores to any sudden, uncharacteristic law-enforcing by the Met. ' 'Scuse me, Eddie. Hey! Those ear-rings really suit you.'

'Thanks,' said Eddie unselfconsciously. Having searched through Dawn's impressive collection of jewellery he'd at last found a pair of ear-rings, the size of small chandeliers, that he rather thought were him.

'Keep them. Bit ostentatious for me.'

'Ta. I will, then.'

'Drives up in a Ford Cortina, does this particular busy,' continued Dolores, deep in her outsider's world of us and them, of sudden inexplicable demands and early-morning raids, 'and comes head-first through the door without knocking.'

'Who?'

'D/S Pyle. Chelsea. Take Tuesday.'

'What?'

'She's watching *Newsnight*, is Pretty Marie – punter of hers being interviewed, Falklands unsung hero, wasn't he? – when BANG! Her front door only comes down off its hinges.'

'Him? Pyle? The high-flyer?'

'Her mother. Wants to know why she hasn't written.'

'Mothers! Still. She should keep in touch.' Dawn was meticulous in this respect, travelling to Yorkshire once a month to see her widowed mother. Her mother thought she was doing well in catering, which was more or less the truth and accounted conveniently too for the close relations her daughter so obviously enjoyed with the rich and powerful. She was always pleased to see her, though Dawn sometimes wondered whether she might not have been just as happy to have received the cheque by post.

'Then Friday,' said Dolores, 'she's listening to *Today In Westminster* – BANG! Shit, it happens again! She nearly died, man. I tell you.'

'Her mother?'

'Drugs Squad. Straight through the front door, search warrant in one hand, ounce of shit in the other, abracadabra, snatch it out of thin air, don't they? Cost her two fifty to straighten. Plus she had to give one to the bloke in charge.'

'Wasn't Pyle, then?'

'No. I *told* you. He's straight, isn't he? Really bad news. Produced the stuff out of thin air, did these old Bill, like Channing Pollock and his fucking parrots. "Here," said Pretty Marie, "that's not my gear and well you know it." "Actually, darling," says the head old Bill, "we were hoping to find some coke." "Run out, have you?" said Pretty Marie. That didn't please them, so then she had to give one to the other three as well. Leery sods.'

'Doves,' said Eddie unexpectedly.

'Pigs if you ask me.'

'Not pigs. Doves. Channing Pollock didn't produce pigs out of thin air, did he? Channing Pollock and his fucking doves, wasn't it? I rated his act, as it happens.'

Dolores, pulling at her haggis-sized joint, her face pursed with disapproval at the Drugs Squad's time-honoured means of

23

securing, if not a conviction or a pay-off, at least an improvement in their love-lives ('How else,' Toby had once asked, 'can they hope to lie down with their social superiors except by breaking down doors in the middle of the night and running among them with the evidence?') failed to register the correction.

'Straight through the front door. BANG! I tell you.'

'Only trying to run a business, same as anyone else,' said Dawn, whose instinctive sympathy with those fuelled by the profit-motive had always co-existed uneasily with her distaste for anyone whose calling it is to get others into trouble. Her father had been a policeman on the beat and this had been a source of shame until she discovered that he'd never arrested anyone and had only joined the force for the free drinks and small backhanders that had been the norm before corruption became properly organized.

'Well, Eddie and me aren't into being busted at the moment. We're splitting to Ibiza maybe to think things over.'

'You'll like it,' said Dawn, who in the late sixties had done her nine months in Ibiza with a Belgian on the run. 'Loco, the lot of them.' In her field, nine months in Ibiza with a Belgian on the run was a necessary, though by no means sufficient, qualification. Indeed, on its own, it was a rather mediocre one, like a third in PPE at Oxford; helpful if coupled with having been a *Penthouse* centrefold (appearances in *Men Only* and *Mayfair* were best kept secret, like a pass in Business Studies at the South London Polytechnic); more impressive on its own than having been Miss Ipswich, but not as good as having lived for at least a year with one of the Moody Blues (the equivalent of a first in English at Downing College, Cambridge). Pretty Marie had all these feathers in her cap and was therefore considered to be, if not over-qualified, at least rather suspect – like a man with seventeen 'A' levels: an achievement likely to give rise to the suspicion that only someone who'd been in prison could have had time to take so many.

'Great,' said Dolores. 'Better than sitting here waiting to be turned over by sodding Pyle.' She glanced apprehensively towards the bedroom-door as though a bullet-head might suddenly reduce it to dust and splinters before her eyes.

'You know what? You're becoming paranoid.'

'No. I *see* things, don't I?'

'Yeah? Like what?'

'I've met the devil, me.'

'Get away! What's he like?'

'Ugh!' Dolores grimaced as though a dead rat had been held under her nose. 'Nasty, stinking little man, squat and green and scaly with little evil eyes looking you up and down.'

'Wow. In a discotheque, was this?'

'*No.* Followed me home, didn't he?'

'Here. You'd do better to concentrate on Pyle.'

Dolores moaned pitifully and her eyeballs shot up into her skull. 'You *do* think he's going to bust us, then?'

'*Course* he isn't going to bust us.'

Dolores glanced fearfully towards the bedroom-door. 'Straight through the door, I tell you. BANG!'

'I wish you'd stop going bang like that,' said Dawn sharply. 'You're making me and Eddie smudge our lipstick. Right, Eddie?'

'Right.'

2.40 p.m. Chelsea Police Station.

Detective-Sergeant Arthur Pyle strode into the squad-room at Chelsea Police Station. 'Right!' he barked, 'let's get moving here.' One of those people who assumed that nothing of consequence could happen in his absence, he had, since an early age, always announced his arrival on a scene with a brisk, up-socks injunction. 'Smiley! Perks! Perhaps you'd be good enough to shift your backsides over here. *If*, that is, I wouldn't be interrupting your close perusal of that highly improving literature. *The Times Educational Supplement*, is it? Prospectus for the Open University, perhaps?'

Detective Constables Smiley and Perks suspended their sniggering assessment of some Swedish porn (booty from a raid the night before) and ambled over to Pyle's desk, while a third member of the group – a rock-hard little man in a tight suit – conjured himself miraculously from the room, though not quite magically enough to escape Pyle's notice.

'Receiving visitors, are you Smiley?' he asked. 'Inspector of Constabulary, was it? Dropped in to seek your advice on community policing in the eighties?'

'Snout of mine, wasn't it, skip? Ronnie Snipe.'

'A snout! My goodness me! Next you'll be nicking villains.'

His expert grasp of leaden irony apart, Pyle was confusingly unlike most detectives. Someone so shamelessly after results rather than earners agitated those around him – villains as much as colleagues – and, worse, his notion of what reasonably constituted evidence was bewilderingly fastidious. This latter, entirely original, perception of his duties compelled detectives working under him, like Kevin Smiley and Trevor Perks, to expend more energy than they'd have wished, forcing them often, to discover which villains had actually committed which offences, rather than to follow normal police procedure, known as balancing the books, which would have been to fit them up in strict rotation.

Nor did he look quite right. Detectives divided, traditionally, into two classes: the Flash Harrys and the Slobs. The Flash Harrys were the more dangerously ambitious, the more audaciously corrupt, putting themselves about with insolent disregard for anyone who might wonder how they could afford three hundred and eighty pound suits, hand-stitched Gucci shoes and Cartier watches. The Slobs, sweaty and easy-going, could easily be confused, on the other hand, with the small-time villains they sometimes captured and were content, on the whole, to trouser an extra hundred notes a week to augment their pitifully meagre wage packets (pitifully meagre, in their assessment, bearing in mind the risks of the job – specifically the risk that they might themselves be nicked). Pyle fitted into neither group. Tireless and unbending in pursuit of results, he looked and behaved less like a detective than a young accountant due soon for a partnership, if not in the City, at least in that area north of Oxford Street where the rag trade's profits are totted up.

'Okay,' he said, 'we're going to bring a little distress into the lives of some very naughty girls, aren't we?' He seemed delighted at the prospect, in a thin-blooded, quite unlascivious way. 'Take a look at this photograph and tell me whether you recognize anyone.' From a group of ten-by-eights, fanned out like a poker-hand, he passed one across the desk to Smiley.

'Phew!' Smiley, an experienced Flash Harry, fed piggily on the photograph for longer than Pyle's impatiently drumming fingers suggested was altogether in the line of duty. 'Fucking tasty, isn't she? *Very* fucking tasty.'

'Never mind the obscenities,' snapped Pyle. 'Do you recognize her?'

'I think so, skip,' said Smiley, handing the photograph back to Pyle. 'Lewis Collins, isn't it? Want me to give him a pull? I reckon he's long overdue.'

Detective Constable Perks, an unusually nervous Slob, risked a tentative snigger, which quickly became a cough when caught in the draught of a freezing glance from Pyle. Far more frightened of Pyle than Smiley was, he fervently hoped that his notoriously reckless side-kick wasn't about to cause unnecessary grief for both of them.

'Oh dear,' said Pyle. 'Oh dear, oh dear. It had quite slipped my mind that in Detective Constable Kevin Smiley we are fortunate to have an accomplished comedian in our midst. No, Detective Constable Smiley. I was rather hoping you might direct your attention towards the big jungle-bunny lying naked on the bed.' He passed the photograph back to Smiley. 'Perhaps you'd be so good as to take another look. It is her, you see, rather than Mr Collins, who interests me at the moment.'

'Is that right, skip?' said Smiley innocently. 'Well *chacun à son gout*, as the woman said when informed that the Dirty Squad wanted her daughter.'

Mad prat, thought Perks, he'll have us both back as

wooden-tops if he goes on winding the sergeant up like this. To seem keen, he tried to take the photograph away from Smiley, but Smiley held on to it.

'Oh yes,' said Smiley, having scrutinized the picture for a moment or two longer, 'I do have to admit that she's nice too. Very nice indeed. Okay, Trevor, you can have your thrill now. Fancy a choc-bar from time to time, do you?'

Perks glared at him.

'That's enough of that,' said Pyle. 'We can get along quite adequately without your prurient comments, thank you very much, as I inferred previously.'

'Sorry, skip. Didn't realize she was a friend of yours.'

'She's not a friend of mine, Kevin.' When addressing a subordinate by his first name, Pyle always managed to catch exactly the tone of chilling familiarity ('you've been a naughty boy, John, a very naughty boy indeed') with which a detective lets a villain know that it's his turn to go in the frame. 'Not a friend of mine by any means. Do you happen to know who she is?'

'Can't say I do, skip,' admitted Smiley cheerfully. 'Actress, is she? Looks like a still from *The Professionals*, this. A shocking programme, if you want my candid opinion, glamorizing nudity and mindless violence.'

'No, Kevin, we don't want your candid opinion, thank you very much. And she isn't an actress. She's a wrong-doer, Kevin. A hooker. A brass. A tom. A slag. Know what I mean by that, Kevin?'

'I don't think I do, skip.' Smiley had managed to order his sharp, wide-boy features into an expression of bumpkin innocence. 'Care to explain?'

'She's at it, Kevin.'

'*At* it, skip? At what?'

'Immorality, Kevin. She sells her body, doesn't she?'

'Oh – got you! You mean she likes it. But charges up front instead of brassing her husband on the side and putting in for maintenance when he can't get it up any more.'

Even Smiley wouldn't normally have tried to provoke Pyle, a

28

furiously married man, quite as brazenly as this, but he'd heard the day before that Pyle had passed his Inspector's board and he reckoned he'd soon be out from under the thin-lipped fanatic. Only Pyle would give a monkey's whether the jungle-bunny was at it or not, he thought. Sinister fish-eyed bastard. Like any detective's, Smiley's only interest in hustlers in the neighbourhood centred on the possibility of blackmailing them into coming across on the house. Since being a call-girl wasn't in itself an offence, this usually involved 'more in sorrow than in anger' threats that he might feel obliged to have a little word with the girl's parents, or, if she still refused to see reason, that he might have to ask awkward questions at the school where her children were being educated, giving rise to a visit from the child welfare inspector. At the moment he had half a dozen tasty little numbers well tucked up in the area, but he didn't have a spook, never mind a looker like this one.

'You don't have her phone number by any chance, do you, skip?' he asked, his expression still gravely innocent.

'As it happens, I do, Kevin, yes I do. But I don't think we'll be calling her up. We might be paying her a litle visit, though. Not altogether a social one, mind.'

'Oh yes? She doing something wrong, then?' Smiley widened his street-shrewd, totter's eyes into saucers of artlessness.

'Doing something *wrong*, Kevin? Goodness me no! Nothing wrong at all. What we want here in the Royal Borough of Kensington and Chelsea is mad-looking knickerless spooks trawling the streets with their tits hanging out so that decent women and children don't care to go about their lawful business unaccompanied.'

He's a basket-case, thought Smiley. A million for the funny-farm. 'But skip. . . .'

'You got children, Kevin?'

'Can't say I have. Not that I know about, at least.'

Pyle frowned primly at the flippancy of this. Mary fucking Whitehouse, thought Smiley, a prim detective sergeant. Whatever next? Must have lost his bollocks in an accident. If he'd ever had any.

'Well I have.'

Fuck me, thought Smiley. Must have one bollock at least.

'Two little girls. And I don't want them set upon by the likes of this big jungle-bunny, do I?'

'I dare say not, skip. On balance, I dare say not.'

Poor little sods. With a freak like Pyle as a father they were odds on to be doing it upright in Argyle Square before they hit fifteen.

'Nor by the likes of her boyfriend,' continued Pyle, too indignant now at the prospect of what might happen to his little girls at the hands of hooligan-hairstyled spooks to notice the contempt in Smiley's voice. 'Here,' he said, passing another photograph across the desk, 'take a look at this. Her ponce, isn't it? Known in the environs in which he frequents as Steady Eddie.'

'Bloody hell,' said Smiley. 'Looks like a shirt-lifter to me.' He shared the distaste all policemen feel for ponces, an attitude less grounded in moral scruple than annoyance that anyone except them should be getting it for nothing. 'Here,' he said, handing the photograph to D/C Perks, 'cop this one, Trev. He's wearing enough personal jewellery to open a boutique in the Balearics. Must know his business, Steady Eddie.'

An exaggerated wink in the direction of his colleague suggested that there'd be earners in pulling this one. Smiley was something of an authority on the Balearics, in fact, holidaying there once a year with his friend Honest John the thief. He and Honest John had a nice little business going. When Chelsea residents were reckless enough to inform 'B' Division that they planned to leave their houses unattended for a while, Smiley would tip off Honest John, who could then effect an easy entry and gut the place, no bother. Even after the third member of the firm, Ronnie Snipe the stand-over man, had got himself nicked, the caper had been so profitable that they were thinking of up-marketing their holiday this year, maybe going to Marbella. Perhaps he'd take the big spook from *The Professionals* in return for not nicking her boyfriend, the rear-gunner. No he wouldn't. Coals to Newcastle. He'd never had trouble pulling arse off the beach, specially when he flashed his warrant-card. 'I'm apprehending you, darling,' he'd say, 'for being a definite provocation in that cerise thong to clean-living country boys such as I myself,' and giggling audio-typists from the North would tumble over one another to get to his bedroom via a Bacardi and Coke at *Los Dos Caballeros Ingleses*, their pleasure being only slightly clouded on arrival there by the discovery that they had to accommodate Honest John as well. What a day this was proving to be. First Ronnie Snipe turns up demanding twenty grand when he was owed, by Smiley's reckoning, at least twice that amount, and now Pyle drops this highly fuckable spook in his lap. He must remember, by the way, to get that info Snipey was after. Whereabouts of some fraudulent theatrical who'd done him up for a cool ten grand. Toby Danvers. Shouldn't be hard to run down. Anyone fly enough to tuck old Snipey up had to be on the computer. He wouldn't want to be in Toby's boots. Snipey had had a naughty look in his eye. Last time he'd seen that look Scotch Jack had shortly thereafter lost his cheque-writing arm.

'What do you reckon, then, skip?' said Perks, thinking that one of them at least should seem keen to rid the Royal Borough of this dangerous-looking twosome. 'Do we go for a result or what?'

'I'm coming to that, Trevor, I'm coming to that. But first have a look at this.' Pyle passed the last of the photographs across the desk.

'Here,' said Smiley. 'This is *Oliver*, isn't it? I really reckoned that.' He broke loudly, and rather impressively, into song. 'As long as *he needs me*, as long as *he*. . . .'

'Thank you, Shirley Bassey, that will be enough of that. Look at the tall girl in front, second from the left. Recognize her?'

'Can't say I do. But she's nice, isn't she? *Very* fucking nice. I could give her one, as it happens.'

'No, Kevin,' said Pyle wearily, 'she is not nice. She is not nice at all. She's at it too, isn't she? But big-time. She's the one I want. Name of Dawn. Dawn Codrington. Lives just across the road in Nell Gwynn House, doesn't she?'

That's handy, thought Smiley. Might drop in later; warn her that this basket-case was after her. That should get her leaning in his direction. Christ she was nice, though: legs that went on forever and a cheeky fucking look in the eyes. She was a definite promise, this one. You could tell she knew what it was for. Never mind the big spook. This one was class. A five-star bird, no argument. He'd hop over later with his handcuffs and smack her arse for being a naughty girl. Perhaps she had a boyfriend too. 'Here, suck my cock, darling, else the boyfriend does six months down the river, doesn't he?' That should get her seeing things his way.

'Here, skip,' he said. 'She got a ponce too, then? This Dawn?'

'Not exactly,' said Pyle. 'Odd set-up. Lives with someone, but he couldn't be her ponce. Not the type. University-educated, isn't he?' To Pyle ponces were either black and knife-scarred or big girls like Steady Eddie. 'Has some loose connection with the theatre. Name of Danvers. Toby Danvers.'

'Bloody hell!'

'What?'

'Nothing, skip.' He'd keep this tight for a while. He didn't want Pyle to know of Snipey's interest. Pyle didn't favour stand-over men pursuing their civil claims with boot and knuckleduster out on the cobbles. Come to that, he might keep this info from Snipey too, at least until he'd bagged Big Dawn. Hardly the way to ingratiate himself with her, grassing up her boyfriend to his creditors. It was another good lever on her, though, if she proved difficult to crack. 'There's this hard-case looking for the boyfriend, darling. Drop your drawers, there's a good girl, else I might have to steer him in this direction.'

'What's the connection, then,' asked Perks, 'between this Dawn and the other one.'

'Known associates, aren't they?'

'Good heavens!' said Smiley. 'Known associates, eh? That's naughty. Like Knight, Frank and Rutley, you mean?'

'No Kevin. I don't mean like Knight, Frank and Rutley. I mean that they conspire, contrary to Section 32 of the Sexual Offences Act of 1956, to introduce people to one another for immoral purposes. And that, Kevin, though it may have escaped your notice, happens to be an offence. But I'm only interested in Steady Eddie and the jungle-bunny in so far as they can drop Dawn in it. Now, bearing in mind that it's Dawn I want, we've got two options, haven't we? One and firstly: we can lean on the jungle-bunny, tell her that unless she grasses up her friend Dawn we'll capture her ponce for living on the earnings. Or two and secondly: we can watch the jungle-bunny, wait until she turns a trick at Dawn's, then raid the place. Running a brothel and/or influencing the movements of prostitutes, isn't it? But we've got to tread leery.'

'Oh yes? Why's that, skip?'

'She's connected, isn't she? Got influential friends in high places.'

I bet she has, thought Smiley. Probably the local DCI among them, if not the DCS. That would put this sanctimonious fanatic back on the beat double quick, busting the DCI's girlfriend.

'Here, skip,' he said. 'The DCI know about this, does he?'

Pyle looked up sharply. 'No he doesn't. And I don't want him to, right?'

That's the weight of it, thought Smiley. Pyle didn't trust the DCI, a well-known sugar-bags, and he planned to get this Dawn nicely tucked up before the DCI could intervene. He'd play this one very careful for a while, see which way the wind was blowing, find out just how heavy this crazy-looking Dawn's connections were before putting the black on her himself. Depending on what he discovered, he could either drop Pyle in it with the DCI, or tip Dawn off – drawing a nice little dividend for himself – or let Pyle nick her while he sat back pissing himself when the shit hit the ceiling.

'So,' continued Pyle, 'we won't shoot off all over the place like four-bob rockets, will we? We'll make double sure we've got a case against Dawn that'll stand up in court before we start running through doors. Here's what we do. Smiley, you take Harris and watch the spook. I want to know where she goes and if her ponce is living in. What would really suit me, however, would be to catch her turning a trick at Dawn's. Dawn would be running a brothel, right? Simpler than getting the spook to give evidence against her. In the latter case she'd be an accomplice, and what are magistrates in their infinite wisdom beginning to do, Kevin?'

'Cast an unfriendly eye on evidence supplied by an accomplice, skip?' They're also casting an unfriendly eye, he thought, on dirty-minded detective-sergeants wasting valuable manpower watching harmless tarts, most of whom were close friends of the said magistrates anyway, when they'd be better employed trying to stop proper villains nicking the magistrates' valuables.

'Exactly,' said Pyle. 'Anyrate, the spook's bottle might not go quite as double quick as is the norm with her ethnic type. So, Perks, you take young Blagden and keep a watch on Dawn's place. If the spook turns up dressed like something from a Barcelona brothel, let me know immediate. With her inside Dawn's place we'll watch out for visiting johns. When they arrive, in we'll go, bang, no messing about. Any questions?'

'Just one, skip,' said Smiley.

'Yes? What's that?'

'You been to a Barcelona brothel, then?'

'Get out of here,' snapped Pyle.

2.45 p.m. Nell Gwynn House.

'Here,' said Dolores. 'Who you seeing in Dolphin Square, then?'

They were still in the bedroom of Dawn's flat, their dispositions hardly changed. Dolores was still stretched on the bed, Dawn was naked at her dressing-table attending to her face, while Eddie, dressed now in skirt and blouse, gazed fondly at his image in the mirror.

'Mount-Hugh,' said Dawn. 'MP. Monday Club and that. Expect you've heard me mention him. Wanker.'

'Oh him. Law and order freak, right?'

'That's the one. Bring back the noose. Britain for the British. Likes me to go as an English lady. Last time it was Katie Boyle. Time before that Raine Spencer. Time before that Princess Anne.'

'Princess *Anne?*' Dolores was shocked, reacting like a musician with perfect pitch, affronted by a duff note. '*She's* no lady. Her language!'

'Right. But she's the easiest to do. Hope he doesn't want me to go one time as Princess Di. Stretching it a bit at my age. Mind you, they've all diddled themselves sightless. Did you hear about Pretty Marie?'

'Yeah. I just told you, didn't I? She got busted.'

'Not *that*. Pillock – ex-2 Para, banged his head in the Upland Goose, now with British Intelligence – wanted a sixteen-year-old as per usual, didn't he? So I sent Pretty Marie. Well, he did that thing of his, you know, suddenly asking what year you were born. I'd warned Pretty Marie about this, but the dopey thing hesitated, not being able to subtract sixteen from 1983, right? So he sent her away and phoned me for another girl. I put Pretty Marie into a dark wig and sent her straight back, having told her to rehearse saying "1967" all the way in the taxi. Well, it all went smooth as clockwork this time and Pillock was delighted. "You're a lovely little thing," he said, "*so* much nicer than the girl who was here an hour ago." '

'Well, she would have been, wouldn't she?' said Dolores. 'Stands to reason. Pretty Marie must be twenty-eight, right? Couldn't get away with sixteen.'

Dawn swivelled on her dressing-table stool and stared at Dolores disbelievingly.

'Christ! It *was* Pretty Marie. That's the point.'

'Yeah. No wonder she got sent away.'

'Oh, what the hell.' Dawn readdressed herself to the business of putting her face together. 'Anyway, today I've got to go as Jane Baker.'

'What? From *Nationwide*?'

'Right.'

'Wow.' This information roused Dolores to an unusual degree of animation. 'That's more like it. I fancy her, as it happens.'

'She is nice, isn't she? Do I look like her, then?'

Dawn stood up and did her impression of a Jane Baker pose: weight on the left leg, right leg placed behind it, left arm supporting the opposite elbow, an imaginary clipboard in her right hand; her expression inquisitorial but unchangingly sweet; there'd be no hard-nosed quizzing here. Dolores studied her carefully, head on one side, then the other, leaning back then zooming in, eyes narrowed critically beneath a thoughtful frown, like an enthusiast for art pondering a purchase at the summer exhibition.

'Hard to say without your clothes. Yeah, you do, as it happens. Turn round.'

Dawn stood with her back towards Dolores for some time while the thoughtful scrutiny continued.

'Yeah, you definitely do. Wow. That's really nice. I could give you. . . .'

Dawn spun round. 'Leave off! You're just feeling horny.'

'Well put your clothes on, then.'

'I would if Eddie'd take them off. Here, give me those, Eddie. It's my Jane Baker gear, that.' As Eddie handed her the clothes, she began at last to get dressed. 'What do you think, then, Eddie?'

'I don't think you do,' said Eddie.

'Oh. Thanks very much.' Dawn was crestfallen.

'Need a bottom-lift,' explained Eddie. 'You said you did. I reckon not.'

'That's as may be. But do I look like Jane Baker or what?'

'As it happens,' said Eddie, 'I reckon you do.'

'Eddie fancies her too,' said Dolores. 'Don't you, Eddie?'

Eddie, exhausted by the unusually heavy contribution he'd just made to the conversation, was unable to muster a reply.

'That's funny,' said Dawn. 'So does Toby.'

Here was a thought. If she was still done up as Jane Baker when he got home perhaps he'd fuck her. He hadn't fucked her for two weeks and three days. She would normally have thought it demeaning, unnatural even, to mount the fatuous performances at home that were necessary to get a punter going, but two weeks and three days was far too long to go without social sex, particularly when you'd been fucking as much as she had recently. Eddie wouldn't be giving Dolores this sort of problem, that was for sure. In his business, if you didn't service the account you'd come home one day to find the locks changed and your sounds, ear-rings and high-heeled boots in an untidy pile on the doorstep.

'Here,' she said. 'When did you last fuck, if you don't mind my asking?'

'What? Like socially?'

'Of course like socially. I'm not prying into your business, am I? That's your affair.'

'Who with?'

'With Eddie, of course.'

'With *Eddie*? Wow. What are you asking me? You're throwing some pretty heavy questions here. Wow. With *Eddie*. I don't know.'

Dawn was encouraged. Perhaps she had less to complain about in this department than she'd supposed. At least she could remember the last occasion with Toby, and the six occasions before that too.

'Try and think. It's important.'

Dolores, as instructed, fell into a thoughtful trance, nodding and muttering to herself as she totted up on fingers and thumbs. From time to time she swore softly and returned to square one in the calculation, like someone interrupted in the counting of banknotes. The harder the arithmetic became, the higher Dawn's spirits rose.

'Shit,' said Dolores at last. 'I can't do it. Eddie, when did we last fuck and all that stuff?'

Eddie either didn't hear or preferred not to think about it.

'*Eddie*!'

'Yeah? What?'

'Dawn wants to know when we last fucked. I can't

remember, can I?'

'Christ, I don't know,' said Eddie, who was now trying on a black Saint Laurent two-piece, rejected earlier by Dawn as being a trifle too severe for her coming rendezvous.

'*Think*!'

'This morning, I reckon. I don't know, though.'

Dolores seemed amazed. 'This *morning*? Never!'

Dawn began to feel as though she was caught up in a game of the good news and the bad. Either way she now thought she couldn't lose. Or win either, she supposed.

'Yeah,' said Eddie. 'Definitely this morning. Then again just before . . . no we didn't.'

'Just before what?'

'That's right. Then again just before coming over here.'

'*Did* we? Hey, I think you may be right.'

'No we didn't.'

'Thought not.'

'Yes we did, though. Definitely again just before coming over here. Remember now.'

'Take your word for it. Crazy.'

Dawn, her mind reeling as she tried to process all this information, decided that it pointed fairly to only one conclusion: Eddie would be back on the open market any day now. Only had himself to blame, of course. If he'd got busy with Dolores at least twice in the last twenty-four hours and she couldn't remember either occasion he was hardly keeping to his side of the bargain. That was the trouble with these self-absorbed professional boys. The whole performance was as smoothly uncommitted as a turn in a floor-show. Afterwards you were left feeling they could have phoned it in. They were all like bloody girls anyway. If the price was right they could manage it with anyone. At least her Toby made it fiercely clear that it was *you* he wanted, even if his demands were somewhat occasional and a trifle unconventional – particularly as to time and place. He would, when she least expected it, tackle her angrily from behind, grunting with intention, often in the kitchen. After years of choreographed sex with flaunting boys who performed like skaters aiming at artistic merit she rather liked his sudden squirarchical demands. Bloody professionals, you could keep them.

'Golly,' she said, 'must have been good. Anyway, that's me finished. If I don't look like Jane Baker now I reckon I never will. Plain skirt, fairly drab, worn just below the knee. Non-matching top. Sensible jacket. Brown boots unlikely to have been acquired at Liberated Lady. Minimum of make-up and accessories. What do you think?'

'Give us a twirl.'

'Don't be soft. Jane Baker doesn't do twirls. I'm not going as Anthea bloody Redfern. I'm going as a lady, me.'

'Show us your knickers, then.'

Dawn pulled her skirt up to her waist. 'There. Marks and Spencer's. Sensible. Right?'

'Hey. That's nice. Come here. I could really. . . .'

'You'd be lucky,' said Dawn. She frowned thoughtfully. 'I don't know, though.' It had, after all, been two weeks and three days. She took a pace forward and then stopped, shaking her head. 'No. Nothing to write home about last time, as I recall. Anyway, my car will be here in half an hour.' She pulled her skirt down and picked up a pair of glasses that were lying on the dressing-table. 'Here,' she said, putting them on. 'Do these look like glasses?'

Dolores stared at her in amazement. 'Of course they look like glasses.'

'Oh. I hoped – you know – that they might look like accessories. In LA they're wearing them as accessories, you know.' She had become so embarrassed recently by the fact that she could only read menus and telephone directories if she held them at arms' length that she had finally overcome her fear that glasses might be ageing and had visited an oculist. Now she put them back in a drawer in the dressing-table. 'Anyway, don't suppose I'll need them on this gig.'

'Never know,' said Dolores. 'He may want you to read a script or some damn thing, Pillock, ex-2 Para.'

'I'm not seeing Pillock, am I? I'm seeing Mount-Hugh. I told you.'

'Oh yeah. Well, *he* may want you to read a script. Happening more and more, you know.'

Punters, it was true, were increasingly finding it more erotic to leave typed instructions in the hall than to forfeit all semblance of spontaneity by holding face-to-face rehearsals of the coming drama. The perils of role-confusion were avoided and the method aborted passion-dousing small-talk too, making it impossible for the business-girl, her clock ticking away at a fiver a minute, to spend the first half-hour of a sixty-minute turn discussing last night's episode of *Minder*, while her hot-eyed host sucked in his stomach and rattled ice-cubes in detumescing agitation. But Dawn had played her unvarying role so faultlessly and on so many occasions in the Wanker's fantasies that it seemed unlikely that he would suddenly feel the need for printed cue-cards.

'Never,' she said. 'I could do his thing and count the laundry at the same time.'

'Please yourself. But did you hear what happened to Pretty Marie?'

'Golly. I just told you, didn't I? She saw Pillock as two different girls in the space of an hour.'

'Did she? Well I never. No – she's going blind like you, isn't she, and. . . .'

'Watch it,' snapped Dawn. 'I'm not going blind.'

'Okay. She's getting a bit short-sighted or whatever. Well, last week she visited that photographer – you know, the one that does royalty and so forth from time to time – in his studio-cum-home thing over in that mews. She only confused the script with some instructions for preparing a Norfolk turkey, didn't she?'

'Bollocks!'

'No. Straight. Told me herself. Trussed him up, stuck an onion up his arse and put him on a shelf in the larder, didn't she?'

'Bullshit!'

'Only passing on what she told me. Discovered there the next day by one of his assistants, the Honourable Tara Tattersall or somesuch, who had a nervous breakdown and went home to her mother in Northamptonshire or some fucking place.'

'What a load of old pony.'

Dawn hadn't given Pretty Marie's stories any credence since the day she'd claimed she'd seen Reginald Bosanquet and Sandy Gall dancing together at the Gateways. Nevertheless, she now had second thoughts. A staunch Tory, she didn't want the government to fall thanks to her failing eyesight. If, through a misreading of the script, she were to abandon the Wanker, compared to whom Norman Tebbit was about as dry as a reservoir, in a position that was even wetter than the one he'd intended, some of the ignominy would inevitably attach itself to Mrs Thatcher. Since being filmed three-in-a-bed (as the tabloids had put it at the time) with Lord Lambton, Norma Levy and enough restraining equipment to bring down a rodeo steer – a mishap that had brought an expensive visit from the Serious Crimes Squad – she had always tried to calculate the unintended political consequences of her practice. Now she once again took the glasses from the dressing-table drawer and put them in her bag.

2.15 p.m. Old Scotland Yard.

In his office in the Norman Shaw Building, Old Scotland Yard, Nigel Mount-Hugh MP was completing an article – 'In Defence of Inequality' – for that week's *Sunday Express*. Since he was unable to compose except in preassembled blocks of words – the knee-jerk clichés of the trendy right, which were as comforting to him as they were to his decrepit editor – his method was to stride around the room, floating oratorical lead balloons, which Miss Bark, his devoted secretary for fifteen years, caught on her dictation pad. Later, at her typewriter, she would blend the disconnected parts into an almost coherent whole before despatching them by messenger to Fleet Street.

'So,' said Mount-Hugh, 'deedum deedum deedum and then, perhaps, that bit about confetti money being the root-cause of all our present ills, including the tidal wave of mindless lawlessness that threatens to engulf the land. Have I mentioned soft options?'

Miss Bark consulted her pad. 'Er – yes you did. "The nostrums and soft options of the so-called progressive left." That came after "compassion on the rates" and "concern for the criminal rather than for the victim of his crime".'

'Good. Good.' Mount-Hugh, a bone-dry Tory, had taken on board every item of the Thatcherite cargo, from macho economics to a lustful taste for Old Testament retribution. Why a liking for tight money should entail enthusiasm for the rope, first-strike capability and tighter controls on coloured immigration might seem unclear to some, but Mount-Hugh had always found it simpler to accommodate himself to one of the available political caricatures. 'Where were we, then?' Searching for inspiration, he gazed out of the window on to the courtyard below, from where, it pleased him to think, re-assuring Homburg-hatted Chief Inspectors had once set forth in ancient Wolseleys to apprehend burglars with names like 'Lefty'. There'd been no confusion then between cops and robbers – merely mutual respect. 'You're nicked, chummy,' kindly Inspector Fabian would have said, and an unprotesting Lefty would have replied: 'It's a fair cop, guv.' There'd been a few bent coppers then, of course, just as there were a few bent coppers now. He wasn't stupid. He knew what went on. But he lived, he liked to think, in the real world, and those who inhabited the real world rather than cloud-cuckoo-land knew it was better if occasional police malpractice remained a secret shared only by those with enough experience of life to keep such matters in perspective. It was not in the public interest that ordinary people should be privy to such disagreeable knowledge. Knowledge, in the wrong hands, was a two-edged sword. This wasn't censorship, merely commonsense. His hostility towards permissiveness had similarly paternalistic roots. What sickened him most about the progressive, liberal cant of the past twenty years was that it had made pictures of naked women available to the broad mass of humble folk, who, if encouraged to have desires which, in the very nature of things, they were unable to understand or, economically, to satisfy, were bound to become over-stimulated, discontented, work-shy and neglectful of the family. 'Have I mentioned "mush-rooming massage-parlours"?'

'Oh!' Miss Bark gave a little start and then consulted her pad. 'Er – in fact not. But you wanted to return to your central thesis.'

'Ah, yes.' And what on earth was that? Mount-Hugh was finding it more than usually difficult to concentrate today. Miss Bark had noticed this, and assumed that his thoughts were flying forward to his participation that evening in a law and order debate on *Nationwide*. 'Er – just recap for me, would you, Miss Bark?'

'You were developing the idea that ordinary people don't in fact *want* equality. You'd opened with a quotation from Shakespeare. "Take but degree away, untune that string. . . ." '

'Of course, of course. Let's see how this sounds.' Mount-Hugh crossed the room and stood behind his desk, leaning forward on his knuckles, jaw thrust belligerently out, as though addressing a rally of the faithful. ' "A classless society",' he boomed, ' "no less than a multi-racial society, is seen by the masses as something alien, even a bit foreign. Better by far. . . ." No, hold on a moment there. Not "the masses". Got rather a patronizing ring to it, "the masses", unless I'm mistaken. Make that "ordinary folk". So – here we go. "A classless society, no less than a multi-racial society, is seen by ordinary folk" – yes, that's better – "is seen by ordinary folk as something alien, even a bit foreign. Better by far an *unjust* society that has grown out of British history than an equal society which exists only in the minds of so-called intellectuals of the *Guardian*-reading sort." How's that?'

'Excellent!' cried Miss Bark. 'Really very good.' She hadn't heard a word of it. She'd been doing this for so long that, just as a person can drive a familiar route almost unconsciously, so could she transcribe him faultlessly while letting her mind play freely elsewhere. An assembly-line of prefabricated verbal building-blocks journeyed smoothly from Mount-Hugh's mouth, across the room, down her right arm and on to her dictation pad without disturbing her mental processes any more than they had his.

'On we go, then,' said Mount-Hugh. ' "Like it or not, the class system *is* Great Britain, as much as the White Cliffs of Dover, the Queen Mum, *Sunday Night At The London Palladium*. . . ." '

'Excuse me, Mr Mount-Hugh.' Some hiccup in the assembly-line had automatically caused Miss Bark's hand to suspend its scribbling. She glanced down at her pad to identify the fault. Ah yes, there it was. 'You usually insert "God bless her!" after any reference to the Queen Mother,' she said, 'and perhaps *Sunday Night At The London Palladium* is no longer the happiest of references. It's been off the air, as far as I know, for many years now.'

'Is that so? You're quite right, then. And of course we want to insert "God bless her!" after "Queen Mum". Where *would* I be without you, Miss Bark?'

Miss Bark ducked her head into her dictation pad so that Mr Mount-Hugh wouldn't see the hot flush of excitement that spread uncontrollably upwards from her bosom, turning her face prawn-pink with pleasure. She'd been in love with him since her first day as his secretary, not that she had dared suppose for a second even then that anything could come of it. He was a devoted, four-square family man, and had he been otherwise she would have thought less of him. His reputation as a ferocious upholder of the old standards was such that some of her sillier colleagues in the building gigglingly referred to him as 'Old Stonebottom', but he was twice the man, in her opinion, than the heavy-breathing old Romeos for whom they worked and by whom, if they could be believed, they sometimes allowed themselves to be clumsily fumbled in nearby service-flats. Craggy-faced and broad-shouldered – he'd once propped for Saracens' third XV – he didn't have to prove his masculinity to her by furtive disloyalty to his wife: an invariably graceful, if rather wistful-looking English beauty, whose photograph with labradors he kept on his desk and whom he always telephoned at home in Wiltshire when his parliamentary and other duties kept him unexpectedly in town.

'So,' continued Mount-Hugh. ' "Like it or not the class system *is* Great Britain, as much as the White Cliffs of Dover, the Queen Mum, God bless her, and . . . and . . . and" – er, what? – I have it! "As bangers for tea." '

Mount-Hugh, treading back and forth, head down in thought, hands clasped at buttock level, like a Rear-Admiral on his quarter-deck, halted suddenly in mid-stride.

'I wonder, in fact, whether the lower classes *do* have bangers for tea. Do you happen to know whether the lower classes have bangers for tea, Miss Bark?'

'Oh. I'm not certain, to tell the truth. Perhaps not.'

'Hm. Better make that bangers for breakfast. Everyone still has bangers for breakfast, surely?' Mount-Hugh resumed his measured pacing. 'Let's see. Bangers for breakfast. Bangers for breakfast. Doesn't sound like fireworks, does it? Beginning to sound like fireworks.'

'No no. I'm sure it doesn't.'

'Good. Leave it in, then. So, on we go. "Ordinary people accept wealth and privilege far more readily than they accept, for example, coloured immigration, because . . . because . . . because." Why *do* they accept wealth and privilege? Why do they? Why do they?' Mount-Hugh looked hopefully towards Miss Bark.

'Oh! Perhaps because wealth and privilege are part of the British heritage?'

'Of course! Excellent! "Because wealth and privilege are part of the British heritage in a way . . . in a way. . . ." ' Mount-Hugh, back at the window, gazing downwards, was silent for a while, his thoughts elsewhere. ' "In a way," ' he said at last, ' "that pictures of naked foreign actresses in newsagents' windows can never. . . ." Er – was I in fact dealing with the

45

rising tide of filth which is turning Soho, once the most agreeable of London's many little villages, into an unfit place for decent women and children to walk in safety?'

'In fact not, Mr Mount-Hugh. You were dealing with coloured immigration.'

'Of course, of course. "Because wealth and privilege are part of the British heritage in a way that coloured immigrants are not. Everyone loves a lord. But no one likes a coloured neighbour." Got that?'

Miss Bark consulted her pad. 'Yes, yes. I've got that.'

'Perhaps after "coloured neighbour" we'd better add "however cheery and well-mannered". Don't want to provoke the usual parrot-cries of "racist" do we? Er – you told the BBC to send the car to the flat, did you?'

This was the fourth time he'd checked with Miss Bark that the BBC car would pick him up at his flat in Dolphin Square rather than at his office or the House. He really was unusually distracted this afternoon, she thought, jumpy almost. No doubt his appearance on *Nationwide* was on his mind, but his edginess surprised her. An experienced TV performer, he had never, in her experience, been as nervous as this before.

'Yes, it will be there at 5.15,' she said. 'They want you to be at Television Centre by 5.45. You'll be on at 6.20. I'm so looking forward to it. Who are the other experts?'

'The Commissioner of Police – Sir Angus McDuff – and Dame Letitia Merryweather.'

'Oh, I *do* like her. I must have seen *Springtime In Mayfair* umpteen times. It was on again last Sunday. Sheer escapism.'

'Yes, a splendid old lady, quite splendid. Must be on the wrong side of seventy now, but she still does invaluable work for the silent majority. A great patriot. And what an agreeable change that makes! An entertainer speaking up unashamedly for Britain rather than for whales or pacifism. A truly marvellous old lady.'

'One of the old school, Mr Mount-Hugh.'

'Indeed, indeed. So how's the enemy now?' Mount-Hugh glanced at his watch. 'My word, it's gone 2.30. We'd better

46

crack on. I want to be at the flat by 3.15. One or two things to see to before tomorrow. Angela's half-term, you know. With my wife in the country it falls on me to see the place is shipshape. So – where were we?'

Miss Bark looked at her pad. ' "But no one likes a coloured neighbour, however cheery and well-mannered".'

'Good, good. Let's see how this sounds. "For humble people a sense of nation remains more precious than social justice, equality or even freedom itself, none of which abstractions" – no, make that "windy abstractions", would you?'

Miss Bark, on automatic pilot, consulted her pad and was pleased to note that "windy" had already been inserted. Its absence, since there'd been no warning spasm in her writing-arm, would have signalled a major breakdown in the system.

' "None of which windy abstractions," ' continued Mount-Hugh, ' "so popular with so-called academics and the professional do-gooders of the compassion lobby, have any meaning for ordinary folk except in terms of essentially *British* experience." What's that slogan people daub on walls?'

'Oh dear, I'm sure I don't know. Blacks go. . . .'

'No, no. Not that one. Drat. On the tip of my tongue. Got a colloquial ring to it. Please old Junor if I could work it in. Always complaining that my stuff's too intellectual. OK Steve Davis or something.'

'Oh yes. George Davis is innocent – OK?'

'That's the one. Well done, indeed, Miss Bark. Whatever whatever whatever – OK. Let's try something on those lines." Mount-Hugh glanced at his watch again and hurried on. ' "*British* inequality – OK. That's acceptable to the broad mass of humble folk. A recognition that inequality is part of Britain's heritage to be defended not on the grounds that inequality is necessarily good – although it may be – but on the grounds that . . . on the grounds that. . . ." ' On what grounds? Mount-Hugh, his thoughts becoming more and more scattered, looked to Miss Bark for inspiration.

'On the grounds that it is British?'

'Excellent! "To be defended on the grounds that it is British.

The same rule applies to the monarchy and all our other institutions and national rights – such as the basic British right not to live in a multi-racial society – without which ordinary folk would feel cut adrift from their roots." ' Mount-Hugh was proceeding at such a pace now, the connections becoming so far-fetched, the inferences so bizarre, that a fuse in the system seemed inevitable. ' "Those with drive, talent and the advantages of birth will always come out on top",' he declaimed. ' "That's the way of the world and no amount of bleating from woolly-minded enthusiasts for equality can change it." I wonder whether we might not include here that bit about there being more class-consciousness in the Soviet Union than you'll ever find in White's?'

'I think you used that last week, Mr Mount-Hugh.'

'Really? Well, mustn't repeat ourselves. Let's see. Have I mentioned Colonel H this week?'

'No, not yet.'

'Good. Here we go, then. "Only nationalism offers glory – albeit vicariously – to all. Enables the humblest in the land to walk like a hero – to walk with Colonel H" – no, better make that Mrs H. She has the higher profile at the moment. "Enables the humblest in the land to walk with Colonel H's widow. At the deepest level of welfare, which transcends mere economics, Mrs Thatcher has done more for the pride of humble folk than any of her predecessors since. . . ." '

'Er – excuse me,' Miss Bark's writing arm had suddenly bucked and writhed like a divining rod, alerting her to the expected blow-out in the system.

'Yes?'

'Shouldn't you perhaps say something about the plight of the unemployed?'

'You're right, of course. Make that "Mrs Thatcher has done more for the well-being of humble-folk, even for those who have the tragic misfortune to be unemployed, than any of her predecessors since Winston Churchill, by restoring their pride in being British." I wonder if we might not wind up by quoting from that article young Scruton had in last month's *Salisbury*

Review? Do you know the piece I mean?'

'I don't think I do, Mr Mount-Hugh.'

'Excellent stuff. Something about national consciousness providing one of the strongest experiences of the immanence of God. Points out that a person who willingly sacrifices himself for the sake of his country represents the most vivid human example of the sacred. Of the temporal order overcome by transcendent meaning. Relevant to what I'm saying, if I'm not mistaken. Clever chap. Can't remember the precise words, alas.'

'Shall I look the copy out?' asked Miss Bark. 'I'm sure we have it.'

Mount-Hugh glanced at his watch. 'By jove! No – I tell you what. We'll use it next week. Make it the basis of a piece called "God is British" – something like that. Type up what we've done, if you would, and I'll run my eye over it tomorrow. I'd better be pushing off. Can't keep Jane Baker waiting, can we?'

'She'll be chairing the discussion, then?'

'So I gather, so I gather. Got to get the flat ready too. For Angela, that is. See you tomorrow, then.'

'Good luck!'

What a splendid man he is, thought Miss Bark. With so much on his plate he could still find time to organize everything for his daughter's half-term.

2.55 p.m. Nell Gwynn House.

'Okay,' said Dawn, 'that's me done. Think you can make it to the other room? And put those down, Eddie. I've got a Chief Inspector on the Porn Squad really likes me in those.'

'Yeah? Not surprised.'

'DCI Daphne Appleyard. Silly cow. Janet Reger, aren't they? Cost me over two hundred pounds, those did.'

'Do you have a receipt, then?' asked Eddie.

'Course I've got a receipt. I'm not stupid, me. Here – are you

49

taking the piss, or what? Careful!'

They followed Dawn through to the living-room, with Dolores, like a marathon runner reaching for the tape on filleted limbs, just making it to the enormous Habitat sofa before her legs went ga-ga under her.

'Phew! Let's have some sounds, then,' she said. 'Put me in the mood. Know what I mean?'

'What mood?' said Dawn. 'You're not doing anything.'

'Hey. That's right.'

'It's me working, isn't it? Still. Not a bad idea.'

Dawn walked over to a sound system that looked sophisticated enough to launch a moon-rocket. It had been painfully extracted from a Sony executive who'd imagined that she'd endure the stupefying boredom of his company and doddering demands (he'd tried to kiss her, she recalled) in return for a long weekend in Acapulco in 1976. Back in London he'd discovered otherwise.

'Any preferences, then?'

'Whatever you say. Your sounds.'

'Okay – you asked for it.' Dawn put on a tape, which failed immediately to please Dolores.

'Bloody hell!' she cried, her face pursed in disapproval, as though detecting a sudden gas-leak, 'can you dance to that?'

'It's not for dancing, pot-head,' said Dawn, joining Dolores on the sofa, 'it's for listening. *Side By Side With Sondheim*.'

'Christ. Dead, is he?'

'Don't think so. One of Toby's, isn't it?'

'Not surprised.'

'Nothing wrong with Toby's taste,' said Dawn sharply. She wasn't having that. She wasn't having aspersions cast simply because he was articulate and that. 'Sophisticated. New York chic, isn't it? Cecil Bernstein and so forth.'

'Leonard,' said Eddie, who was wandering around the room, searching for a mirror in which to continue his thoughtful self-appraisal.

'Him too, I dare say. People *do* listen to music, you know. Right, Eddie?'

'Eddie's not into music any more,' said Dolores.

'No? What happened to the group?'

Eddie, like everyone else, had been part of a group, more or less, since 1968, at a staggering cost to his several benefactors in rehearsal fees and demo-discs. It had even performed professionally once, filling in for a whole evening at a pub in Hammersmith while the resident group was helping the police with their enquiries following some unpleasantness involving three off-duty nurses behind the municipal rubbish-tip. The group had been reluctant to prosecute, but the police had charged the nurses anyway and had held the group as witnesses.

'Left it, didn't he?' explained Dolores. 'I told you. He's not into music any more. Says it's finished. Like Hollywood. I mean Hollywood was the thing, right? Burbank. Beverly Hills. Malibu and that.'

'*Malibu*? I've been to Malibu, me. Middle of nowhere. It can make you very nervous if you're fucking people you don't like, Malibu can.'

'That's as may be,' said Dolores. 'But it doesn't alter the fact of what I'm saying, does it? What I'm saying is that film stars were where it was at and that. Lana Turner and so forth.'

'Golly,' said Dawn. '*She* wasn't very nice. I've been reading a book about Lana Turner, me. *She* certainly put herself about.'

'Responsibility to her public, wasn't it? Anyway. Then music took over from films, didn't it? Now music's finished.'

'Get away! What's taking over from music, then?'

Dawn was interested. She didn't want to be left in the starting-stalls when the new thing took off. Some years previously she'd had her mind on other matters and had, in consequence, missed the whole meditation thing – eating seaweed, taking the phone off the hook and standing on your head in canary yellow tights and that. Still, she didn't really regret that. She'd had enough to worry about at the time, she recalled, what with her personal life being at sixes and sevens, as per usual in those days. She'd been trying to shake off some moody little boy who sat around all day sewing roses on to his handbag. Thank God those days were over. Golly she must have been vulnerable then, when any pretty boy with head-phones and a bulge in his trousers (which deep surgery might have revealed to be his brain) could take root in her hall with his bongo-drums. She'd been lonely, she supposed. Racketing round London till all hours, trying to postpone that frightening moment when the lights would have to go out, and preferring to come home to any little rotter, however heartless, than to no one.

'Seb Coe and that, isn't it?' said Dolores.

'What? Bloody runners?'

'That's what Eddie says. Athletic young bodies. That's what the viewing public wants to see on its TV screens now. I mean, they're making films about it, aren't they? *Chariots On Fire*. And that thing with Dudley Moore's old lady.'

'What? Tuesday Weld?'

'*No*. Not Tuesday Weld. The other one. Big girl. Blonde. Not bad at all. Susan Anton. That's the one. Runs fast, doesn't she? Dare say that's how she got the part.'

'I'd run fast if I was with Dudley Moore,' said Dawn. She thought about this while Dolores, who, though bombed already, had not yet reached that haven of oblivion in which thoughts of Pyle and sudden busts could no longer snag the outer fabric of her consciousness, began the laborious business of building herself another jumbo-joint. 'I don't know, though.'

'She wasn't running away from Dudley Moore,' said Dolores. 'She was in this film about running, wasn't she?'

'I thought you said films was finished. And don't set fire to the sofa with that thing. Cost me a thousand pounds, did this sofa.'

'I didn't say they don't still *make* them, did I? They'll still go on *making* them. Same as there'll always be music. It's just that music won't be where it's at any more. That's what Eddie says at any rate.'

'Golly,' said Dawn. 'I've never heard Eddie say so much. But then you know him better than me, of course.'

'No I don't,' said Dolores.

'Here. That's right! Small world.'

Dawn had indeed done her turn as Eddie's provider some years before and it came as quite a shock to be reminded of the fact. Now that she had entered what she thought of as her 'mature English gentlemen phase' – a fundamental change of style which had allowed Toby to enter her life – she found it humiliating to think that once she'd have felt undressed in public unless accompanied by a vain little boy who matched her handbag.

'Don't suppose you want him back, do you?' asked Dolores.

'No thanks. No offence, Eddie. Here, what do you think you're doing? Put that down.'

Eddie had come across a pile of old clothes stacked in a corner of the room and, with an opera hat on his head at a jaunty angle, was now inspecting a twenties evening-dress, having it in mind to see whether the two went well together.

'What's all that then?' asked Dolores. 'Opening a jumble sale, are you?'

'A *jumble* sale? Do you mind? Hermione Gingold wore that dress in *Fallen Angels*. It's historical stuff, that. And take that hat off, Eddie. That hat was Fred Emney's, wasn't it?'

'Client, was he? Left his hat behind?'

'*No*. That's Toby's memobeelia, that.'

'Oh.'

'Mind you, there are advantages, I suppose.'

'To what?' Dolores, inhaling deeply, had lost touch with the conversation, floating away on another level, in an opposite direction, eyes closed, stilling her present worries.

'In being with someone like Eddie.'

'If you say so.'

'One thing – and put that down, Eddie. Dame Merryweather wore that dress in *Cavalcade*. I *am* out of date. I didn't know any of that stuff about music not being where it's at any more. Came as a bolt from the blue to me. Something happened the other night made me realize just how untrendy I am. Remember Them, do you?'

'Them what?' said Dolores sleepily.

'Not them what. Them the pop group.'

'Can't say I do.'

'There you are. Very big in the sixties.'

'Yeah. Heard you were.'

'Not *me*, coke-brain. *Them*. Irish, weren't they? Had a lot of hits. Number ones and all that. I mean, they were really successful, right?'

'If you say so. Here, you sure you don't want a pull of this? It's good gear.'

'No. Working, aren't I? My car will be here soon. Coming at three-thirty, isn't it?'

'Yeah?' Dolores's eyes suddenly clicked into focus and a deep internal rumbling, like an eruption in a drain-pipe, caused her to clutch her stomach and sway backwards and forwards on the sofa, her legs stuck rigidly outwards, parallel to the floor, as though she might be having a fit. Gradually the rumbling gave way to a raucous, high-pitched farmyard whooping in the throat. A joke was straining to be laid. 'Your car,' she wailed at last, 'oh shit! – your car will be coming at three-thirty, right?'

Dawn glanced impatiently at her watch. 'Yes? Get on with it.'

'And the Wanker – oh dear! – and the Wanker will be *coming* at *four-thirty!!*'

Dawn glared at her in disgust. 'You know something?' she said. 'You can be really coarse, you black chicks. Anyway, I was with this bass guitarist for a while, wasn't I?'

'What bass guitarist?' Dolores, honking and gurgling, her mind, in its stoned condition, still locked into her witticism, was rolling around on the sofa, her legs shooting convulsively in all directions, like those of a Cup Finalist with the Wembley cramps.

'Christ! The bass guitarist of sodding Them!'

'Thought you said they were good.'

'So they were. He had an Alfa Romeo, did the bass guitarist of Them. Some weekends we used to drive up to Lancashire to see his mum and dad. That was all right. Well, usually when you drive up north it's business, isn't it? But in an Alfa Romeo

54

you're having a good time, right? I don't know what his mum and dad thought. I mean, they were working-class people, weren't they? He'd fall out of his Alfa Romeo, stoned legless, and it would be "Hey!" – with an ear-ring and that, you know. I mean his mum and dad were simple people, right? Anyway, I was in the King's Road the other night and. . . .'

'Here. Eddie was a bass guitarist.'

'Look, Dolores! Do you want to hear about my experience or what?'

'Sure I do.'

'Well, I was in the King's Road, as I say, when I bumped into him. Mickey he's called. Hardly recognized him. Well, he must be forty.'

'Christ.'

'Nothing wrong in being forty, darling, as you'll discover soon enough.' Dawn used 'darling' only as a rebuke, launching it like something nasty from a blowpipe. Touchy though she was about her age, she was, on this occasion, defending the absent Toby's standing in the *milieu* rather than her own. 'Anyway, he's become all respectable, hasn't he, wearing a suit and saying "after you" and that and opening doors and so forth. Doing well selling double-glazing or some damned thing. Well, we go and have dinner for old time's sake and later he's driving me home when we see this young bloke in the middle of the road with Police in fucking great letters on his front and he's waving us down, isn't he?'

'Wow. Heavy.'

'Right. Mickey and me fly into the horrors, of course.'

'Not surprised.'

'On top, right?'

'Yeah.'

'Mickey starts yelling.'

'Bet he does.'

Dolores was following the story with only that degree of attention that good manners seemed to dictate, easing it along with a vaguely appropriate comment here and there while she organized herself to roll another joint. The sharp edges of the world outside and sudden raids and bullet-heads still lurked in corners of her mind.

' "FUCK ME IT'S A BUST. . . ." '

Dolores went rigid with shock, like a cartoon cat that's stuck its tongue into a light-socket. 'JESUS WHERE?' she shrieked, trying in her panic to clear up the debris of her joint-rolling efforts and, at the same time, to get to her feet – failing, through a malfunction in that part of the brain that co-ordinates movements of the arms and legs, in both endeavours. 'For Christ's sake! Let's get out of here!'

'Not *here*, you dozey dollop! I'm telling a fucking anecdote, aren't I? It was Mickey who shouted, "It's a bust", wasn't it?'

'Oh.' Dolores relaxed a little, but she breathed heavily for a while, muttering to herself and, from time to time, spinning round to check her rear, like a panto comic lost in the Forest of Horrors.

'You all right?'

'Phew. Guess so.'

'Anyway. "It's on top," shouts Mickey, and throwing a packet out of the window, which must have been his gear – so perhaps he's not so respectable after all – he puts his foot down and pisses off at seventy miles an hour. Wasn't till we reached Sloane Square that we realised that it had only been a pop-fan in a Police T-shirt. Well, I mean Mickey's had number ones and that but he'd never heard of Police. Makes you think, doesn't it?'

'Wow. Narrow squeak. Just as well he got rid of his stuff.'

Dawn glared at her in disbelief. 'Christ! You're missing the point, aren't you? It wasn't *really* the. . . .' Oh fuck it, waste of time telling these chicks anecdotes. At least Toby had liked her story. He'd laughed so much he'd had to sit down and undo his waistcoat and then he'd had one of his choking fits, bless him, and she'd had to fetch him a glass of water from the kitchen. He always appreciated her stories, unfailingly got the gist of them.

Dolores, meanwhile, had fallen into a state of agonized concentration, like a contestant on a quiz show trying to conjure up the answer that will win the Austin Allegro, rocking backwards and forwards, hands clasped between her knees, scanning first the ceiling and then her boots for inspiration, mewing quietly. Dawn assumed that she was trying to puzzle out the meaning of her Police anecdote.

'Here,' she said at last. 'What's memowhatsit then?'

'Memobeelia?'

'Yeah. What's memobeelia then?'

'Stuff from Toby's old shows. Props, costumes, posters, special effects and that. He's planning to open a theatrical museum, isn't he?'

'What? *Here*?'

'Of course here. Where else? It's his home too, you know.'

Dawn hadn't the slightest intention of letting Toby open a museum here, or anywhere else, if she could help it, but that was nobody's business but hers. They never took her Toby into account, these silly girls, seemed to think that he was merely passing through, that his living here was some sort of joke, a source of embarrassment to her just because he'd read books and that, and used words in a peculiar way. Time they learnt, these chicks, that just because you were educated it didn't necessarily mean you were stupid. This defensive arching of the back, this instant edginess, brought on by the merest whiff of implied criticism of Toby or his various schemes, was caused, she realized, by her loss of confidence, her unworthy ever-present fear that she'd be thought less of in her circle, lose status because she lived with a man likely to be dismissed as a most unflattering accessory. None of the girls she knew would have given Toby the time of day unless there was money involved. She told herself that they were just silly chicks with their values between their legs, but she knew what they were thinking, because ten years ago she would have thought the same: poor old soul, she'd have thought, he's probably the best she can get. She knew better now, of course, and she was right to defend her Toby against criticism from empty-headed chicks. It was a mistake, however, to display her own anxieties so revealingly. Even Dolores, stoned senseless, could pick up on that. She wished she hadn't been so quick to point out that this was

57

Toby's home too. Dolores, after all, had said nothing to suggest it wasn't.

'Yes, but I *mean*,' said Dolores. 'A working flat, and Toby plans to show the public round! "Step this way folks. Here we have the hat Fred Emery wore in whatever and here we have Miss Dawn enjoying a relaxing moment with – oh bollocks! We seem to have strayed into the the private quarters." I *mean*.'

'Good cover when your friend Pyle busts us. Door comes down and he finds he's in a theatrical museum.'

Dolores reacted to the word 'Pyle' like the victim of a behavioural experiment, jumping like a rat with an electronic device in its brain. 'Shit!' she cried. 'Why did you have to mention Pyle? You *do* think he's going to bust us, then?'

'*Course* he isn't going to bust us, you great loon. Why should he? We're not doing anything wrong. Anyway, it may have escaped your notice that this isn't a working flat any more.'

Dolores looked bewildered. 'It isn't?'

'Well. Hardly.'

Dawn's gradual realization that Toby wasn't just passing through (brought to dinner one evening by a mutual friend, he'd fallen asleep over the soup and had thereafter simply stayed on, gathering in his various effects, transported in carrier bags, from previous ports of call) but had added a comforting dimension to her life, had made her determined to turn what had virtually been an office, where all had been subordinate to function, into a home for two. The sitting-room, which had once been as welcoming as the waiting-room in an abortion clinic, was now a cheerful confusion, with Toby's accumulated paraphernalia (tatty-theatrical, late fifties, early sixties: books, a tin deed-box, posters, bulging files marked 'Creditors', family albums, binoculars, his father's shooting-stick) blending oddly with Dawn's Habitat-late-brothel *circa* 1969. And the bedroom, which, out of deference to the upper-class Englishman's preference for being suspended from the ceiling and otherwise restrained, had once resembled the business quarters of a health club, would no longer arouse a flicker of suspicion. The giant four-poster bed with handcuffs at the corners, upon which many a toff had been spread-eagled after hours, had been removed, as had the racks, pulleys, ropes, straitjackets, masks, wet-suits, rubber sheets and whips with which a working girl has to equip herself if she means to make a go of it with the ruling class. On the whole she only took outside bookings now, and while this had caused a drop in her income she was hardly on the breadline. She owned this flat and three others that only she and her accountant knew about; she had £35,000 with the Abbey National; £20,000 in unit trusts; £25,000 on deposit at the bank; and £30,000 in the money market. Making money and hanging on to it had never been a problem; the difficulty had been to discover why she drove herself to such frenzied feats of accumulation. Now the compulsion had left her. Protecting Toby from himself, trying to cure him of his lust for catastrophe, had given her a sense of worth she'd never known before. What she didn't need now was trouble. She didn't want to fall foul of the law (she'd been more alarmed by the news of Pyle than she'd let Dolores know – and intended later to make some phone calls) and she didn't want Toby to take another embarrassing prat-fall in the theatre. That he needed to, and inevitably would, hadn't perhaps occurred to her.

'Anyway,' she said, 'running a museum's better than if he was still producing shows, right?'

'Yeah. Wow.'

'Yeah. Wow,' echoed Eddie, who, in spite of Dawn's previous warning, was now dressed for a revival of *Cavalcade*, and looking good.

'Never mind the "yeah wows",' snapped Dawn, reacting sharply to this implied criticism of Toby's track-record, in spite of her earlier resolve not to display her insecurities. 'He had his hits, you know.' She got up and went over to the corner where Eddie was still rummaging around among Toby's theatrical remains and produced a poster from the sixties. 'Here,' she said. '*Over The Edge*. Those four clever young dentists. Ran for five years, didn't it? Anyway, things are looking up. Right now he's being interviewed.'

'Yeah? What for?'

'A job. Teaching. He's gone to see Gabbitas and Thing. Educational agents, aren't they? He's got a degree and that, you know. I'd really like him to be a teacher.'

She imagined cosy evenings at home cooking and watching *Coronation Street*, while Toby, pipe-smoking, slippered and patched at the elbow, corrected exercise books. She smiled in a fond, thoughtful, sentimental way. Perhaps it wasn't too late to make a go of things. 'Life's bad enough when you've nothing to lose,' Toby had said the night before. 'Imagine how sad it would be if things were going well.' But he'd been disconsolate at the time, in one of his silly moods. Everything would be all right. She'd see to that. Dolores had noticed her contented smile.

'Here,' she said. 'You think the end of the world of your Toby, don't you?'

'Shit,' said Dawn casually. 'Maybe I do. Well I never.'

'That's great.'

She's not such a bad old tart, thought Dawn.

3.00 p.m. The Ivy Restaurant.

'Channel-Four-Letter-Word, that's what I call it,' said Scott-Dobbs, nearing the end of a long exposition of what, in his view, could be counted as acceptable family entertainment. 'Take last night's agenda for instance. Programme after programme about the so-called rights of "concerned" minorities. Gays, blacks, Asians, lesbians, feminists, the disadvantaged – well, I don't want all that garbage stuffed down my throat after dinner, and nor does Jennifer. This fellow Isaacs seems to be hopelessly out of touch with what the ordinary viewer wants. "At this rate," I said to Jennifer, "he'll have a new minority on his hands. Himself!" Ha!' Scott-Dobbs whinnied briefly at his *mot*, and then noticed that Danvers was strangely silent. He leaned forward and peered at him closely. 'I say, are you all right? Toby? Toby?'

Great heavens, the man was asleep! Here at the Ivy in the middle of the day, snoring softly, his chins resting on his chest, in mid-sip too, his glass, held in a chubby fist, precisely equidistant between table-top and mouth. Queerest thing he'd ever seen. And what a shambles the fellow was, what a dog's dinner he'd made of his life after a promising start. Unshaven, wearing odd shoes, one black, one brown, living with a dancer in a dream-world, drug-induced, no doubt, about as socially unreliable, if this lunch was anything to go by, as Pillock's incontinent, one-eyed bull terrier which had bitten Jennifer above the knee only the week before. No, to be fair, and taking considerations of breeding and education into account, Pillock's bull terrier would have made the more acceptable lunch companion. True Toby hadn't bitten him yet, but he'd called him a drain-pipe, he'd insulted Jennifer, he'd sent the wine-waiter flying and, worst, he'd embarrassed the other customers, not least the sensible-looking couple at the next table, who, if he wasn't mistaken, were friends of the Grafftey-Smiths and might, for all he knew, be staying with them this weekend in Cookham. He glanced in their direction, caught Fish-face's eye and exchanged a sheepish smile. A short series of coughs and grunts and nasal honks quickly established tribal contact.

'Whawhawha.'

'Whawhawha.'

'Scott-Dobbs,' said Scott-Dobbs.

'Swainston, ' said Fish-face. 'This is my wife, Susan.'

'Whawha,' said Caroline.

'The Grafftey-Smiths. Right?'

'Absolutely right!'

'Whawha!'

'I say. Your friend. A bit the worse for wear.'

Scott-Dobbs might have disowned Toby, claimed him as a mere acquaintance, or an inmate of an insane asylum in his charge for the day, perhaps, had he not been genetically endowed with the quality of loyalty to his kind.

'Taken a knock or two of late,' he explained. 'He'll be all right.'

'Hope so. Sad to see a fellow run out of road like that.'

Sad indeed, thought Scott-Dobbs, and frightening too; a glimpse of chaos, of a life without rules, without coherence. And yet Toby had had the advantages, come from a good family, been to a decent school, married soundly, had a son. And what would become of *him*, poor little devil, with a father like Toby as an example? Further polite enquiries as to the lad's where-abouts and current form had elicited nothing but an off-hand reference to religion. 'Joined up with a group of cranks,' Toby had said. 'Roman Catholics I wouldn't wonder. No, that can't be right. Last seen at the "Mind, Body and Spirit Festival" dancing for peace in bottle-green tights under the sign of the Purple Pansy. Happened to be there with Dawn – she's my young lady, do you see? Believes in such nonsense. I boxed him to the ground, of course, and told him to get a job, whereat I was set upon by a dozen or so of stone-bald Buddhists, clutching tiny cymbals. Might have suffered damage had not Dawn passed among them with her handbag, laying six out cold and scoring technical knockouts against the rest. Now, where was I? Ah yes, about your investment in *Satan's Daughter*. . . .'

It was now clear to Scott-Dobbs that the man was demented, off the rails and heading for a frightful prang, and of one thing he was absolutely sure: to give him money, of which he was all too obviously in desperate need, would not be the act of a friend. Charity would merely speed him on his irresponsible way to the inevitable shunt, taking others with him. That was the trouble with basically unsound types: they always involved others in their calamities. No, what the poor chap needed was the name of a good trick-cyclist. Who was that foreign fellow in Harley Street 'Niffy' Pillock, ex-2 Para, had been persuaded to visit after he'd tried to garotte Vanessa with some cheese-wire when, in a fit of pique, she'd swept his toy soldiers to the floor, disposed as they'd been to re-enact the Battle of Goose Green under his command? Vanessa had suddenly appeared in the war-room, dressed in the early afternoon, for strange, female reasons of her own, in a black suspender belt and lace-up boots acquired by mail-order from a Soho sex-shop, and Pillock, naturally, had told her to buzz off. Funny thing about Vanessa: perfectly sound background – an Annoir, of the Annoir millions – but she'd never seemed to understand that men prefer to pay for that sort of nonsense, to have it on rented premises, with a Maltese maid in the other room, not with the mothers of their children dressed like tarts. But then she'd been a dancer too, of course, like Toby's friend, taking her holidays only grudgingly in Scotland and once, so rumour had it, spending a whole weekend in a Bayswater boarding-house with a pansy colleague from the old days, a frightful sewer whom she'd once partnered in the dance of the bluetits, or some damn thing. Nor had this been the only time she'd slipped. Once Pillock had come home early from manoeuvres to find Vanessa receiving an Australian in the bedroom. Bare-arsed and, according to Pillock, as erect as a telegraph pole, he'd introduced himself as the Chairman and Managing Director of Pardoe International Metals Pty and had persuaded Pillock on the spot to invest £10,000 in a hole in the ground in New South Wales. (Pillock had been slow on the uptake even then, of course, and this had been before he'd banged his head in the Upland Goose, after which a Board of Enquiry had reported that, though his men still followed him, they seemed to do so only 'out of mild curiosity' and had then recommended that he be transferred to British Intelligence.) Pillock, wishing to spread the risk, had insisted that *he*, Scott-Dobbs, should meet Pardoe, bringing him one afternoon to chambers. A plausible rogue, likeable even, and conceivably attractive to the Vanessa type of woman, but he'd shown him the door in very short order.

Meanwhile, should he wake Toby or – here was temptation – pay the bill and quietly steal away, released at last from what had been the most damned awkward lunch he'd ever had? He'd have been up and away countless times already had he not been schooled since birth to see a matter through and, more relevantly, had not a deranged glint in Toby's eye, as in that of

Pillock's hooligan bull terrier, made him fearful that any sudden, unexpected move on his part might give rise to a retaliatory act of such social inexcusability that much of the resulting ignominy would descend on him as well. Dogs, they say, can smell fear, and without a doubt Toby was blessed with this instinct too. To sit tight and keep calm had been the wisest course. But now, he thought, he'd better wake him. After all, they'd been friends once – not that Toby seemed aware of the fact – and you didn't scarper, leaving a friend to be taken prisoner. And asleep, in his velvet jacket – a size and a half too small, asymmetrically buttoned and fertile enough, in his judgement, to grow potatoes on – he looked quite harmless, vulnerable even. Who knows, perhaps he'd set off for this lunch thinking his luck had changed, sallying forth quite bravely, assuring his dancer friend that they'd be eating that night for the first time in God knows how long.

Compassion suddenly flooded into Scott-Dobbs's honest heart, drowning self-interest. What a hideous ordeal the lunch must have been for the poor fellow – trying to keep his dignity while brandishing the begging-bowl – and how shamefully self-absorbed of him not to have assessed the occasion from Toby's point of view. How insensitive he'd been, how un-imaginative his objections to Toby's assinine but, in the circumstances, excusable proposition, and how forgivable, bearing in mind the humiliating situation in which he found himself, Toby's behaviour. He knew suddenly that he couldn't let him down. He would, after all, have to give him money, disguised, for the sake of Toby's pride, as an investment in this crackpot revival thing. Five hundred pounds, say, or perhaps a thousand even. Money down the drain, of course, but what the hell? Perhaps it would be deductible. He'd consult young Marco, the expert in chambers in such matters. No, he wouldn't. What a thin and paltry thought to have at such a time. What was money compared to friendship? He'd cut short this embarrassing charade, release Toby from his agony at once, write the cheque out on the spot. It would be nice to see Toby's face when he handed him the money. His look of relief would be all the thanks he'd need. On second thoughts, perhaps he'd make it two thousand pounds. Yes, two thousand pounds it would be – a punishment to himself, perhaps, for having that thin, unworthy thought *re* tax deduction. He took out his cheque-book and filled in the sum without a qualm.

Outside, not half a mile away, Ronnie Snipe was circling the Ivy in a tight, diminishing orbit. Since his board meeting with D/C Smiley, the firm's deputy managing director, he'd been making himself busy in the West End. He'd bought some shirts at Cecil Gee and was now on his way to Gerrard Street to capitalize on some useful contacts made in prison. Banged up as he'd been for the past four years with key personnel from both the Vice and the Drugs Squads (he even had an intro to the face at Scotland Yard who'd inherited the concession on the recycling caper, the DCI who now put the seized substances back on the market once they'd appeared in court as evidence), he was handily placed to do some sharp deals in that maze of shady side-streets south of Shaftesbury Avenue. With the twenty grand of accumulated dividends due from Smiley and the proceeds from the business he was about to do in Gerrard Street, he'd be back in funds the following day and able to concentrate full-time on running down that fat theatrical, Toby Danvers. He chuckled wheezily to himself at the prospect of mayhem to come – a sound like an old whaler creaking at its moorings on a dark night.

Back at the Ivy, a short, introductory series of nasal honks suggested that Fish-face was about to re-establish contact with Scott-Dobbs. 'Going to the Grafftey-Smiths this weekend?' he asked.

'Matter of fact we are, yes. And you?'

'Certainly. See you there, then.'

'I'll look forward to it. Just going to wake my friend.'

'Well done.'

Scott-Dobbs reached across the table and shook Toby gently by the sleeve. 'Toby, old fellow, are you quite okay?'

Toby, in the thrall of a hideous dream in which the General Secretary of Equity, no less, had, seconds before the curtain was due to rise on his triumphant revival of *Satan's Daughter*, arrived backstage, disguised, confusingly, as Ronnie Snipe and wielding a butcher's knife, opened his eyes with a bellow of rage.

'Leave my theatre this instant, Plouviez, you abominable pig!' he roared. He dropped his glass and struck like lightning across the table, gaining a hook-hold on Scott-Dobbs's head and driving it hard into the table-top, like an auctioneer bringing down his gavel.

'Good heavens!' said Fish-face.

'I say. Whawha,' said Caroline.

Scott-Dobbs, grinning wildly and far from certain where he was, rose to his feet with a cry of 'Objection, me lud!' and, clutching the cheque made out to Toby, fell backwards into the pudding-trolley. Fish-face and Caroline picked him up and placed him in his chair, while suave, impassive waiters rallied round to sweep up broken glass and change the table-cloth, their smooth attentions rousing Toby from his dream.

'Hullo?' he said. 'What's up? Been an accident, has there?' He rubbed his eyes and stared around him, and then focused, first with surprise and then with mounting disapproval, on Scott-Dobbs, who was slumped in his chair, still grinning idiotically, a deposit of whipped cream with a cherry in it sticking to the tip of his nose. 'Oh dear, my friend seems to have fallen in the trifle. Probably had a bit too much to drink.'

The waiters backed away, their faces non-judgemental masks.

'What happened?' moaned Scott-Dobbs, groping for his forehead, on which a bump the size of a plover's egg had now appeared.

'You spilt your wine,' said Toby. 'Slight *faux pas*. No need to reproach yourself unduly. Could happen to anyone. But kindly remove that cherry from your nose. You look like a circus *auguste*.' He turned to Fish-face and Caroline, who were hovering on the outskirts of the incident, ready to step in if violence flared again. 'Can't hold his drink, the poor old fool. Pray don't concern yourselves. I can cope.'

He leant across the table, meaning to remove the cherry from Scott-Dobbs's nose, but Scott-Dobbs, interpreting this move as another assault, recoiled too violently, the sudden backward-jerking of the head causing a wrecking-ball to swing inside his skull. The pain was shattering, but its very intensity cured his amnesia.

'I remember now,' he said, his voice rising with indignation. 'You crazy bloody fool! You damn near knocked me out!'

'Nonsense! And kindly watch your language.' Toby lowered his voice and leaned forward confidentially. 'Between ourselves, I'm trying to impress the fellow at the next table.' He tapped the side of his nose and jerked his head in the direction of Fish-face. 'Silly-looking ass, but a money-bags, if I'm not mistaken. May do business with him. He's leaning my way, I think, but you're hardly helping – spilling your drink, taking a header into the trifle and sitting there with a cherry on the end of your nose. Get a grip on yourself, for goodness sake.'

'I spilt nothing!' yelped Scott-Dobbs. He swatted at the cherry, meaning to dislodge it, but, due to some damage done to his sense of spatial relations when his head had struck the table-top, merely fetched himself a frightful crack on the right temple. 'Aaahhhhggghh!'

'Careful!' warned Toby. 'You'll knock yourself out, you silly old fool.'

'*Me*?' Scott-Dobbs was gibbering with fury. 'Knock . . . silly . . . *look*! You were sound asleep. Foolishly, I tried to wake you. Next thing you rapped my head on the table.'

'*Really*?' Toby was astounded. 'Asleep, you say? I can scarcely credit it.' He frowned and drummed his fingers on the table-cloth, the insistent rhythm causing Scott-Dobbs to wince and clutch his eyeballs. 'Ah! I suddenly have it! It all comes back to me. I was having this dream, do you see?'

'You called me Plouviez and then. . . .'

'That's right. The General Secretary of Equity, but disguised, can you beat it, as Ronnie Sni . . . oh! oh! Here we go.'

He rose inches off his seat and back-fired preposterously, causing Fish-face and Caroline to throw their napkins on the table and call it a day. Fish-face asked for his bill, while Caroline tried to hide her embarrassment by groping under the table for her bag. 'There you are!' cried Toby triumphantly. 'Happened again, do you see?' He turned to Fish-face. 'Please excuse me. Oh – are you off? Well, you've got my card. Give my secretary a ring.' He readdressed himself to Scott-Dobbs. 'Well. Stop pissing me about. Are you in or out? Delfont's in.'

Scott-Dobbs squinted at him disbelievingly. He's round the bend, he thought. Certifiable. A danger to the public. He'd rapped his head on the table – a potential investor – and now he was telling him not to piss about.

'If I live,' he said, ruefully touching the lump on his forehead, 'which, I may say, is most unlikely, I'll think about it.'

Despite his previous charitable intentions, he was less inclined now to invest in *Satan's Daughter* than he was to vote for the Workers' Revolutionary Party at the next election, but he was eager to get out of the Ivy more or less in one piece. An unambiguous suggestion as to where Toby could stick his absurd revival might, he felt, give rise to further violence. Though the pounding in his head was easing slightly, he doubted whether he'd survive another full-frontal assault.

'I can give you precisely a week,' said Toby, as brisk as a mongoose now after his little nap. 'I'm capitalizing the venture at £50,000 and selling minimum units of £1,000. I'll be observing the customary split between investors and management of forty per cent to the investors and sixty per cent to the management, so each unit, as will be immediately clear to a man with a laser-beam mind such as yours, will carry ten per cent of the net profits. Fair enough?'

'Er – more than fair,' said Scott-Dobbs, calculating that Toby was proposing to give away five hundred per cent of the show's profits – the most blatantly fraudulent offer he'd come across since that Australian horse-player, Ken Pardoe, had promoted poor old Pillock to the tune of £10,000. What a combination Pardoe and Toby would make. They'd swindle each other dizzy. Perhaps he'd introduce them. That would be some revenge, at least, for his throbbing head.

'Excellent!' cried Toby. 'I'll instruct my secretary to put an investor's agreement in the post tonight. If you're in, simply sign one copy and return it to me with your cheque. WAITER! Ah, well done. My bill, if you'd be so good.'

'No no,' said Scott-Dobbs, 'it's my lunch, I insist.' He would happily have bought the Ivy had that been the one condition under which he could bring this absurd charade to an end, and he doubted, anyway, whether Toby was carrying enough cash to recover his parcel from the cloakroom, let alone settle the enormous bill, for which, thanks to his repeated demands for further bottles of *Sancerre*, he was largely responsible. Nor did it seem likely that any cheques or credit cards with which he might attempt to cover their departure from the room would hold up for the time it took them to reach the exit. Scott-Dobbs had suffered enough humiliations for one day without being held as an accessory to a pecuniary advantage.

'My dear fellow,' said Toby with relief, 'how very good of you.' Dawn had capitalized him that morning with a hundred pounds with which to buy a new shirt, a tie and a pair of shoes at Fortnum and Mason, but on an impulse he'd spent the lot on a bag for her that had taken his fancy in Gifts and Accessories. And the prospect of trying to bluff the Ivy's management with a cheque drawn on the Bank of Rotterdam, Straabe Knottenbelt Branch and stamped 'Hair – Investors Account' had quite clouded his enjoyment of his second brandy. 'But the next one's on me. I insist. At my club, perhaps. They do a very decent spotted dick.'

That will be the day, thought Scott-Dobbs. And what sort of dingey clip-joint would Toby's club be? That cellar in Beak Street, perhaps, where Pillock caught crabs from a lunchtime dancing partner and passed them on to Deirdre.

He paid the bill by cheque, and when the waiter returned with a ten-pound note on a plate he pushed it back across the table, saying, 'No no, that's for you.'

'Thank you very much,' said Toby, scooping the money off

the plate, which had come to rest nearer to him, admittedly, than it had to the hovering waiter, whose own scoop had to be altered in mid-action, for suavity's sake, into an adjustment to the table-cloth.

Toby pocketed the tenner, delighted at first with this sudden windfall, but gratitude soon gave way to indignation. How typically clumsy it was of Scott-Dobbs, he thought, to assume that he'd be impressed by such a derisory handout. The man had no sense of style at all. Though subsidizing the activities of creative people like himself was, he supposed, one of the few functions that the Scott-Dobbs's of this world could still usefully perform, rage at the fellow's impudence exploded in his head. There was nothing for it but to get out of here before he did something silly: hand the money back, for instance, or suddenly bring his hand down in a whistling karate chop on the back of Scott-Dobbs's neck, thus causing him to falter, perhaps, in his intention to invest. Already he was calculating angles, measuring the distance to that pink inviting target, so he hurriedly pushed his chair back and got to his feet.

'Well, I must be getting along,' he said. 'Other fish to fry. Ball's in your court. My regards to Marion.'

It was an abrupt farewell, he realized, brusque even, but it was wiser to leave now, having made a good impression, than to hang around and do something he might later regret. He gave a perfunctory nod and, congratulating such of the staff as had seemed to him to have performed their duties adequately, he waddled from the room, leaving a startled Scott-Dobbs searching for notes with which to square the waiter.

Meanwhile Ronnie Snipe, with a couple of useful orders in his pocket, emerged from a porno bookshop in Little Newport Street and walked briskly towards the Charing Cross Road. He was on his way to a drinking club behind Cambridge Circus, from where he intended to phone D/C Smiley. Smiley would have had time by now to check out Danvers on the police computer. If he'd drawn a blank, Snipe reckoned he'd go on the search himself, calling back-stage at a few theatres in the area until he found someone with knowledge of Danvers's current whereabouts. If he was still in London he'd have his bollocks and the ten grand back by nightfall. He punched his right fist into the palm of his left hand with such a crack that a nervous, bowler-hatted City gent dropped the copy of *A History of Corporal Punishment in the Army, Navy and Airforce*, which he was perusing outside S. Solosy (Educational and Medical Books) Ltd, and scuttled off towards Trafalgar Square.

Back at the Ivy, Toby, having claimed Dawn's present from the cloakroom, was delighted to discover that Fish-face and Caroline were still on the premises, and grateful for this chance to repair some of the damage inevitably done to their opinion of him by Scott-Dobbs's buffoonish behaviour. He now had an opportunity, he realized, to explain to them that he and Scott-Dobbs were scarcely more than acquaintances and that he had been lunching with him, and letting him in on a business venture, only as a favour to a mutual friend. He addressed himself first to Caroline, who was holding the front door ajar and peering into the street, while the cloakroom attendant was helping Fish-face into his coat. 'Pissing down as usual, is it?' he said chattily. 'What a confounded nuisance.'

'Oh!' yelped Caroline, giving a nervous little start. 'Er – yes it seems to be. Just a thin drizzle actually.'

'Looking for a cab, are you?'

'Yes, actually,' lied Caroline, stepping quickly into the street, eager not to be confined indoors with Toby. 'I'd better go and get one.' She planned, in fact, for safety's sake, to move smartly ahead of Fish-face to the haven of a nearby car-park where they'd left the family Rover.

'Leave this to me, my dear,' said Toby helpfully, and with one foot still inside the Ivy he suddenly yelled 'TAXI!' with such unexpected force that the cloakroom attendant, who'd boxed at heavyweight for the Royal Marines but who'd filled out considerably since then, jumped high and backwards like a mountain goat, landing heavily on Fish-face's foot, while out in the street, Caroline, hurrying towards St Martin's Lane,

71

turned to see what the commotion was and stunned herself against a lamp-post.

'Do look where you're going, my good woman,' said Toby, stepping outside and hauling her to her feet, but failing in his efforts to keep her upright since her legs, sturdy as they were through constant yomping after game, no longer seemed able to carry her enormous weight. 'At your age you should be more careful.'

After she had slipped through his fingers for the third time, he abandoned her abruptly, the sudden withdrawal of his support causing her to sit down so sharply that she seemed to bounce a little on the pavement.

'Did my best for the silly woman,' he said to the cloakroom attendant, who had come outside to see what the fuss was about. 'Here, see to her, will you?' He handed him Scott-Dobbs's tenner and, as an afterthought, Dawn's present too. 'And give her this, will you? I've decided it's a trifle vulgar for my young lady. More the kind of thing you'd expect to see the Queen Mother carrying at Cheltenham races.' Then, still bellowing 'Taxi!', he swung off towards the Charing Cross Road with such purpose that he concussed himself against the same lamp-post as had downed Caroline. She, in fact, recovered first, and, having kicked the unconscious Toby viciously in the groin, swayed groggily towards that confluence of meagre side-streets behind the Cambridge Theatre, where she was later to be found, squatting on the pavement talking to herself. Fish-face, meanwhile, limping out of the Ivy to seek revenge for his damaged in-step, assumed that Toby had been mugged and, feeling that a kind of rough justice had taken place, was inclined to leave him lying in the gutter. Then it struck him that he ought, perhaps, as a church warden and trustee of many discretionary interests, to take a more responsible line, so he approached Toby and, mindful of the damage done earlier to Scott-Dobbs, prodded him cautiously with his toe-cap. At first there was no response, but while Fish-face was wondering whether, by bending over and tapping Toby lightly on the cheek, he would run the risk of being seized in a wrestling-hold and brought to the ground himself, Toby opened an eye.

'Are you in or out?' he asked. 'Minimum units of. . . .'

'Take it easy now,' said Fish-face soothingly. He got a grip under Toby's arms and managed, with difficulty, to haul him to his feet. 'Gently does it. There's a good fellow.'

'. . . agreement in the post. Cheque made out in my name, do you see? Hell. Don't feel too clever. AAAAGGGGGGHHHHH!'

Messages from Toby's horrifically abused groin had at last carried to that section of the brain that deals with such things. A look of astonishment spread in slow motion across his face, then, squinting with pain, he clutched his parts and doubled up. Fish-face, stricken with sympathy – though unaware that his own wife had done this dreadful thing – went at once to his assistance, whereupon Toby, with a sudden bellow of rage, straightened up, lifting his knee as he did so into Fish-face's undefended balls. Fish-face went down croaking.

'What's your game?' he gasped.

'Thought you attacked me in a cowardly fashion. Went for the waterworks.'

'Not me, you fool. I found you lying on the pavement.'

For a while a shared agony caused the two of them to hop around in tiny circles, bending slightly at the waist, knees locked together like men competing in a sack-race, their antics, unbeknown to them, being observed incredulously from across the road by a bullet-hard little man in a cheap suit. Then, propping one another up, like two drunks held together by each's need of the other's support, but with Fish-face taking responsibility for the steering since Toby's collision with the lamp-post seemed to have impaired his sense of direction – causing him to veer off suddenly at right-angles like Charlie Chaplin in an old two-reeler (one such swerve, happily for Toby, dummying Ronnie Snipe up a side-street and causing him to lose contact temporarily just as he was going to belt Toby from the rear) – they made their way painfully to Trafalgar Square, where Toby at last managed to find a cab.

'Take me home, my good man,' he said to the driver. 'Been mugged from behind, do you see? The streets aren't safe.' He clambered inside, where he squatted like a man at stool, a position caused by the fact that he had, on attempting to sit down, missed the seat by a foot or more, and now he didn't care to aim at it again.

'And where might that be, guv?'

'Of course. Not for you to know. Nell Gwynn House in Sloane Avenue. Flat 2004 to be precise, though that's no concern of yours. On the way I'd be obliged, however, if you'd stop off at the German Food Centre in Knightsbridge. I must stock up with wine and comestibles. Do a lot of entertaining in my game. The live theatre, you know.'

'Is that so, guv?'

'It certainly is, my good man, it certainly is.' Toby, the better to bid farewell to Fish-face, stuck his head out of the window precisely as Ronnie Snipe came panting round a corner. Growling with rage, Snipe ran towards the taxi, bunching his right hand into a rock-hard fist as he weaved his way between the traffic. 'Can I give you a lift, Fish-face?'

'Oh! I say. What! Ha! ha! Actually no. Better go and find Susan.'

'Susan, eh?' chortled Toby. 'You rascal! Your secret's safe with me. Not a word to Caroline.'

'Caroline?'

'Your wife.'

'No no. That's Susan.'

'If you say so. Well done anyway. And don't forget to ring my secretary. Minimum units of a thousand pounds.'

'Of course, of *course*,' said Fish-face placatingly. He wanted no more trouble today.

'Home James!' cried Toby, withdrawing his head as Ronnie Snipe let go a right hook that would have dropped an ox. Fish-face, left in the firing-line and beaming reassuringly, took it full in the mouth and was lifted six feet backwards, landing, as Toby's taxi sped away, among some dustbins in a doorway. Nor was this the end of his troubles. When he came to it was to

74

find himself being questioned painfully below the rib-cage by a complete stranger who seemed to find it hard to credit that he didn't know the address of his departing friend.

Scott-Dobbs, meanwhile, having at last managed to settle matters at the Ivy (even retrieving the cheque made out to Toby – quite forgotten until that moment – as it was about to be served, stuck like a flag in a portion of *gâteau*, to a man in a brown suit who travelled in industrial detergents), walked thoughtfully up the Charing Cross Road towards Cambridge Circus with a cherry on the end of his nose. It was now 3.35. Nothing on the agenda until a late conference in chambers at five o'clock. Old Harbottle bringing round some unfortunate woman involved in a messy divorce. Husband, a Toby type, had suddenly lost his marbles in middle age, diving into the Clients Account and taking off with his secretary for foreign parts. Wife left without a bean and three children to educate. Always the children that suffered of course. Like Toby's boy. That was the tragedy. Frankly he blamed Roy Jenkins and his so-called 'civilized society'. Civilized indeed! Nudity and granny-bashing; flying pickets and galloping herpes; public schoolboys walking the streets with needles through their noses; their randy, flint-eyed sisters on the pill; sex education televised in the early evening; the family sneered at, religion mocked; morality no longer based in authority, but a matter of individual choice; pleasure and self-indulgence off the leash; the arts a desert of obscurity and dirt; the country's architects mere vandals, plunderers of the skyline; its painters hawkers of ugliness and outrage; its poets, with the exception of the Laureate, purveyors of mystification and aggression, delighted not to be understood, or even read, except by northern academics spreading their filthy jargon south. Scott-Dobbs stopped outside the Queen's Theatre and, on an impulse, stepped inside and bought two stalls for a new boulevard comedy ('Agreeable nonsense' – *Daily Telegraph*, 'The fun is fast and furious' – *Daily Mail*), starring Kenneth Williams. It would be a nice treat for Jennifer's birthday. Kenneth Williams made her roar with laughter, and him too, come to that. There'd be

75

no gratuitous nudity here, or schoolboy allusions to matters below the belt, just healthy vulgarity and saucy fun. That was the mistake that people like Toby made. On his uppers after twenty years trying to shock people with pornographic plays like *Satan's Daughter*, yet here was a piece of family entertainment absolutely coining it. Infantile hedonists like Toby failed to grasp that ordinary people weren't *shocked* by blasphemy and filth and naked women, they were merely bored. Scott-Dobbs turned left into Old Compton Street and then left again into Greek Street, noting sadly, but without surprise, that the agreeable little French bistro where he'd proposed to Jennifer eighteen years ago almost to the day, had become a Gay Nude Encounter Parlour. No doubt it enjoyed a GLC grant by order of the supreme Soviet of Central London under Chairman Livingstone. Perversion and squalor on the rates. Scott-Dobbs quickened his step as he headed towards Soho Square, as though fearful that by loitering he might fall victim to one of the garish opportunities advertised in every doorway. In the middle of the road, a little further on, two cheery coloured gentlemen were leaning into the back of a Mini, clearly intending to give it a push-start, while a pretty blonde waited to engage the gears. Keen to prove that a sense of community still existed, even in these unsalubrious parts, Scott-Dobbs stepped into the road and, with a cry of 'Put your backs into it!', launched his full weight up the boot of the Mini precisely as the blonde, who had only stopped to pass the time of day, drove off, leaving Scott-Dobbs face down in a puddle. 'Looking for a naughty girl?' asked one of the cheery coloured gentlemen, who seemed greatly amused by the incident. 'Certainly not,' said Scott-Dobbs haughtily. 'How dare you!' He picked himself up and marched off towards Soho Square, reflecting that he'd only been trying to help, just as earlier he'd been trying to help Toby. No doubt Toby was laughing at him too, but Scott-Dobbs knew in his heart which of the two of them would end up looking sillier. Toby would discover soon enough that you couldn't alter the rules, deny your obligations, do the dirty on your background and get away with it. The punishment would be sudden, swift and terrible. Outside No. 18 Greek Street Scott-Dobbs paused, sighing at the madness of it all. This had once been The Establishment, where, in the early sixties, before obscenity became the fashion, those clever young chaps from Cambridge had poked tongue-in-cheek fun at authority without ever going too far. They'd known where to draw the line. Now there were several little business-cards pinned to the doorway, one of which read: 'Miss Fatima. Young Turkish model. Full theatrical wardrobe. 4th Floor.' Scott-Dobbs went in and climbed the gloomy staircase. At the top he paused briefly to catch his breath before knocking on the door. After a few seconds it was opened by a tall lady no longer in her first youth but gamely attired for all that in crutchless knickers and a pink suspender-belt. Scott-Dobbs greeted her warmly.

'Afternoon, Pillock,' he said. 'Long time no see!'

'Scott-Dobbs! What a delightful surprise.'

'You ahead of me in the queue?' asked Scott-Dobbs. 'Mind if I play through? Conference in chambers at five o'clock.'

'Help yourself, my dear fellow,' said Pillock obligingly. 'Just leaving, as it happens.'

'What? Like *that*?'

'Of course not like *this*, you silly bugger. About to change when you knocked. Miss Fatima, on the mat with some funny little man, asked me to take the door, do you see?'

'Well done.'

'How's Jennifer?'

'Great form. And Vanessa?'

'Much better, thank you.'

'Just had lunch with Toby Danvers. Remember him? Off the rails. Wearing odd shoes. One black, one brown.'

'Poor Sod. Well, don't stand there like a spare prick. Better come in. Going to the Grafftey-Smiths this weekend?'

'Certainly. And you?'

'Indeed, indeed. By the way, have you been to Nell Gwynn House yet? The girl I told you about. Dawn. Pop along some time. Mention my name. I say. You've got a cherry on the end of your nose.'

'I've had second thoughts, haven't I?' said Dawn, getting up and walking towards the bedroom. 'I'm going to wear my Janet Regers after all.'

'Great.'

'May be out of character.'

'Great.'

'But what the hell.'

'Great.'

'Not going for the *Evening Standard* Most Promising Actress award, after all.'

'Great.'

'Never get it ahead of Eddie, anyway.'

'Great.'

'Afternoon Mr Pyle.'

'Gre . . . whooooaaaaah!' Dolores, moaning like an air-raid warning, rose unsteadily to her feet and crashed into the coffee-table. 'Shit! What's your game?' Having established that Mr Pyle wasn't in the room, she stared accusingly at Dawn. 'That's not funny.'

'Just checking.'

'On what?'

'Whether you were paying attention.'

'*Course* I was paying attention.'

'Good. What am I going to do now, then?'

'How should I know?'

'I'm going to wear my Janet Regers after all.'

'Oh. Great.'

Brooding, as she'd been for the past half-hour, on what she hoped were Toby's fantasies rather than the Wanker's, Dawn had decided that it would be more exciting for him, once he'd wrestled her to the floor and peeled away her outer garments, to discover that the demure and blushing Jane was daringly attired beneath her modest, early-evening interviewing clothes. So aroused had she become by the prospect of playing the lovely, wide-eyed Jane for Toby that the realization that she must first stage a sneak preview for the Wanker had quite unsettled her usual, impeccably professional refusal to let thoughts of pleasure interfere with business. Still, if the Wanker's form was anything to go by he wouldn't actually *touch* her, the silly old sod, so that the Janet Regers, once on, would only come off at the urgent insistence of the sexually infuriated Toby. Her plan was that, maddened by her adorable, eyes-cast-down demurring – 'No *no*, Mr Danvers! Really! Please! We must stick to the question on the clipboard' – he would actually tear them off in an explosion of desire. As she reached the bedroom, there was a sudden, unusually insistent ring at the front-door, causing Dolores once again to wail with siren-like alarm.

'Oooooh! It's them! Old Bill. Must be.' She would have got off the floor and made a move for safety had she been able to operate any muscles except those that controlled her spinning eyeballs.

'Don't be soft. It'll be my car, won't it? Daimler Hire. They don't ring first if it's a bust, pot-head. It's straight through the front-door with a search warrant in one hand and the evidence in the other. You said so yourself. Take it, will you?'

'What? *Me?*'

'Yes *you*. If it's not too much trouble, of course.'

'I'm not into opening doors at the moment. What about Eddie?'

'You're joking!' Eddie dressed now in the actual gym-slip and white socks that Jane Birkin had worn in *Passion Flower Hotel*, was mesmerized before a mirror. 'Don't want Daimler Hire to think I live with a weirdo, do I? Taking a risk with you.'

'Right.'

'No offence, Eddie. Remind me to send you to see Pillock some time. He'd do his nut. Go on, Dolores, tell him I'll be ready in a minute.' She disappeared into the bedroom, closing the door firmly behind her to cut out any further protests.

Dolores, mewing at the injustice of it, managed to lift herself off the floor and then to swerve on spaghetti legs towards the front door, propping herself against it while she peeped cautiously through the spy-hole. Outside, humming cheerfully to himself, stood a tanned, piratical-looking fellow in his early thirties, dressed with the studied casualness of those King's Road fantasists who ran around Chelsea in 1973 pretending, not without success, to be something in the world of music. He didn't *look* like a chauffeur, thought Dolores, but he had none of the blatantly criminal appearance of old Bill either. It couldn't be Pyle, was her immediate, relieved reaction, but who on earth could he be? He wasn't a friend of Dawn's, as far as she knew, and he was far too at ease with himself to be a punter. She decided to take no chances, so she bent down and addressed his crutch through the letter-box.

'She'll be ready for you in a minute.'

The fellow outside lowered himself so that his eyes were in line with hers. They were blue and rascally, beaming mischief, but quite unthreatening. They were the undesperate eyes of a man you'd accept an approach from in the street, thought Dolores, the eyes of an optimist, to whom little had happened to make him think less of his chances. Framed by the letter-box, their impact in the darkness had the intensity of searchlights, causing her to blink and stagger back, shaking her head.

'Is that right, darling?' he said. 'She'll be ready for me in a minute, will she, the cheeky sheila? This is my lucky day and no mistake! Could I possibly lob inside meanwhile? Very fucking stylish out here – like the decor a lot – but it's as draughty as an Abo shit-house.'

Could be Australian, thought Dolores, returning to the letter-box. Yeah, with his broad shoulders and bandit moustache, he could be one of those badly behaved Australian cricketers; or a male model and part-time shop-lifter, taking orders door-to-door. They could be handy them. Highly accomplished and no messing about with poachers' pockets and sleight of hand. Having jotted down the client's requirements, they'd run straight into the nominated boutique, king-punch the sales-staff into submission and wheel a whole rail of clothes into the street. She'd once acquired her entire winter wardrobe, evening-gowns and all, from just such a fellow. Better be on the safe side, though. They were as cunning as rats, the fuzz these days. He might be an Australian old Bill over here on an exchange scheme, working under cover, like you sometimes saw on telly. On the other hand, old Bill on a bust would always come mob-handed. She decided to lay a trap.

'Here. Are you old Bill?'

The mischievous blue eyes six inches from her own momentarily took on a calculating look. Here was a poser. Who the hell was old Bill? Would it be to his advantage to take on the fellow's identity? A moment's thought and then he decided against it.

'No, darling, I'm not old Bill,' he said, adding, as a catch-all rider, just in case old Bill had the entrée to this mad household, 'and more's the pity. Yes sir, more's the pity. Pardoe's the name. Pardoe International. Call me Ken.'

Dolores decided to chance it. She opened the door and Ken sprang over the threshold like a two-year-old out of the starting-stalls, hopping and chortling and gleefully rubbing his hands together. He cast a quick appreciative eye around the room and then beamed in with full force on Dolores.

'Well blow me over!' he cried, actually recoiling a pace or two, as though literally knocked off balance by the impact of her beauty. 'You're a looker for a razor-blade and no mistake! This *is* my lucky day!'

Dolores, squinting at Ken in stoned confusion and reeling from this sudden eruption of energy into the room, began to sway alarmingly and would have gone over had he not stuck a forefinger into her chest, like a comic in a silent movie holding up a house.

'Phew. Ta. Here. Are you Daimler Hire or what?'

Stone me, another poser. This crazy spade certainly tossed them in from left-field. Which way to play it? He was on to something here and no mistake. This one wasn't bad at all – maddest fucking thighs he'd ever seen, he could duck his head in there right now – and there was the other sheila who'd be ready for him in a minute. Christ, she might be even better.

'Well, darling, yes I am.'

'Great.'

'But on the other hand, no I'm not.'

'Oh.'

With a sudden conjuror's flourish he produced a handful of business-cards from the hip pocket of his immaculately faded jeans and, after a quick shuffle, selected the two he thought most suitable.

'Darling,' he said, handing Dolores one of the cards, 'this is your lucky day. I represent the "Mobile Model Agency Of Mayfair", which happens to be amalgamated with' – and here he suddenly dropped his voice and spoke in an urgent stage-whisper out of the side of his mouth, as though fearful that eavesdroppers in the woodwork might take advantage of the top-secret info he was about to impart for her ears only – 'fucking *amalgamated* with, mind you! – "Photography In The Home". Here.' He handed her the second card. 'Two brand new dodges saving top-drawer molls like you no end of heartbreak. I take it you are a model, darling?'

'Oh well, yeah, I've done some, yes,' said Dolores. 'Bit heavy on my head, though. All that standing around. I don't need the aggravation, me.'

'Ex-*actly*!' Ken beamed and slapped his thigh with a clap that sent Dolores reeling back towards the sofa. She didn't go down, but she propped herself against the arm, like a groggy boxer clinging to the ropes. 'Pre*cisely* why my associates and I instigated "Mobile Models" and "Photography In The Home". With us the aggravation's over. *We* come to you! Yes sir! How do you like that?'

'Crazy,' mumbled Dolores, utterly bewildered and reckoning that she'd have to lie down unless this engaging stranger stopped hopping in her line of vision.

'No more punting around the West End carrying your portfolio and a suitcase full of fucking wigs. No sir. We offer a complete and highly confidential service in the privacy of your own home. Now. You've got an up-to-date set, I take it?'

'What? Photographs? Haven't had any done lately, no.'

'Incredible!' Dolores braced herself against another thunderclap wallop on the thigh, but Ken merely recoiled a yard, as though blasted back by the coincidence of his having lobbed at such an opportune moment. 'Best thing that could have happened to you, darling, my hopping through your door like this.'

'Yeah?'

'I should say so! Here's the deal. It's a hundred on the table fully clothed or nothing' – and here Ken dropped suddenly into his highly confidential, out-of-the-side-of-the-mouth routine, as though tipping the runner at Haydock Park that's had a shot of chemicals with its breakfast – 'and I have to point out that most top-drawer sheilas are going for this one – fucking *nothing*, mind! – stark fucking naked! *And* you get a set of prints! How do you like that?'

Like a Safari Park invalid coming round after a shot from a valium gun, Dolores, thanks to the high-voltage shocks she was receiving from Ken's electric personality, was gradually achieving some sort of mental and physical cohesion, but she had to sit down to work this one out. Where the hell was Dawn? She was clever at this sort of thing.

'Here,' she said. 'Let's get this straight. You're a photographer, right?'

'What!' Ken seemed amazed that she should need to ask. 'You know who I mean by Bailey?'

'Yeah, I've met him. Only socially, mind.'

'Oh.' Ken was momentarily derailed, but he soon recovered. 'Terence fucking O'Donovan?'

'Never met him, no.'

'My partner. Set him up. Taught him everything he knows.' Dolores was impressed. 'So. You're a photographer. . . .'

'You know it, darling!'

'. . . and it's a hundred on the table in my gear?'

'Right!' Ken beamed encouragement.

Dolores grappled with the next stage in the calculation. She wished Dawn would hurry up. Dawn could work these things out in her head.

'But without my gear I pay nothing?'

'That's the deal, darling. Which is it going to be?'

Two considerations seemed to Dolores to weight decisively against the first offer. One, she didn't have a hundred on her and, two, she didn't fancy doing it on the table (last time she'd been talked into that had been on a snooker table at the Monday Club with a guy in a ginger toupee and afterwards she hadn't been able to walk for a week).

'I'll go for the nude, then,' she said.

'That's my girl!'

Ken clapped his hands together and, whooping jubilantly, did a little celebratory shuffle on the spot, like an All Black before the kick-off. He was about to arrange a time when the session could conveniently take place for both of them (you couldn't rush these demure English sheilas) when he noticed with some surprise – indeed he took two or three smart steps backwards – that Dolores had got to her feet, removing her skirt as she did so, and was now unzipping her USAF master-sergeant's combat tunic. Within a second she stood before him in nothing but her postage-stamp size knickers in British racing-green.

'Holy *Christ*!' cried Ken. 'Will you cop that fucking body! Will you cop those fucking legs! Will you cop that fu . . . Je-*sus*! This I have to get on film!' He banged himself urgently about the body back and front, suddenly producing from nowhere a cheap instamatic camera. Then he quickly removed his trousers, folding them neatly before hanging them over the back of a chair.

'Okay,' said Dolores, taking off her knickers, 'where do you want me, then?'

'Where do I want you? Where do I fucking want you? Yow-*eeeee*! Don't tempt me now you rascal! Let's see.' Ken suddenly assumed the serious demeanour of an artist about to go to work. 'First we need some atmosphere in here. Appropriate fucking sounds and so forth. What's that on now? No offence intended if

84

it happens to be one of your favourites, darling, but it's hardly conducive to the sort of shots I have in mind.'

Dolores pulled her dead-mouse-in-the-woodwork face. 'Know what you mean, man. *Highlights From Rigoletto – Various Artists*, isn't it? One of Toby's.'

'Ur-huh, ur-huh. Various fucking artists, eh? Well, I'll tell you this, darling. If *Rigoletto* was currently playing in London wild horses couldn't keep me away, but right now I need something a little more sensual, if you catch my meaning. And – 'scuse I for asking, darling – who might Mr Toby be?'

'He's with Dawn. She'll be ready for you in a minute.'

'Ur-hur, ur-hur. He's with Dawn. Got you.' Ken began to show small signs of unease, glancing round the room and moving casually nearer to his trousers. 'And Dawn will be ready for me in a minute, eh? Er – he's with her now, is he, Mr Toby? On the premises, I mean?'

'Oh no. He's out with Gabbitas and Thing. You know.'

'Good good. Out with Gabbitas and Thing. Got you.' Ken relaxed again. 'Perhaps I could look through your tapes, then, darling? Find something a little more appropriate?'

'Help yourself, man.'

Dolores, beginning to enjoy herself and already moving rather unsteadily into her somewhat dated repertoire of glamour poses – pouting wetly, eyes menacingly half-closed, bumping and thrusting here and there, knees together, bottom out, an index-finger archly at the chin – waved a free arm in the general direction of the sound-system, its wide arc happening at its furthest extension to alert Ken at last to the presence in the room of Steady Eddie, still dressed as Jane Birkin in *Passion Flower Hotel*.

'Right. Leave this to ... FUCK ME DEAD! Who's the horse's hoof?'

'Oh,' said Dolores, not looking up from a suggestive yoga crouch she'd now assumed, 'that's Steady Eddie. He's my personal life.'

'Stone me! You certainly drew the short straw there, darling. Steady Eddie, eh? Stone *me*.'

The discovery that there was a man, of sorts, on the premises after all, brought the powerful forward momentum of Ken's intentions to a gear-grinding halt. Mr Eddie didn't look a threat, but you could never be a hundred per cent in a situation like this. They all looked like benders, these poms, but they could suddenly go the other way when least expected. There'd been the occasion with that mad Vanessa out at Aldershot, for instance. What an insatiable old auntie she'd been! Fucking her had been like painting the ceiling of Sydney Opera House. As soon as you'd finished you had to climb up and start again. He'd been attending to her privately one afternoon when her husband, Pillock, ex-2 Para, lobbing unexpectedly, had beaned him from behind with an electric frying-pan, causing him, as it happened, to climax with Vanessa for the first time in weeks, but it had been an unpleasant experience for all that, alleviated only fractionally by his having been able to tug ten grand off Pillock for investment in Pardoe Minerals International. He'd better not take any chances with this Mr Eddie fellow, better move fucking suavely in the opposite direction. He put his camera away and, going through his wallet, selected another card from the pack.

'On second thoughts, darling,' he said, 'perhaps you – and, er, Mr Eddie too, of course' – he beamed at Steady Eddie and bowed politely in his direction – 'might be more interested in another of my services. "The Park Lane Pebble Dashing Dodge". Yes sir. Driving past this block just now with my colleague Bruce the Goose I happened to notice that it's in terrible fucking shape.'

'Is that right?' said Dolores, vaguely. She'd failed to register Ken's change of course and was still going through her model poses, facing away from him now, jack-knifed over, peering up and backwards between her thighs, like an American footballer ready to deliver.

'It certainly is, darling,' said Ken, wanting urgently to spear her from behind right now, but exercising massive self-control. ' "Pull over, mate," I said to my colleague, Bruce the Goose, "a gust of wind and this building would come down faster than

86

Miss Australia's knickers after half a Fosters. We'd better alert the tenants." '

Dolores suddenly got the message. 'Shit man!' she cried, snapping out of her suggestive crouch with a suddenness that would have hospitalized a less supple person. 'We'd better get out of here!'

She zig-zagged unsteadily towards the door and would have been outside and on her way to safety had not Ken headed her off in time and grabbed her in an arm-lock.

'Plenty of time for that, darling,' he said, lifting her back into the room – Christ she was tasty though, this mad spade, hard, silky-firm; he'd throw one up her right now if it wasn't for the fellow in a gym-slip preening in a corner – 'plenty of time for that. But what you *do* need' – he kept the arm-lock on with one hand and started a leisurely body-search with the other – 'what you *do* need – Holy *Christ*! – as a matter of fucking *urgency*, however' – his right hand sped urgently over her thrusting breasts, palming and juggling them in turn, as though testing avocados for ripeness in a market, and then slid downwards across the smooth curve of her stomach, moving in for the full frontal delve between her thighs – 'Jes-*sus*! What you do need is a first-class fucking pebble-dashing job to protect you – ugggghh! – against the elements. Tch*oooo*!'

'We do?'

'That's right, darling.'

Placing himself behind her in the frog-march position, he lifted her across the room, like a window-dresser positioning a naked dummy, and bent her over Dawn's glass-topped dining-table from Peter Jones.

'But this is the eighth floor, man,' protested Dolores, rather indistinctly, since her face was jammed hard into the table-top.

'Set an example, darling.' His right hand played busily now in the warm tunnel of her thighs – 'fucking hell!' – while his left, being no longer required for the maintenance of the arm-lock, since she showed no inclination to throw him off (and anyway he had her pinned with the cunning application of a grape-vine hold on her left leg with his), moved down the silky valley of her

87

back towards her cheekily up-thrust buttocks. 'Set a fucking example. Someone's got to.'

'I suppose you're right.'

'Too fucking right I'm right!' Both hands had now achieved full penetration, front and back, and were pumping urgently in perfect synch. 'My colleague Bruce the Goose is outside with his pebble-squirting machine just waiting for the go-ahead. A signal from me – he'll point his nozzle up here and let fly. Whoosh! Rocks. Cement. Shit. Dead rats. When my colleague Bruce the Goose has finished the fucking *owner* of this block won't recognize it!'

'Wow.'

'So. Do we have a deal!' Ken removed his left, buttock-probing hand and slid it round to join his right for the full, two-handed frontal goose. 'It's a monkey on the table and another monkey spread over six months. Easy terms. What do you say?'

'I guess it's the sensible thing to do, then.'

'Too right, darling!' Without releasing his grape-vine hold, Ken, by leaning gymnastically sideways, managed to reach his trousers and, with his left hand produce a contract from a pocket, while his right hand didn't falter in its rhythmic clitoral massage. 'Sign here.'

'That's better,' said Dawn, opening the bedroom door, 'I feel much more sex ... GOD ALMIGHTY! That's not very nice!' It seemed to her that her friend Dolores, naked over the dining-room table, was being penetrated from behind by a tall stranger so devoid of *savoir-faire* as to have removed his trousers only, attending to her in his cowboy-boots and boxer-shorts. 'Here! I've got to eat my dinner off that table tonight!' She appealed to Eddie, who, among the present company, seemed for once to be the most innocently occupied. 'Eddie! What's going on here?'

'It's Mobile Models, Pornography in the Home, Daimler Hire and the building's falling down,' said Eddie.

'Do *what*? You're never Daimler Hire, young man! And where might your trousers be? We'll have nothing explicit here, if you please. Are you from the Continent or what?'

Ken, looking up, was so enraptured by the sight of Dawn that he released his right, buttock-delving hand and held it out in greeting, continuing to goose Dolores only with the left.

'Christ darling!' he cried. 'You were worth waiting for and no mistake. Allow me to introduce myself. Pardoe International. Call me Ken.'

Unable to believe the evidence of her eyes, Dawn reached for her glasses and, vanity forgotten, together with the fact that they were for short rather than long-range work, put them on. The obscene display was still there, but happily somewhat blurred around the edges.

Ken was captivated. Here was a top-drawer moll and no mistake. The spade was okay, no complaints, but a bit of a push-over, a trifle lacking in feminine modesty and restraint. He liked molls to be decently reserved, to hold out for half an hour or so. This one looked the type, real class, with a haughty fucking look in her eyes behind those mad specs. To get this one's gear off finesse would be required. It was an occasion for his most sophisticated opening line. He abandoned Dolores and moved in Dawn's direction.

'Here. Don't I know you, darling? You're that mad Italian movie star. . . .'

'*Piss* off!'

Dawn could scarcely believe her ears. Last person to use that tired routine had been a bald old disco-hustler claiming to be Jack Nicholson. Joke was it *had* been Jack Nicholson.

'No! Don't tell me! Simone . . . Sylvana . . . got it! Claudia. . . .'

'Stroll on!'

'And don't you deny it, darling! This is my lucky day and no mistake. Here I've stumbled quite by chance on two top movie stars living together incognito!'

'Dolores! Who *is* this clown?'

'He's Ken, man,' said Dolores, still bent double over the table, waiting patiently for the resumption of her modelling career, her buttocks tipped invitingly upwards like those of a sprinter at the starting-line. 'Ken – this is Dawn.'

'*Dawn*,' cried Ken, sorting with disbelief. '*Dawn*? Don't jerk me off here, darling. That's just her fucking aliarse for smudging the paparellis!'

After a quick flip through his bulging wallet, he now produced his best card, the one kept in reserve precisely for occasions such as this, and handed it to Dawn.

'My card, darling. Pardoe International Productions Inc. Hollywood, Rome and Hong-fucking-Kong.' He narrowed his eyes craftily and dropped into his race-course tipster's, for-your-ears-only routine. 'Over here between ourselves from LA on the search for two top types. You could be the ones, yes sir. This I have to get on film.'

Dawn let out a shriek of horror. 'You're not filming here, young man!' She wasn't having that. She'd been caught like that before. Trusting a fellow once – he'd been to public school and that – she'd been persuaded to pose for some Polaroids. Next thing she'd known she'd been showing her tits on the cover of one of them dirty magazines. All right, that sort of thing, for topless models and *Sun* Page 3 girls. If they didn't mind married men wanking secretly over their pictures in the bathroom after breakfast, that was their business. But she had her self-respect.

Ken ignored her. He took up his instamatic and, oblivious to her cries of protest, began to snap away at random, bending slightly at the knees, shooting upwards from the squat, as he'd seen professional photographers do. Dawn – eager to intervene decisively but equally keen to stay out of focus – was forced to dart in and out, snatching vainly at the camera, but Eddie, intrigued by all this activity across the room, tried to get into the picture – 'Fuck off Phyllis or you'll get the toe of my boot up your arse!' – while Dolores, delighted to be back at work, went at once into her old routine, leering crazily and bending her body into its full repertoire of suggestive squats and thrusts.

'Fantastic!' cried Ken. 'Spot on perfect! Now, I want you to imagine that you're making love to the camera!'

Dolores responded by leaning backwards into a limbo-crouch, hovering gymnastically just off the floor, inching towards Ken, making it seem likely that he and his camera would be swept into the dark mysteries of the huge V formed by her advancing thighs.

'You've got it, babe!' he growled, stepping back a pace for safety's sake. He'd seen a documentary on ITV starring Lord Lichfield, so he wasn't strapped, thank God, for the appropriate patter. The spade would never spot a phoney, but the fiery one, glaring at him through those mad specs, hopping out of camera-range each time he swung in her direction, would sus a bull-shitter a mile away. He must keep the chat *ultra*-fucking sophisticated, cool, classy, Lichfield-suave. 'Great, babe! Too much! Now – I want you to run your hands down towards your cunt and veeee-ry gently. . . .'

Dawn, utterly aghast, had had enough. She stepped forward and, her fear of being photographed forgotten, planted herself squarely between Dolores and the crazily snapping Ken.

'Cut that *out*, you great Australian clown! Dolores! Stop that daft posing about the place. And put your knickers on! You look . . . you look. . . .' Crouched for the scorpion thrust, the most venomous, the most instantly lethal insult in her repertoire, she suddenly uncoiled it. 'You look like a fucking *model*, for Christ's sake!'

She seized Dolores by the shoulders and shook her so hard her brain must have pinged inside her skull like a pellet hitting a spittoon. Dolores, bending at the knees as though from a short, mind-scrambling tap to the jaw, grabbed Dawn round the waist and held on, their sudden Sumo-like proximity causing Ken to yelp and hop about the room, cursing with excitement.

'Fucking *hell*! You've got it at last! *That's* the shot I want. I tell you, when Spielberg sees this set he'll do his fucking lot! Yes sir! Now, Dolores, I want you to grab Big Dawn as if you're fucking *enraged*!'

Dolores, her brain unscrambling, took Dawn in a hold and scrummaged her, spitting protests, against the sofa, tipping her, legs in the air, over its arm. 'Hey man,' she cried, straddling the furiously bucking Dawn, 'are these for *Harpers*

Queen, then?'

'You know it! *Harpers Queen*, yes sir!' Ken moved in for a close-up, zooming in so tightly that his camera disappeared between Dolores's magnificent upturned buttocks, glistening like toffee-apples, perfectly rounded. 'Front fucking cover!'

'*Harpers Queen* my foot,' gasped Dawn, squirming helplessly under Dolores's enormous weight. 'Get *off* me, you great black loon! *Harpers Queen*! Lonely wives section of *Fiesta*, more like!'

Ken was on fire. Holy shit, why didn't he have a film in his camera? This was the maddest scene he'd had since Malcolm Fraser's political beach-party back in '76 when he'd got a half-nelson on Miss New South Wales and Bruce the Goose had got likewise on her chaperone and they'd both gone for the violet crumble behind a sand-dune. They'd been molls, though. Low-life broads. This was a different situation. Dawn was a classy bird, a top-drawer type. He had her leaning his way and he mustn't blow it now. He must keep the tone ultra-sophisticated.

'Fantastic!' he cried. 'Now, Dolores, I want you to put your hand inside her blouse and grab her tits!'

'You've got it, man!'

'Incredible! Now. Get her fucking skirt off!'

Dawn screamed but Dolores had her pinned. Whipping her over on to her front, she unzipped her down the back and removed her skirt with one deft tug. When Ken saw the Janet Reger underwear he swore with delight, quite drowning out Dawn's cries of fury.

'Jesus fucking Christ! Will you cop those mad brown fucking silky thighs!'

He'd been a hundred per cent that this one would be sensational without her gear. She had that smooth over-all fucking crazy nectarine-like bloom that had made her seem suggestively naked even *in* her gear. He must keep his head now. One false move and you could lose these dee-mure, ultra-classy English sheilas. You had to keep it light, keep them guessing.

'Now. Get those mad knickers off and bite her in the box!'

Dolores peeled the Janet Regers off with the deft expertise of a fisherman skinning a skate, but outrage that they should have been removed by anyone but Toby gave Dawn the strength to heave Dolores to the floor with one maddened shove.

'Get fucking *off* me, you great cackling loon!'

She struggled up and went in search of her clothes, whimpering with indignation, while Ken, his loins in an uproar, and quite unimpressed by her apparent coyness – they all liked it really, these haughty top-drawer English sheilas, only the day before he'd speared his tongue straight up a Sloane Ranger within minutes of pulling her in the Health Juice Bar at Harrods – began to track her round the room.

'Here,' screamed Dawn, backing away and trying to put her knickers on at the same time, a perilous manoeuvre, making it seem likely that she'd up-end herself plumb in his path. 'Don't you get busy with me, young man!'

'Come on, darling,' chortled Ken, delighted that she was putting up more resistance than the spade had, 'stop pulling my prick here!'

'Pulling your . . . oh! . . . how *dare* you?'

'Come on! Tell me who you *really* are. Christie Brinkley? Jerry Hall? Cheryl Tiegs? Lauren Hutton? Margott fucking Hemingway? You can't fool me! No sir! You're both top models, aren't you? Admit it now, you rascal!'

The slander stopped Dawn dead in her tracks. '*Models*? *Us*? *Models*? How *dare* you suggest such a thing!' She was crouched, fists clenched, spitting with rage. Ken began to suspect, for the first time, that something had gone wrong. Doubts gathered heavily in his mind, dragging at his confidence, anchoring him foolishly in no-man's-land.

'Only after a little fun, darling.'

'Fun! You've come to the wrong place for that, *darling*. This is a brothel.' She started to get dressed.

'Stone me!'

'That's right. We're call-girls, us, and we expect to be treated as such.'

'I. . . .'

'And we're not attainable at the moment. You want to get more *au fait* with the English way of doing things, *darling*.'

Ken, utterly bewildered, still wearing the silly half-smile of a man who's run aground, was trying to work this one out – was it a smart new brush-off line, perhaps, one he'd not come across before? – when there was a loud ring at the front door.

'It's them!' wailed Dolores. 'The fuzz!'

Ken reacted to the word 'fuzz' as though a thunder-flash had gone off between his legs. Wild-eyed and spinning on the spot, searching for a blunt instrument to crack down on the head of any uninvited constable, he grabbed a table-lamp and sprang towards the door, in the process disconnecting the lamp so violently from its socket in the wall that its long extension-lead, snaking across the carpet, whipped Steady Eddie's legs from under him – 'Sorry Phyllis' – bringing him crashing to the floor.

'Good grief, calm *down*!' screamed Dawn. 'What's the matter with you all? And put that lamp down, you great prat. It's my car, isn't it!'

She walked over to the front door and opened it to Fred the porter, who took in the scene with one impassive sweep of the room. Nothing unusual here. Miss Dolores in the nude, a gentleman without his trousers brandishing a table-lamp, and another gentleman in a gym-slip and white socks, writhing on the floor, clearly the victim of some new bondage technique. He'd seen it all before.

A discreet clearing of the throat behind the hand. 'Ahum. It's your car, madam.'

'Thank you, Fred. Tell him I'll be there in a minute, will you?'

'Very good, madam.' Fred withdrew, his face an uncensorious blank.

'Right,' said Dawn, turning to Dolores. 'Are you coming with me or what? If you are, get your gear on quick. I'm late already, aren't I?'

'Think I'll hang on for a while,' said Dolores, who was slumped on the sofa once again, brought down by the shocks of the last few seconds. 'Get my head together and then split. Okay?'

This seemed a very bad idea to Dawn, but a glance at Steady Eddie, whose frantic efforts to unwind himself had only caused the extension-lead to hold him more tightly in its coils, convinced her that waiting for these two would make her unpardonably late for her appointment.

'Oh shit, I suppose so,' she said doubtfully. 'Not much option, have I?' She turned to Ken. 'Right, Ned Kelly. You're coming with me. So put your trousers on.'

'But darling, uncompleted business with. . . .'

'Look! Do I have to spell it out? You – are – leaving. *Now.*'

Ken got the picture. There was no mistaking the authority in this one's voice. Big Dawn knew the score. If he wanted to keep an entrée here he'd do well to retire gracefully while he was still ahead. He'd made an impact, no doubt of that, and he'd be a fool to foul it up now by outstaying his welcome. He urgently wanted to throw one up this mad, fiery Dawn. Perhaps he'd manage it going down in the lift. They liked it in lifts, these posh English sheilas. Christ, he'd had an auntie coming up. Forgotten all about her. What number had she said she lived at? Didn't matter. It was Dawn he wanted. He'd hand her a new line in the lift. Something a trifle more substantial, perhaps. What did he have left? Merchant banker? Property tycoon? Film director? She'd been leaning his way when he'd mentioned Spielberg. Art dealer? Literary agent?

'Right, captain,' he said. 'You're the boss, yes sir.' He threw his arms up in surrender, the gesture, since he was still holding the table-lamp, once again up-ending Steady Eddie – 'Sorry Phyllis!' – who had just managed to struggle, trussed like a parcel, to his feet. 'On my way. Yes sir!' He put his trousers on and then pulled one last card from his pocket, handing it to Dolores. 'Another of my services, darling. The Ken Pardoe International Literary Agency. Any time you want to write your meemores, just let me know.' That would impress Big Dawn. 'Represented in Beverly Hills, New York, Paris, Rome, Toronto and. . . .'

'Come *on,*' screamed Dawn.

'Ta,' said Dolores.

'So long, then, sweetheart.' He gave her a big wink.

'Bye darling. Keep in touch.'

'You know it!' Ken glanced at Steady Eddie, writhing in desperation now, like an escapologist whose act has gone disastrously wrong. 'Bye Phyllis.'

'Yeah. Shit.'

'Okay,' said Dawn. 'I must be mad to leave you here. Don't let *anyone* in. Understand?' She looked pointedly at Ken.

'Got it. No one in.'

'Come on then, Jolly Roger. And grab that.' Dawn pointed to a small black case of the sort that a country physician in the old days might have carried on his rounds.

'What's that, then?'

'My props, isn't it?'

'I *knew* it!' cried Ken in triumph, picking up the case and following Dawn into the passage. 'You *are* a top fucking actress! Darling this *is* your lucky day! I happen to have lobbed from Paris on the search. . . .'

As Dawn closed the door behind them, Dolores lit a joint, which she found abandoned in an ashtray almost unsmoked, then, getting to her feet, she swayed towards the sound-system, on the way stepping over Steady Eddie, who was hopelessly enmeshed now, flopping around pitifully like a mackerel at the bottom of a boat.

'Think I'll put some sounds on,' she said.

'Great. *Hell*.'

Dolores chose a disco-tape and, having slotted it into the deck, began to dance in front of the mirror, self-absorbed, hardly moving, admiring her body, running her hands lovingly over its surfaces.

'What do you reckon, then?'

' 'Bout what?'

'That fellow. Literary agent. Think he liked me? I quite fancy the idea of being a writer, me.'

'Seemed like a nice guy. Shit. I'm in trouble here.'

'Yeah. I'd definitely like to be a writer.' Dolores tried out a series of writer's poses, stroking and fingering her declivities, as writers will, but froze with sudden horror when a loud scratching noise outside the front-door suggested that someone was trying to open it with the wrong key.

'Oh Christ! It's them! *Must* be.'

'Guess you're right.'

'Hide yourself!'

Dolores ran to turn the music off and was about to conceal herself behind the sofa when she noticed Eddie squirming at her feet. Bending down she plucked him off the carpet and running with him like a caber tossed him into the bedroom, returning just in time to squat behind the sofa before the front door opened.

Toby walked in, a huge cigar clamped between his teeth, puffing slightly under the weight of loot acquired at the German Food Centre, but in the best of spirits. He'd prevailed up west, acquitted himself brilliantly out-of-doors, in daylight too: something he hadn't done since he'd suddenly realized some years before that nearly all the nastiness in life happens during office hours and that by refusing to acknowledge the world between 9 a.m. and 6 p.m. a great deal of unpleasantness – accountants' meetings, phone-calls from banks, nuns collecting, special deliveries, shopping with women, meeting babies – could be avoided. He was a little tired, of course, and looking forward to a nap, but first he must make an important call. He put down his parcels, walked over to the telephone and dialled a number.

'Hullo. Hullo. Lord Delfont, please. Mr Danvers. Toby Danvers. Thank you.'

While Toby waited, Dolores, realizing who it was, came out of hiding, a hand aloft to slap him on the back.

'In a meeting? Well get him out of it, my good woman. Yes of course it's important. It's not my habit to waste time on trivialities.'

Dolores approached silently from behind, her hand beginning its descent.

'Bernard, my dear fellow, I just wanted to say – BOLLOCKS!'

The impact of her greeting caused Toby's cigar to fly from his mouth like a missile, he dropped the phone and spun round, fists up.

'Hi man,' said Dolores, collapsing on the sofa, 'it's only me.'

Toby peered down at her. 'So it is. Well well.' He lowered his fists. 'What's your game? Creeping up behind a fellow's back? Gave me the devil of a turn. Been mugged from behind today already. Damn lucky I didn't knock you cold. Captain of Boxing at Shrewsbury. Don't mention it much.'

'Sorry man. Thought you were old Bill didn't I?'

'Yes? Why's that?' Toby recovered his cigar from the floor and, quite forgetting his important phone-call, sat down next to Dolores on the sofa, placing his cigar beside her joint in the ashtray. 'Expecting a visit, are we?'

'It's Pyle, isn't it? Running through doors and that?'

'How tiresome of him. But don't you worry, my dear. You're quite safe here.' He patted Dolores reassuringly on the knee. 'He won't come running through our door, I assure you. Dawn has made certain . . . er . . . *investments*, you understand? Not for us to know the details, of course.'

'No good, man,' said Dolores miserably. 'Pyle can't be straightened, can he?'

'Really? That is bad. Still, plenty of time to worry about him later. Sufficient unto the hour, what?' He picked up Dolores's joint and pulled on it deeply. 'Damn good cigars, these. Get them at the German Food Centre in Knightsbridge. Well, it's been a long day. Bit whacked, to tell the truth. Got mugged, do you see? Think I'll have an early night.' He tried to get to his feet, but gave up after three attempts. 'Give a chap a hand, will you, my dear?'

Dolores, now smoking the cigar, helped Toby to his feet.

'Thank you, my dear,' he said, walking unsteadily towards the bedroom. 'Legs not what they were, do you see? Ankles swollen like blood-puddings. Strong as dancers' in the old days, but now, alas. . . .' He opened the bedroom door and disappeared inside, leaving Dolores muttering to herself on the sofa.

'Yeah. I'd really like to be a writer, me.'

After a minute or two, the bedroom door opened and Toby emerged. He returned to the sofa, still smoking the joint, and sat down looking thoughtful.

'Hi,' said Dolores. 'Quick nap. Feeling better?'

'Indeed, indeed,' said Toby vaguely. He shook his head and passed a hand across his eyes.

'Great.'

'I say.'

'Yeah?'

'Between the two of us, there's some fellow in a gym-slip trussed like a chicken on the bed.'

'Right.'

'Ah! You knew.' Toby looked relieved. 'Afraid I might be seeing things. Funny thing exhaustion. Been up all day, do you see? Client of yours, is he? Should have twigged you were in the middle of something, sitting there without your clothes. Clumsy of me. Must apologize.'

'No. Eddie, isn't it?'

'*Really*? Good gracious! I'd no idea he went in for that sort of thing. Funny old world. Not for us to criticize, of course.'

Dolores, pondering her new ambitions, wasn't listening.

'Yeah. That's it. I'll be a writer. Do my memoirs.'

Toby, still puffing at the joint, nodded politely. 'Why not indeed? Many have. Mynah Bird. Sir Robert Mark.'

'Met this fellow just now,' said Dolores. 'Literary agent, wasn't he? Don't know how to reckon him. Left me his card.'

'Perhaps I should have a look,' said Toby. 'Know a thing or two about literary agents.'

'Sure. Here.' Dolores handed Toby the card that Ken had left.

'Let's see. "The Ken Pardoe Litery Agency Worldwide". Hm. Spelling not a hundred per cent. Perhaps he's dyslexic. Could be a disadvantage in a literary agent, I suppose. Ah – what's this? He seems to have left a message on the back. "I'd love to talk to you about your career, darling, but right now I want to fuck your brains out." Well, I hardly know what to think. He certainly expresses himself unambiguously enough. The direct approach. I like that in a man.'

'Here. You could help me. If I wrote my memoirs. With the words and that.'

'It would be my privilege, naturally, my dear,' said Toby. 'But – just a thought, you understand – with your looks, well, frankly I'd stick to acting. Become a movie star. A household name, perhaps.'

Dolores was unimpressed. She pulled a face.

'No. I've done film work, me. Met Lewis Collins and that.'

'Of course. Say no more.'

'Mind you.' Dolores had had a sudden thought. 'You could help me with that too. You were in showbusiness.'

Toby was appalled. '*Were* in showbusiness? *Were* in showbusiness? Oh dear, oh dear. Allow me to correct you. . . .'

'Sorry.' Dolores was accustomed to Toby's pedagogic ways, having been present on many occasions when Dawn had had to endure small lectures. 'Was in showbusiness. You was in showbusiness.'

'No no. You quite misunderstand me. I wasn't correcting your grammar. Wouldn't presume. No no. It was your use of the past tense to which I took exception. I *am* in showbusiness, my dear. Or rather the live theatre. There is a difference, you know.'

'Yeah? Doing anything now, are you?'

'There's my museum.'

'Right. Dawn told me. Bit spooky, if you ask me.'

'And there's my revival.'

'Yeah? Feeling better, are you?'

'Of a play. *Satan's Daughter*. But not a word to Dawn, you understand. A grand girl in every respect – pure gold, in fact – but not *of* the theatre, if you understand me.' Toby patted Dolores confidentially on the knee, including her in the magic fellowship. 'Not one of *us* in that respect. I can rely on your discretion?'

'I'm cool.'

'They think it can't be done, do you see?' Toby began to work himself into an indignation at the memory of the cretinous reception *Satan's Daughter* had received on its last outing. 'Bone-heads! Philistines! Mor . . . by jove! Can you lend me a tenner?'

'Some revival, man!'

'No no. A different matter. I left this taxi downstairs with the metre running. Better make it fifteen.'

'I don't know,' said Dolores. 'Vice Squad breaking down doors at all hours, Drugs Squad doing their thing, Dawn the only person hustling and you're driving round London in a taxi. Doesn't seem right to me.'

'In a good cause, my dear, in a good cause. It just so happens that I've been negotiating a substantial deal over lunch at the Ivy. An angel from. . . .'

'Here,' interrupted Dolores. 'Dawn said you were being interviewed. For a teaching job.'

Toby started guiltily. 'Ah – well, yes. I – er. . . .'

'I don't know. Dawn out hustling her arse off for you and you're living it up at the Ivy!'

'Not living it up, my dear. Securing a capital advance. This angel from the old days. And he very much liked my concept. He'll be taking up two units towards the initial capitalization, if I'm not very much mistaken. After lunch at the Ivy it is not customary for a gentleman to depart on a bicycle. Hence the taxi. You don't suppose Lord Delfont pedals himself home after lunch at his club, do you? Good gracious! I was speaking to him on the phone. Said bollocks to him.'

'He'll have had that said to him before.'

'More than likely. However. . . .' Toby got up and picked the receiver off the floor. 'Hullo! Hullo! Damn fellow seems to have hung up. Typical. Oh well.'

'There you are.'

Toby sat down again. 'About that twenty-five pounds, then?'

'Sorry darling. Haven't got a bean. Honest. I told you. Dawn the only person hustling, Pyle busting down. . . .'

Toby nodded towards the bedroom. 'What about Eddie?'

'What!' Dolores raised her eyes ceilingwards. 'You're joking! Gave him his allowance Monday. He'd spent it Tuesday having a facial. Men! Know what I mean?'

'I certainly do. Not working, eh?'

Dolores let out a snort of derision. '*Working*? What are you saying, man? Eddie was unemployed in 1977, before it was fashionable. *Work*? Never has. No – I'm wrong. Needed cash urgently once. Got a job on a building-site. Carrying bricks up a ladder. Ony lasted ten minutes.'

'My word. That's not long. Why was that?'

'When he got to the top of the ladder he just stood there. "Yes?" said the brickie. "Well?" said Eddie. "Well what?" said the brickie. "What do you say when I bring you your bricks, then?" said Eddie. The brickie stared at him. "You say thank you," said Eddie. "Fuck *off*!" said the brickie, and he pushed Eddie off the ladder, didn't he? Hasn't worked since.'

'I'm not sure I altogether blame him. A most disagreeable experience.'

'Mind you,' continued Dolores. 'I tried to get him into the family business once.'

'What? Yours?'

'No. Eddie's. Hustling, isn't it?'

'Really? I'd no idea. His mother on the game, is she?'

'No. His father. Greek Street. Fourth floor. Miss Fatima, isn't he? Young Turkish model.'

'You astound me! What a ball-breaker for his clients, though. When they discover Miss Fatima's a fellow.'

'Don't suppose they ever do. Turkish method, isn't it?'

'Of course, of course. Er – what's that then?'

'Discipline, isn't it? Followed by relief. All diddle each other senseless, the Turks, don't they?'

'Is that so? Probably accounts for their poor showing in the Eurovision Song Contest.'

'Yeah. You may be right. Anyway. Quick in and out, isn't it? Don't suppose Eddie's father ever has to take his gear off.'

'I'm with you. Still. Suppose a punter – persistent little man, let's say – not *au fait* with the Turkish preference, has other ideas. Respectable little fellow, insurance salesman from the provinces, let's suppose. Wears brown nylon socks with a motif up the side, do you see? Been looking forward all year to his trip to London. He's read the literature on Soho, saved up, got into shape. He comes to town, randy as hell, heart beating like a road drill, creeps up Greek Street, dives in and climbs to the fourth floor. Bangs his money on the table and demands that Miss Fatima reveals all. Miss Fatima demurs, for reasons that our friend could never guess. But he persists. Miss Fatima finally accedes to his demands. Strips off. Reveals all. Nasty. Hell of a shock. Hardly like to think about it. The mind recoils.'

'Here. I don't suppose Eddie's father's that bad.'

'Indeed not. But he's been saving up all year, do you see? Pumped up with desire. Been reading the literature. Nothing there about the Turks. Still. That's how knowledge advances. Our expectations thwarted. The refutation of our theories. Popper, my dear.'

'No thanks,' said Dolores. 'Not while I'm smoking. Give me palpitations, don't they? Care for a pull?'

Dolores handed the cigar to Toby, who was still drawing deeply on the joint.

'No thanks,' he said. 'Very rarely do. Have to keep my wits about me in my game. Can't afford to forget things. Mind like a lobster-pot, thank God. Once in, nothing can escape.'

'How you going to pay it off, then?'

'Pay what off?'

'The taxi, man.'

'Bless my soul! Forgot all about it! Have to get a sub from Dawn, I suppose.'

Toby struggled to his feet and started to bang around the flat, opening and shutting doors, bellowing for Dawn.

'Drat,' he said at last. 'She doesn't seem to be here.'

'Right.'

'You don't happen to know where she is, I suppose?'

'Dolphin Square, isn't she?' said Dolores. 'Hitting a guy's prick with a ruler.'

'Ah. The Belgian method, no doubt.'

'No. English, isn't it?'

'Of course, of course. Damn. A bit tricky, this. Don't like to duck my obligations. Not the way I was brought up. Just have to sit it out till she gets back, I suppose. Rather a lot on the clock by then. Still, can't be helped. Bit whacked, as it happens. Think I'll have an early night. Got mugged, do you see?'

Toby turned and walked towards the bedroom, but fell asleep in mid-stride, being unconscious before he hit the floor.

3.50 p.m. Dolphin Square.

In his flat in Drake House, Dolphin Square, Nigel Mount-Hugh MP, hawk, patriot and resident of the real world – bathed, talced and Bruted here and there – stood in naked self-communion before the bedroom mirror. Not an unattractive body for a man of forty-nine, he thought. A little fleshy at the waist, perhaps, but on the whole it was a figure to be proud of. He turned round to view his backside in the mirror. Shanks getting a trifle reedy, but the buttocks, thank God, were still as firm as footballs. Poor old Norman had just had his bottom lifted for the third time, or so the backbench rumour went. Now a smoking-room wag was putting it about that every time he sat down his hat fell off. Poor old Norman. Charming fellow, you had to like him, but no steel, weak as water.

He turned back to face the mirror, his hands straying to his parts, gathering and stroking. His heart beat a little faster, but no erection came. The chain of events leading up to this bleak moment of pre-coital gloom were always the same, thought Mount-Hugh, and yet it always took him unawares. First would come the restlessness one day in the early afternoon, a vague inability to concentrate, unidentifiable at first as the onset of solipsistic lust. Then the feeling focused and settled in the loins, or more precisely in the mind, which refused suddenly to function normally until he'd made that phone-call – a phone-call leading directly to this moment of remorse and apprehension. With Miss Bark out of the room, a hand, not his own, the hand of a stranger without ego or self-respect, a jittery weak-willed lurker who took hold of him from time to time, not the hand of the devoted husband and respected politician, this other damp trembling hand would reach for the private line and a call would go through to Dawn. Once the arrangements had been made, the original symptoms – racing pulse, scattered thoughts, talking and swallowing out of synch – would vanish instantly, to be replaced by feelings of regret and foolishness. For the next twenty-four hours his swings in mood from elation to despair – one moment wishing the engagement had never been made, the next impatiently counting the minutes to its resolution – would be so violent as to make him fear that he might be going mad. But never for a second, once that call had been made – and this was what always confounded him – would he experience the slightest tug of sexual interest. This was the worst moment, waiting for Dawn to arrive. He wasn't in the least aroused, the prospect of sex wasn't so much unalluring as meaningless, yet nothing else had any substance. His normal concerns seemed quite unreal. If the Prime Minister herself rang now, he'd impatiently get her off the line, her words a mad intrusion. He wasn't himself, of course. It wasn't the member for West Wiltshire and contributor to the *Sunday Express*'s opinion page about to do these things; it was that other weak self-abusing creature sweating in his brain.

He shook his head to clear it of morbid thoughts. He couldn't back out now, even if he wanted to. He was out of control. Out of control, but stationary, with the will to move neither backwards nor forwards. He was disconnected but fixed, held in a limbo from which only the arrival of Dawn would release him. Meanwhile, what should he wear? The duck-egg blue jacket in Italian silk he'd bought in Bond Street and never worn? Sarah had said it would better become a Cypriot ponce. No, he wouldn't wear a jacket. It was warm enough for an open-neck shirt and lightweight trousers, a casual and debonaire ensemble, but cut appropriately for a man of his age. You wouldn't catch him making a laughing-stock of himself in jeans with a medallion round his neck. No, he played to his strengths, offering an image of experience, of knowing what the world was about. An older man, a man of power, could be attractive. That, no doubt, was why the girls liked him so much, why they were always glad to see him.

He dressed quickly, feeling more cheerful, and then went into the small, rudimentarily appointed sitting-room. Sarah preferred to stay in the country with her labradors, so this was a bachelor flat, really, in which he did very little entertaining, except of the sort about to take place. And on the rare occasions that his daughter Angela stayed the night, she slept on the sofa here in the sitting-room. He glanced at his watch. Confound the girl, she was late already. At this rate he'd only have an hour with her before the BBC car arrived. Still, she was worth it. A trifle scatty as to time, but incomparable, in his experience, in other respects. You could take her anywhere – not that he did, of course. Far too great a risk for a man in his position. He did, however, occasionally show pictures of her to his friends – those of the same kidney as himself, sports in much the same boat and therefore with as much to lose through gossip. That was harmless enough. 'Dancer I know. What a raver!' And she was. That was the joy of it. She obviously enjoyed these assignations as much as he did. She made that perfectly obvious. She'd probably do it for nothing. An incomparable fantasist, her requirements dove-tailing perfectly with his own. Quite unlike all the other girls he'd tried. Once she'd sent over a friend of hers called Pretty Marie with a five-star recommendation (countless commercials and three appearances in *The Sweeney*). She'd indeed been lovely, no complaints on that score, but she couldn't stop talking. She'd brought her model photographs and made six phone-calls, one to her boyfriend! Nor had she been able to get the hang of the fantasy, showing, for an actress, a quite deplorable lack of imagination. And at one point, a telling moment in the scene, she'd suddenly hooted with laughter, as though the whole thing was some kind of low comedy. He'd never had this trouble with Dawn.

Outside the flat, Dawn took a deep breath, trying to get her act together before ringing the door-bell. He liked her to arrive in character, so to speak, the drama starting from the moment that she crossed the threshold rather than after some moments of sticky cocktail party chatter. Normally she preferred this too – saved time, apart from anything else – but for once she wasn't certain of her role. It was playing Jane Baker that had unsettled her. His requirements usually were quite straightforward. He liked her to be domineering from the start, barking out orders like a deranged animal trainer, sending him cringing into corners at the end of snarled instructions. She was supposed to be unrelentingly imperious, but Jane, bless her, was as imperious as Little Bo Peep. Why had he chosen *her*? Wouldn't say boo to a goose, Jane Baker. Perhaps he wanted some variation in the routine. Hell this was difficult. Should she, for instance, apologize for being late? Normally any kind of apology from her would be disastrously out of character, but Jane *would* apologize – it was her nature, wasn't it? – and Dawn was a perfectionist. Perhaps she should ask him why he'd chosen her. No, that would be wrong. He liked the drama to unfold spontaneously. Jane he'd asked for, and Jane he'd get. He was the customer. She'd tone down her usual performance slightly, raising the dominance level only if he showed signs of dissatisfaction. She stood outside the door practising a range of Jane Baker expressions, finally settling on a sort of semi-cross pout – the sweet Jane in a *rage* – and then she rang the bell.

'Ah, Miss Baker,' said Mount-Hugh. 'Do come in.'

'Hullo,' she said, in a demure, Jane Baker voice, not at all the haughty greeting he usually got. Then, playing it both ways, she handed him her case. 'Here. Take this.' That was the kind of brisk instruction that normally had him mewing with excitement.

'Of course, of course.'

He took her bag and, in a sort of footman's grovel, backed ahead of her into the sitting-room, where they stood uneasily eyeing one another, Mount-Hugh furtively, Dawn trying not to laugh. Better take the initiative, she thought, before she blew the whole number.

'Well?' she said. 'Are you just going to leave me standing here?'

Would Jane have said that? Why not? Jane was as entitled to sit down as anyone. No reason to leave her standing around just because she was sweet and reasonable and that.

'I'm *so* sorry. Please. Here.' Mount-Hugh ushered her to a chair and then cringed and hovered over her.

So he *did* want to be meek, as per usual. But how fierce would Jane be? Perhaps the old freak had confused her with the other Jane, the early evening nutcracker. Now she *would* give you a hard time. Hey, that wouldn't be bad, a hard time from the other Jane. The idea began to unsettle her rather, so she put it from her mind. None of her business to enjoy herself. She'd actually come once with a client in the early days, and the feeling of shame, of unprofessionalism still caused her to blush whenever she thought of it. Mount-Hugh continued to hover over her, gormless, eyes meekly on the carpet, definitely wanting to be ordered about, humiliated. But she wasn't Princess Anne on this occasion, barking at him as though he was one of her horses, causing him to buck and whinny with fear and pleasure. That had been nasty. Nasty but simple, and in her business nasty and simple was better than straight but time-consuming. They came quicker, the perverts. The straights kept stopping and asking what *you* wanted. Pain in the arse, that. What else could you be wanting but to get it over with and go home? Suddenly Mount-Hugh backed away and sat down on a chair on the other side of the room. He'd never done that before. Never been so defiant as to sit down uninstructed. Right. She'd chance her arm.

'Here,' she snapped. 'What do you think you're doing? Did I say you could sit down?'

He sprang up, mumbling apologies. That had worked, thank God. It would be plain sailing now. She'd do her Princess Anne. If he didn't seem to be enjoying it she'd tone it down a bit.

'Get me a drink,' she said.

'Er – yes, of course, Miss Baker. But' – slipping out of

character, almost his normal voice – 'haven't you forgotten something?'

Christ, what had she left out? A missing line, some crisp instruction? She was cross with herself. She didn't normally make mistakes. It was playing Jane Baker that was messing her up. Trouble was she *felt* like Jane Baker, couldn't work up the necessary venom. Perhaps Dolores had been right. Perhaps it *would* be easier with a fucking script. She'd never had to be prompted before. She looked hopefully at Mount-Hugh for inspiration, but his head was bowed, his eyes refusing to meet hers. Nothing for it but to ask.

'Sorry. What?'

'I'm still dressed' – his normal voice, a low aside, an impatiently repeated cue.

Shit, of course. How had she forgotten that? He liked to wait on her in the nude.

She recovered well. 'I was *coming* to that,' she said crossly, like an actress annoyed at being prematurely prompted. 'Take your clothes off.'

'Yes, Miss Baker.'

'Yes, ma'am!' She was doing better.

'Yes, ma'am.'

He cringed and mewed with pleasure, a ghastly sight. He might impress the Tory ladies at the Party Conference, but he didn't impress her. How did they get like this, these men? Decent enough people, probably, might seem quite attractive even, if met in other circumstances. Like that nice fellow, something important in the City, who came to her for half an hour every Monday morning at ten-thirty. Wanted to come at nine-thirty, but she wasn't having that. Liked to be bandaged like a mummy. Swathed from head to foot. Just his cock sticking out. She was a district nurse. Tossed him off. Afterwards he roared with laughter and went back to making executive decisions. Every Monday at ten-thirty. How had he got like that? Oh well. Off came Mount-Hugh's clothes now, quickly, shamefully, dropped in a corner. Then he stood in front of her, head bowed, waiting for the next instruction.

'Well?'

'Madam hasn't told me what she'd like to drink.'

What the hell. 'Champagne.'

Mount-Hugh looked a little startled (Dawn wasn't to know that he had just one bottle on the premises, saved specially for Angela's half-term) but he padded off obediently towards the kitchen.

'I've been rehearsing a new dance,' he said on his return. 'Would madam like to see it?'

Madam would like to throw up. She took a sip of champagne.

'It had better be good. You know what happens if it doesn't turn me on.'

'Yes' – a fearful whisper, the words lost in his manly chest.

'What? I can't hear you. And look at me when I'm talking to you.'

Jane would never have said that, but it was a good touch nonetheless. She'd never said that before. She'd keep that in.

'You'll punish me.' Saying the words caused Mount-Hugh's penis, until now hanging limply and ashamed, to shoot upwards as though released by a spring, a theatrical device for ejecting the Demon King into view from nowhere. 'I have some new music too,' he added.

'Good.'

'I was wondering, ma'am.'

'Yes?'

'Might I dance one evening for your friends?'

Good grief, that was new. No harm in his coming over one evening, she supposed. It would certainly give Toby a laugh. She wouldn't warn him. Just have Mount-Hugh spring through the door during *News at Ten*. And she could get Dolores and Eddie over. Yeah, might be a laugh. He'd have to pay of course. Double, probably, for inconveniencing so many people.

'I suppose so.'

'When?' He seemed very keen. Obviously his latest fantasy.

'Have to be tomorrow night,' she said.

'Oh dear – I'm not sure. . . .'

'Forget it then.'

'No no. Tomorrow night will be fine, ma'am.'

'Good. Ten o'clock. You know my address?'

'Yes, ma'am.'

'Right. Let's see your dance, then. And it had better be good. It's got to turn my friends on, hasn't it?'

Mount-Hugh walked over to the record player and put on Ravel's *Bolero*. A moment *en attitude*, a little jump and he was off, swooping and twirling heavily round the room, sometimes in time to the music, often not, a silly expression on his face, proud, rapt, self-adoring. She mustn't laugh. This was the hardest part. First time Pretty Marie had seen this she'd choked, fell to the floor clutching her sides, rolling around. Very unprofessional, Pretty Marie. She'd never been sent for again. Perhaps she was lucky at that.

'Oh God,' breathed Dawn, 'that's so sexy I can hardly bear to watch. What are you trying to do to me?'

She got up and took her skirt and blouse off. Normally she left her underwear on, but she couldn't risk the Janet Regers being touched, so she took these off as well. Too bad if Mount-Hugh felt upstaged no longer being the only naked person in the room. She groaned a bit and started to play with herself. Mount-Hugh was watching her, his little eyes alert now, checking that she wasn't faking. She squinted so that she couldn't see him properly. Impossible to look at him and not throw up or burst out laughing. Hey, that was a thought. She'd lose him as a client after tomorrow night, that was for sure. Toby would laugh so much Mount-Hugh would never speak to her again. Why hadn't she thought of that before? Never mind, she wouldn't be doing this for much longer anyway. Meanwhile, perhaps she should put her specs on. They'd certainly blurred the disgraceful sight of Dolores and that Australian cowboy. Golly, he'd been a character. Thank God Toby hadn't been at home. He was vulnerable to types like that, was her Toby. They'd be in business together by now, if Toby had been there. She wondered how his interview had gone. She *would* so like him to be a teacher. Nice, Steady. Respectable. She hoped everything was under control at the flat. She'd better get this nonsense over with. The shorter time she left Dolores in charge the better. How much longer could the dance go on? You couldn't tell with this sodding piece of music. Every time you thought it was coming to an end, off it went again, gathering momentum, droaning more insistently. Last week had been a doddle. He'd done the dance of the Sugar Plum Fairy with a rabbit on his head. She'd known that one, had been able to tell how long there was to go. She decided to bring matters to a head.

'I can't stand it any longer,' she said, getting up from her chair. 'I've got to fuck you!'

Mount-Hugh smirked coyly and danced out of reach. She was meant to act now like a sexually enraged punter at a floor-show, out of control, wound up past endurance, leaping over seats into the action. She closed in on him, but he backed away, simpering archly, evading her lunges with a girlish laugh. She tried to grab him, but he was slippery as a bar of soap, glistening from his exertions. Thank God she'd taken the Janet Regers off. Even so, she'd insist on having a bath after this. Normally she waited till she got home, but today she wanted to be sparkling fresh for Toby. As last she managed to back him into a corner, where he suddenly went docile. He'd met his match, his cowed, subservient posture an admission that you couldn't turn people on like this and duck the consequences.

'Go into the bedroom,' she said, 'and lie on the bed.' She gave him a little shove from behind which sent his sixteen stone sprawling on the carpet. He cowered there, looking up at her.

'Why? Why? What are you going to do?'

'I'm going to fuck you!'

'No! *Why?*'

'Because I *need* to!'

'I turned you on?' – an arch upward glance, a self-adoring smirk. Where had she seen that vile kittenish pout before? Was it Hannah Gordon? Diana Rigg? No, she had it. It was Felicity Kendall. She had a heavyweight Felicity Kendall grovelling at her feet. If his constituents could see him now. . . . Mind you, she was well liked in the suburbs, was Felicity.

'You drove me mad! And stand up! I hardly touched you.'

On all fours he skuttled backwards to the bedroom, fearful, it seemed, that she might help him on his way with the toe of her boot. Normally he liked to be left there in suspense for a while, but Dawn didn't have time to piss about today. She drained her glass of champagne, picked up her little visiting bag and followed him into the bedroom. He was standing in a corner, head bowed in shame.

'I thought I told you to lie on the bed?'

'Do I really have to?'

'Yes!'

He lay down on the bed, whimpering with apprehension.

'On your *front*!'

'No! Please! Anything but that!'

She seized him roughly and rolled him over, moaning but offering no resistance. Then she yanked his hands behind his back and tied them together with a piece of rope from her little bag. He whimpered all the time in protest at being used so roughly.

'What have I got here?' she said, taking a dildo from her bag and strapping it on.

'I don't know, ma'am.'

'Yes you do. *What*?' She lifted his arse into the air and slapped his buttocks, causing him to squeal with pleasure.

'You've got a big black prick!'

'That's right.' She was sitting astride him now, riding him like a porpoise in an aqua-show. 'And what am I going to do with it?'

'You're going to fuck me! But why? Why? What have I done to deserve it?'

'You've made me *mad* with desire! That's what you've done.'

'No no! Anything but that!'

'You can't stop me. You shouldn't have turned me on so much. That dance! Oh my God, I'm like an animal!' Was that going too far? She nearly giggled. Good thing he couldn't see her face. 'I'm going to fuck you up the arse!'

He bucked and writhed with pleasure, almost dislodging her.

'Quick,' he gasped, 'the phone!'

This bit always amazed her. She dialled the House of Commons and then leaned forward, like Piggott in a photo-finish, cradling the receiver into Mount-Hugh's chin, enabling him to speak into it, trussed helplessly though he was.

'Hullo, hullo,' he said, while Dawn began her rhythmic pumping, driving forward, like Piggott lifting his horse towards the line. 'The Prime Minister's Office, please.'

'Ugh! Ugh! Ugh!' cried Dawn, cracking his writhing buttocks with deft backward slaps. She should really be wearing spurs, she thought. Perhaps she'd get some.

'Hullo, Prime Minister? Mount-Hugh here. About that amendment to the Obscenity Bill.' He could talk quite rationally to his leader – if a trifle breathlessly – while Dawn drove deeply between his buttocks. The PM probably put the occasional gasps and gobblings down to nerves. And he never climaxed until he'd hung up.

'I'm going to fuck you like I've never fucked you before!' Dawn hissed in his ear.

'*Yes, sir! Yes, sir!* Er – no, Prime Minister. My assistant. . . .'

Sir? Dawn was so surprised that she nearly fell out of the saddle. He'd never called her 'sir' before. Suddenly the penny dropped. Why had she been so stupid? She'd fucked him up the arse as every grand lady in the land and all the time she'd never twigged that for him she was a man, and a black man at that! She was nothing but a substitute! Right! She'd really let him have it, Prime Minister or no Prime Minister on the line. Sodding racist! Blacks go home, indeed.

'Yes, Prime Minister. *Aaaagh!* Excuse me, Prime Minister, I dropped a. . . .'

'Next time,' hissed Dawn urgently into his ear, 'I'm coming round here with a huge black man!'

'*No!*' He quivered like a jelly from top to toe. 'We seem to have a bad line, Prime Minister. Some interference. I was going to say. . . .'

'Yes!' hissed Dawn. 'That's what you *really* want. An enormous black man having you up the arse!'

'*No*! Yes, a crossed line, Prime Minister. *Will I have to dance for him*? Sorry, Prime Minister. I expect they'll clear in a minute.'

'Yes. The Dance of the Sugar Plum Fairy. That was your best. It'll drive him *mad*.'

'*My God*! *Who*? No, Prime Minister, my secretary. . . .'

Christ, who? Dawn's mind went blank. She couldn't think of anyone black except Dolores and she wasn't even a man. Perhaps she could dress her up. No, she was far too dopey. She'd never get away with it. What about one of those footballers Toby made her watch in the winter on Saturday nights? Luther Blisset. What about him? No, Toby, a Watford supporter, wouldn't approve. Hell, who was that other one? Ah – she had it! She leaned forward in the saddle and breathed menacingly into Mount-Hugh's ear.

'Cyrille Regis!'

Christ, she'd hit the button. Mount-Hugh was gripped by a short seismic convulsion, and then lay still, moaning softly. Had he come? If he had, he'd kill her. That wasn't meant to happen while the PM was still on the line. No, all was well. He suddenly lifted his head and continued with the conversation.

'My feelings are, Prime Minister, that the average man, on going into his local newsagent for a packet of Woodbines or his *Sporting Life*, simply doesn't want to be confronted by. . . .'

'Justin Fashanu!'

'AAAAAAAHHHHHGGGHGGGHHHH!'

Mount-Hugh had done something perhaps no man had ever done before. He had climaxed, royally, right in the ear of the Prime Minister seated in her private office at the House of Commons. He roared and gasped and bucked and reared. The room shook. Dawn was tossed, shrieking, to the floor.

4.00 p.m. Westbourne Grove.

'What do you reckon, then?' asked D/C Harris.

'Fucking wank, isn't it?' said D/C Smiley. He and Harris

were in position in their car outside Dolores's flat in Westbourne Grove. 'Pyle's off his sodding rocker. Plus we've drawn the wrong address. I could give that Big Dawn one, as it happens. Still, as long as we're there for the bust.'

'Think we'll be paying her a visit, then?'

'It's a million. Pyle's got that look in his eye. Anyway, I've got to make a call. Keep an eye out, right?'

Smiley climbed out of the car and walked to a nearby phone-box. He stepped inside and dialled his colleague, Honest John the Thief.

'John? Kevin here. Listen, I can't make the meet tonight. That berk Pyle's only got us on sodding tart surveillance, hasn't he? Yeah. What do you mean, sounds all right? I'm sat like a lemon in my car outside a spook's flat in Westbourne Grove, aren't I? Now listen. Snipey's out. Yeah. Thought that would shake you. But here's the good news. He's only asking for twenty grand. Reckon we owe him twice that amount, right? Plus I've got a plan to tuck him up again. He's half out of his box looking for some theatrical con-man who did him over a few years ago. Now, the joke is I know this chap's address. He's only living with one of the tarts we're watching, right? No, of course I haven't told Snipey yet. Can't have him running in there in the middle of the bust, can I? I'll tip him in *after* we've spun the place. He'll tear the arms off this dodgey theatrical and draw another eight years, right? Yeah. Thought you'd like it. I'm meeting him at the Water Rat tomorrow morning. So steer clear yourself. Yeah, better leave this to me. *Course* we'll have to give him the twenty grand, you dozey berk. He must think we're on the up and up else he'll drop us in it after he's torn the arms off the bent theatrical, right? Yeah. Talk to you tomorrow after the meet with Snipey. Bye.'

Smiley walked back to the car feeling well pleased with himself.

4.05 p.m. Nell Gwynn House.

Back at the flat, Toby snored peacefully on the floor, while

Dolores searched, with increasing signs of panic, through her bag. Suddenly the bedroom door opened and Eddie hopped out, still coiled in the extension-lead. He had, by furious contortions on the bed, at last managed to slide it down his trunk, with the result that he now had his hands free but was still hobbled from upper thigh to ankle.

'Oh hi,' said Dolores. 'Here. We've got a problem.'

'Yeah?'

'Yeah. I've run out of stuff.'

'Wow.'

'Better get some more. Think Mad Harry would let us score on credit? I could pay tomorrow?'

'Yeah. Why not?'

'Right,' said Dolores. 'Let's split then.'

'Think we should wake Toby?'

'He'll be all right.' Dolores had once roused Toby unexpectedly and had suffered minor injuries in the ensuing exchange.

'Right.' Eddie hopped towards the tape-deck but half-way across the room was knocked to the floor by Ken, springing suddenly from the kitchen, chortling with glee and clapping his hands.

'Sorry Phyllis!'

'Yeah,' said Eddie, faced with the problem once again of getting to his feet.

'Hi darling!' Ken gave Dolores a big kiss and thrust a hand purposefully between her thighs. Once she had got over her initial shock, she was delighted to see him again.

'Hey man! Great! How did you get back in?'

'Wasn't easy, darling, wasn't easy. Your pal, Big Dawn, seems to have put the black on me at the front. Doorman headed me off as I hopped back through the lobby. Doubled round and up the fire-escape. Uncompleted business!' He took off his trousers and, as before, folded them carefully before hanging them over the back of a chair. Then he spotted Toby's body on the floor. 'Stone me! Who's that? One of your mugs, darling?' He suffered a momentary loss of enthusiasm and moved towards his trousers. 'Here. I'm not second cab off the rank, am I?'

'Course not, darling. He's with Dawn.'

'Got you.' Ken was greatly relieved. 'One of Dawn's mugs.'

'*No*. He's like *with* her, isn't he? It's Toby, isn't it?'

'Oh! Mr Toby. Of course.' Ken bent down and peered into Toby's face. 'Seems a bit whacked. Give him a hard time, does she? Big Dawn?'

'No. He's of the theatre, isn't he?'

Ken was satisfied by the explanation. 'Got you. Of the theatre. Of course.'

'*Over The Edge*.'

'So I see, so I see. Poor old sod. Had it, has he?'

'What are you saying, man? That was one of his shows. *Over The Edge*, wasn't it? He'll be as right as rain after a little nap.'

'*Over The Edge*, eh?' Ken was impressed. He'd heard of *Over The Edge*, its fame having spread to Australia. He must be worth a bundle, the producer of *Over The Edge*. Ken took a closer look at him. His appearance was certainly against him – he looked like a rat-bag, in fact – but that was often the case with these big-time pom entrepreneurs. He'd learned not to write a pom off just because he was wearing sand-shoes and his arse was falling out of his trousers. He'd better get the SP on this Mr Toby. There might be a million pounds lying there on the carpet. 'Er – quite successful, was he, then?'

'Successful? I'll say he was successful,' said Dolores, feeling in Dawn's absence duty bound to defend the sleeping Toby's record. 'Still is, for that matter.'

This Toby was a definite chance, thought Ken. You could make a lot of money in the theatre – or so he assumed – and meet some crazy sheilas too. He'd stick around and get acquainted with Mr Toby, forge an entrée here, before Big Dawn came back.

'Me and Eddie was just splitting, as it happens,' said Dolores. 'Got to pick up at Mad Harry's and then go back to my place. Want to come along?'

Much as he'd have liked to throw one up Dolores, Ken

decided that business must come first. You didn't get an entrée to the theatre every day, and he mustn't blow it. At a theatrical garden party the year before he'd been about to take ten grand off a top producer for a non-existent musical when his eye had lighted on the producer's horny-looking wife. Leaving the producer in mid-sentence ('Hang on a sec, old pal'), he'd speared his wife behind the tea-tent returning ten minutes later to discover that his colleague Ted the Tulip had made off with the ten grand. He wouldn't make that mistake again. 'Normally, darling, you couldn't stop me,' he said. 'No, sir. But perhaps I'll stay here and have a word with Mr Toby. It just so happens that I've got a couple of brand new musicals on the drawing-board that might be of interest to him.'

'That's cool,' said Dolores. 'Perhaps we should wake him, though. Bit of a shock coming round and finding a stranger here.'

'You're right.'

Together they hauled Toby upright. He swayed and would have fallen on his face, but they caught him in time and lifted him on to the sofa, where he stirred and came awake.

'Hullo?' he said, staring round him. 'What's going on? Dozed off, did I?'

'Toby. This is Ken.'

'How do, old pal.' Ken pumped Toby's chubby hand with such enthusiasm that his head shook like a coconut in a storm, causing him to blink with surprise. 'Ken Pardoe. Pardoe Theatrical Productions. London, Broadway, the Champs-a-fucking-lysée and. . . .'

'Pardoe?' said Toby, tugging his hand away. 'Pardoe? I don't think we've . . . ah yes! It all comes back. Mind like a lobster-pot, thank God. Dolores was just telling me about you. Her literary agent, I believe. Can you lend me thirty pounds, by any chance? Got a taxi downstairs with the meter running.'

'Sure thing, old pal, sure thing.' Ken reckoned there was no harm in anteing up for the producer of *Over The Edge*. In this life you had to speculate to accumulate, and this was a rock solid investment. They never had cash on them, these top pom operators. They flashed the old plastics or signed their names. It boded well that his new pal Tobe here didn't have notes about his person. Only back-street types carried cash. He pulled up his shirt, took off his money-belt and tossed it over to Toby. 'Help yourself, old pal, help yourself.'

Toby opened the money-belt and took out an enormous wad of notes. He blinked with amazement. Good God, he hadn't seen so much cash since the day Ronnie Snipe – he shifted slightly on the sofa and broke wind like a mortar-bomb going off ('Stone *me*, old pal!') – took the lid off his shoe-box at the Ivy. He looked more carefully at Ken, and decided that he very much liked what he saw. An alert face, the eyes blazing with integrity, the whole manner suggesting candour, energy and drive. He was a bit rough at the edges, perhaps, sitting there without his trousers, something of a colonial innocent. But he could use him, harness some of that rough, outdoor energy, steer the contents of the money-belt in his direction. He was an excellent judge of character, always had been, and already he knew that he and this charmingly innocent young man could do business together. He'd guide him, tether that rough untutored drive to his own purposes, advise him on how to invest his cash.

'No faith in the British banking system, I see.'

'Too bloody right, old pal,' said Ken. 'Too bloody right. First day off the boat, I hop into Coutts – 'scuse I if it happens to be one of your banks, old pal. . . .'

'Oh – just one of many. Hardly use them.'

' "I want to see the fucking manager," I said. "He's engaged at the moment, sir," said some egg in a top-hat. I wasn't having that. I brushed him aside and ran into the manager's office. "Right!" I said. "Straighten up, John! I want to open an account." I took off the old money-belt and banged it on the table. "We'll need references," said the manager. "*References*!" I said. "Look mate, it's *my* money. It's me who'll need the fucking references!" I wasn't having that.'

Toby beamed with approval. This young man impressed him more and more. 'Entirely right,' he said. 'These minor functionaries must be kept in their place.'

'You're prepared to entrust them with your hard-earned, the whingeing poms – no offence intended, old pal – thirty grand on the table. . . .'

'*How* much?' Toby did a quick check inside the money-belt.

'Forty grand on the fucking table – and they *still* want to look up your arse. "Get fucked," I said. I've relied on the old money-belt since then.'

'Very sensible, my dear fellow, and I can only commend your attitude.' What a splendid young man he was, thought Toby. Very much as *he'd* been in his youth. Spirited, fearless, not suffering gladly the efforts of nincompoops to slow him down. They could do well together, he and this energetic young man. Form a team. With his know-how and Ken's drive, they'd take a few people by surprise – though in which particular field he wasn't yet quite sure. The openings would soon emerge, however. They always did if you kept alert. Damn he was tired. Mustn't drop off at the moment, though. Must make a good impression on this shrewd young man, convince him of his own credentials. He was immediately undone, however, by a sudden torrential haemorrhage of vigour. He yawned hugely and made one vain heroic effort to keep his eyelids up. 'Been a long day,' he explained. 'Big lunch, you understand. By no means a waste of time. Had this fellow over a barrel, do you see? Fell into my trap . . . damn . . . think I'll have a little nap.'

Toby dozed off instantly, clutching Ken's money-belt in a chubby hand.

'Nice guy,' said Ken.

'Yeah, one of the all-time greats,' said Dolores loyally. 'Well, we'd better be splitting. Catch you another time?'

'I certainly fucking hope so, darling,' said Ken, bidding her an affectionate farewell between the thighs. 'I certainly – *Jesus* – fucking hope so!'

'Come on, Eddie. We'll pay off Toby's taxi.' Dolores peeled four tenners off the wad clutched tightly in Toby's hand, waking him in the process.

'Hullo? What's up now?'

'Just splitting, darling,' said Dolores. 'We'll take care of the taxi.'

'Very good of you,' said Toby, rubbing his eyes. Who was that strange young man standing there without his trousers? Ah yes, it was his new partner. 'Been a long day. Got mugged, do you see? Had this fellow over a barrel.'

Dolores turned to Ken. 'Bye then, darling.'

'So long, sweetheart. Bye, Phyllis.'

'Yeah.'

Dolores walked to the door, with Eddie, still coiled and dragging the table-lamp like a convict's ball, hopping after her.

'Nice young couple,' said Toby, as they disappeared. 'Care for a drink?'

'I'd be obliged, old pal, I'd be obliged. Throat's as dry as a nun's nasty.'

As Toby tottered unsteadily towards a tray of drinks, Ken decided it was time to broach the big one – but subtly, with finesse. These worldly, old-school-tie entrepreneurs could sense a bludger a mile off. His new pal, Mr Toby here, could be his route to the try-line and he mustn't drop the pass.

'Dolores was telling me you had some kind of loose connection with the live theatre,' he said casually. '*Over The Edge*, was it?'

'*Over The Edge*?' said Toby vaguely, returning with the drinks. '*Over The Edge*?' He seemed to be leafing helpfully through some mental filing-system of past theatrical triumphs. 'Ah yes! An agreeable little show. Quite a success, in fact. One of many, of course. Ran for six years, if I'm not mistaken.'

'Get away!' Ken exclaimed. Mr Toby must be pissing money. It had been fucking opportune his lobbing here.

'But merely one of many, as I say,' continued Toby. '*Arts And Farces, Wham Bam Thank You Mam*. . . .'

'Not at the moment, thanks old pal. Bit soon after the last one. Coming up the fire escape just now I bagged this mad sheila on the floor below.'

'Annie Ross and. . . .'

'Quite possibly, old pal, quite possibly. Didn't catch her name.'

'A great show. A truly great show.'

Ken was suddenly alarmed. Had he been video'd? You couldn't trust these poms. He didn't want to think ill of his new pal, Mr Tobe, but they were bogglers, the lot of them. 'Here,' he said. 'I wasn't on camera, was I?'

'No, no. Another of my shows. *Wham Bam Thank You Mam.* Annie Ross and Oscar Brown Jr.'

Ken looked puzzled. 'She didn't say anything about that to me. Still, I didn't stay long. Attended to her quickly and then continued up the fire-escape.' He dismissed the incident with a wave of the hand. 'Mad molls. They're all the same.' He leaned forward confidentially and lowered his voice. 'Er – anything substantial in the pipe-line now, old pal? I'm talking theatre here.'

Toby seemed amazed that he should need to ask. 'What! Countless projects!' It was now his turn to lean forward confidentially. They were sitting side by side on the sofa, their noses almost touching, squinting urgently. 'Between ourselves I've just taken a most exciting concept off the back-burner. But not a word to the chief, you understand.'

'The chief, old pal?'

'Dawn. My young lady. I call her that out of deference to her awesome moral authority. The integrity of a De Gaulle, the courage of a Churchill, the strength of a Golda. . . .'

'Got you, old pal. Met her earlier. Awesome's the word and no mistake.'

Ken whistled briefly and shook his head, remembering the mauling he'd received going down in the lift, and then gave an operatic wink, the implications of which Toby quite mistook. He leaned back in order to bring Ken into sharper focus. Odd. He wouldn't have taken him for a punter, even without his trousers. With his bandit moustache and blazing eyes, he looked more like an Australian fast bowler on his rest day, sitting by a pool with an icy-cold in his hairy hand, dreaming about the poms he'd hospitalized the day before. Still, you could never be sure these days – the most unlikely people turned out to be furtive afternoon men – and if Ken *was* a punter of Dawn's he'd have him at something of a disadvantage. Not that he wanted their relationship to degenerate into a squalid jockeying for position at any point, of course, but it was of the essence in business to have the goods on your partners, not least those with profit-participation. Yes, deftly handled, this young man and his money-belt could be good for quite a few units in *Satan's Daughter*.

'Charming girl,' he said. 'Salt of the earth and all that, as you no doubt discovered for yourself.' Toby returned the operatic wink with interest. 'But not of the theatre, you understand.'

'Not of the theatre. Got you.'

'Gave her my word I'd retire, in fact.'

'Retire?' Ken was shocked.

'Er – while I was still at the top,' said Toby hastily. He must be more careful. He'd nearly let himself down there. He patted Ken reassuringly on the knee. 'While the best properties still landed on my desk.'

'Still at the top, still at the top. Got you.' Ken whistled with relief. For a moment he'd thought he'd bagged a has-been.

'But I get these concepts on the side,' continued Toby. He tapped his forehead, suggesting a turmoil of creative activity around the frontal lobes. 'Once of the theatre, always of the theatre.'

Ken endorsed this view enthusiastically. 'Too fucking right, old pal!' Then, leaning forward so their noses nearly touched again, he spoke with urgent confidentiality. 'Er – can you divulge further, or is it top-fucking-secret?' To prevent Toby from proceeding rashly, he put a warning finger to his mouth in a sudden hush-sign, while his craftily narrowed eyes did a quick security check of the room in case rival entrepreneurs had slid in undetected.

'A revival!' announced Toby proudly.

Ken couldn't have been more delighted. 'A revival!' He slapped his naked thigh and hooted with excitement. 'I *like* it!'

He really was a splendid fellow, thought Toby. All the enthusiasm in the world. How different from that cowpat Scott-Dobbs with his middlebrow demurring and philistine objections. He could definitely work with a chap like this. And hadn't he been thinking earlier that he should appoint just such an enthusiastic optimist as his assistant? Ken seemed perfect for the role. Young, vigorous, quick on the uptake with a good appearance and an agreeable manner. And above all – and these were qualities he had learned not to dismiss too lightly, even in business – he exuded honour and good intentions. Even Dawn – not the most reliable judge of character, unimaginative when separating sheep from goats – could hardly fail to be impressed by this young man. With him on the team, even she would support his come-back. He looked forward to her coming home.

'That's right,' he said. 'A *timely* revival. A revival for which the world's been waiting.'

The excitement of the moment had brought Ken to his feet. He was agog, his eyes ablaze with expectation, the weight of his enthusiasm driving him on to the balls of his feet. 'Coward?' he asked. 'Maugham? Terence fucking Rattingdon?'

'Thrush.'

'Thrush, old pal?' Ken sat down abruptly, the wind momentarily out of his sails.

'P. P. Thrush. A modern master. A neglected modern master.' Toby leaned forward and prodded Ken in the chest. '*Satan's Daughter.*'

'Satan's fucking daughter, eh?' Ken still looked puzzled. 'We're talking here about Thrush, are we, old pal?'

'No no,' said Toby. 'That's the name of the play. A modern morality play. An allegory, if you like.'

'An allegory, eh?' Ken's enthusiasm had returned. 'I *like* it!' He rubbed his hands with glee and moved closer to Toby, agog for further details. He could hype a fucking allegory.

'A metaphor for our predicament.'

'A metaphor for our predicament, eh?' Ken chortled with excitement.

'Tried it out years ago at the Criterion. Bad move.' Toby's eyes clouded over at the memory of it and he groaned briefly. 'Wrong theatre. Stage too small, do you see? Couldn't develop the right production values. *Vilely* cramped on that meagre stage.' He groaned again and looked beseechingly at Ken, as though seeking forgiveness for compromising Thrush's vision.

'Cramped, eh?' Ken's eyes bulged with horror, as he imagined how it must have been. 'That *is* bad.'

'Bad? *Bad*? It was a catastrophe! A betrayal of Thrush's dream.' Exhaustion and remembered misery suddenly caused Toby's voice to weaken, forcing Ken to crouch over him as though trying to commit to memory the secrets of a dying man. 'It needed a larger canvas, do you see, to bring out the sheer scope of the concept. The complexities inherent in the theme.'

'The fucking complexities inherent in the theme. Got you, old pal.'

'The sheer audacity of it,' croaked Toby. 'The shocking ethical inversions.'

'The fucking shocking ethical inversions.' Ken had both knees up on the sofa now, athwart his pal in an impresario's straddle, his position likely to suggest to anyone entering the room that artificial respiration was taking place, or something worse. 'Yes? Yes?'

'The moral disjunctions,' breathed Toby faintly. 'The metaphysical extremes. Heaven and hell!' He groaned heart-breakingly and then slumped back into the depths of the sofa.

'Heaven and *hell*!' cried Ken. 'It must have been, old pal, it fucking must have been.' He was seriously alarmed. He didn't want his pal to catch the ferry now. Not when they were about to launch the big one. He didn't like the look of him at all. He'd gone a very funny colour, an angry network of veins covering his face like decorations on a muddy trifle. He picked up Toby's glass and, propping him upright, like a solicitous nurse, held it to his lips. 'Here, cop this, old pal.'

'My dear fellow,' said Toby weakly, managing a sip, 'you're a comfort.' He collapsed again and lay so still that Ken, still perched trouserless athwart his pal and facing him, crouched forward and placed an ear against his mouth, hoping to discover signs of life.

'The Vatican!' bellowed Toby, sitting up so suddenly that

they cracked their heads like fighting rams. 'The Vatican!'

Ken went rigid with alarm, the searing pain between his eyes as nothing compared to his anxiety for his pal. Was Mr Tobe a Catholic about to croak? Did he need a priest? 'The Vatican, old pal?'

'Yes!' cried Toby. 'The Vatican!' The collision of their heads seemed to have brought Toby back to life, so Ken clambered off his pal and moved for safety's sake further down the sofa. 'Imagine trying to convey the splendour, the opulence, the sheer *magnificence* of the Vatican on the stage of the Criterion!'

'Not on, old pal. Simply not on. But perhaps you shouldn't think about it.' Ken didn't want his pal to suffer a relapse. 'Byegones be fucking byegones and all that.'

Toby's self-mortifying tirade wasn't to be checked, however. 'And the papal orgies! Uurrgh!' He groaned disgustedly.

'Orgies, old pal?' Ken was alarmed. He couldn't hype something fucking decadent.

'They should have ravished the eye!' shouted Toby. 'They should have been a sumptuous tapestry of scarlet and gold from which the warm, moist stench of corruption rose – almost tangibly – like some obscene enveloping bog-mist.'

'Like bog-mist, old pal?'

Rum musical, this one. Bog-mist. The devil's daughter. Orgies in the Vatican. Cardinals biting one another in the box. Never mind. These days it was probably easier to hype the rum than the unrum. Standards upside down these days. Hairdressers kissing in the street, sheilas sitting in fashionable restaurants with their skirts round their waists opening their flanges to one and all, fucking couples fucking on the television. To raise the capital for this one all he'd need to do would be to find some rich lascivious auntie who wanted to get her feet wet in a musical. He'd have to get some more cards printed, of course. He'd got nothing in his wallet to cover this one. 'Ken Pardoe International Musicals. London, Broadway and Paris'. He presumed this was a musical. A rich auntie, that's all he needed, just one clean shot at a mad rich aun . . . by God! He had it! That mad Vanessa, Pillock's wife! Crazy about the theatre and money coming out of her arse! Before marrying Pillock she'd been an Annoir of the Annoir millions. He'd unearthed her stock certificates once during a random spot-check in her underwear drawer and, unbeknown to her, had perused them over her shoulder while pumping dutifully away one afternoon in Aldershot, hoping their details would enthuse him to a climax before Pillock got home from manoeuvres. By God he'd promote her for this one – *if* he could still get it up for the insatiable old moll. A glance at his pal, gasping and wheezing on the sofa, stiffened his resolve. By Christ he'd get it up! For the sake of the live theatre, and for the sake of his pal Tobe here.

His pal Tobe, meanwhile, was still in mid-confession. 'And the great Easter orgy,' he moaned, 'a carnal celebration, inextricably and obscenely woven with the spiritual celebration of Mass – had all the divine splendour, all the magnificence, all the sublime moral anarchy of . . . of . . . a wife-swapping party in Dollis Hill. Heart-breaking. *Heart-breaking*.'

Toby, utterly distraught, unable to forgive himself for so vulgarizing Thrush's vision, struggled to his feet and, beating at his forehead, waddled uncertainly round the room. Ken, fearful that he'd knock himself clean off his feet with one of those tremendous thumps to the forehead, hopped agitatedly after him, trying to calm him down.'

'Fucking heart-breaking, old pal,' he said, gathering him as he was about to walk into a wall, 'fucking *heart-breaking*. But try not to think about it. Here. Come and sit down.'

'I blame myself,' groaned Toby, allowing himself to be planted back on the sofa, from the depths of which his stocky little legs failed to reach the floor. 'No! I blame Albery. Talked me into taking it to the Criterion. Talked me into it! *Me*! The producer of *Over The Edge*!'

'I blame this whingeing Allboys fellow,' agreed Ken angrily. 'Where is he now, old pal? You say the word and I'll hop right over and pull his nose.' He'd certainly like to stick one up this Allboys fellow. Just look what he'd done to his pal Tobe. He'd get him for this. He'd give this Allboys a right sledging at an opportune moment.

Toby wasn't to be diverted yet from his lacerating penance. 'Wrong mimes too,' he moaned. 'Flat. Two-dimensional. Mimes with no sense of danger. Alf Garnett as the Pope! Uuhhgh!'

'Alf Garnett as the fucking Pope, eh?' Ken's face wrinkled with disgust at such a lapse of taste. 'Bad move that, old pal. A very bad move indeed. Yes sir.'

Toby, to Ken's alarm, seemed now to be having a relapse sinking more deeply into the sofa, his voice falling to a hoarse whisper. 'A sell-out,' he gasped. 'A vulgarization on a scale scarcely seen before. I betrayed P. P. Thrush. I trivialized his dream. I committed a foul crime against the theatre itself!' He buried his head in his hands, moaning softly.

'Now now, old pal,' said Ken, leaning forward and patting Toby gently on the shoulder. 'Don't take on so. That was yesterday. Think of tomorrow. Think positively. This time we'll get it right. Take special fucking precautions to stop this Allboys bludging us.' He was thinking furiously, trying to hit on a formula that would pump some life back into his ailing pal. With English gents a little past their prime, he'd found that the promise of naked sheilas lobbing unexpectedly often did the trick, but in Toby's case he judged that talk of a sudden capital advantage might prove the better tonic. At this address, sheilas hardly seemed a problem (no one living with Big Dawn could be called deprived in this respect), and Ken was beginning to suspect that in Toby's case appearances might be less than deceptive, that lack of funds rather than of obliging sheilas was the more immediate problem. Either way, he'd offer first the prospect of a financial windfall. 'It occurs to me,' he said, 'that I might be of some assistance here.'

Toby moaned piteously and shook his head. 'Too late,' he said. 'Much, much too late. You mean well, old chap, but. . . .' He made a helpless gesture and then collapsed, eyes closed.

'Rustle up some mugs for this revival,' insisted Ken. 'Help with the *finance*.'

'Finance?' Toby sat up abruptly on hearing the word, his

eyes, which seconds earlier had resembled something floating upside down in a fish-tank, were as bright as a ferret's now. 'You have an entrée to finance?'

Ken was incredulous that he should need to ask. 'Do I!' He pressed on quickly while his pal was on the up. 'Now. How much do we need for this revival? I'm talking money here.'

No other topic could have done more for Toby's health. 'Fifty thousand,' he said at once, 'give or take a few thousand. Price of things these days, it's difficult to keep up. Haven't done a budget yet. Hang on I'll do one now.' He was as alert as a cricket now, brimming with business-vigour. 'Rather a forte of mine, budgets. Have to get the arithmetic right, you know. Oh yes. Many's the enthusiastic amateur who's been brought down by faulty budgeting. Never happened to me, I'm glad to say.' He wagged a knowing finger. 'First lesson of production –get the arithmetic right.'

'Of course, of course.' Ken wore an expression of studious attention, an eager freshman at his first tutorial. He could learn a lot from his pal Tobe. Getting it up for Mrs Pillock was only half the problem; he must be *au* fucking *fait* with the figures too.

'Now then, let's see. Need something to write on.' Toby searched among a pile of neatly stacked papers on the coffee-table. 'Ah, what's this? A rates demand. We won't be needing that. Here we go, then.' He began to jot some figures in its margins. 'Set – say twenty thousand. Costumes – ten. Props – five. Rehearsals – ten. Bonds to Equity etc – say another ten. Advance on a theatre – say fifteen. Misc – another fifteen.'

'Misc, old pal?' Ken had been following this carefully, jotting down the figures on the back of an old race-card as Toby called them out. He had to be on top of the details. There was money to be made here and he didn't want to look a larrikin when it came to raising the capital. He couldn't hope to tug it all off Mrs. Pillock. He might have to hire a bowler hat and run through a few doors in the environs of Gracechurch Street. He didn't fancy lobbing in a banker's office like a raw prawn without the figures.

'A most important category,' Toby explained. 'Catch a lot

under misc. Lunches, taxis, entertaining, general wear and tear, a little something for the ingénue, perhaps.' He winked, judging that with types like Ken, shy country boys who possibly had trouble scoring in the sophisticated atmosphere of town, mention of the ingénue seldom came amiss.

'The ingénue, eh? you rascal!' Ken chortled and beamed, leading Toby to suppose that his hunch had been correct. Truly, there was no substitute for experience. He could handle this delightful young man as a wily angler tickles a novice trout. If he thought girls were in the offing he might be persuaded to cough up the entire contents of his money-belt. 'Now,' continued Ken, doing some quick addition, 'I make that more like eighty-five thousand.'

'*Really*?' Toby seemed amazed. 'Good heavens. I'm not usually as far out as that.' He consulted his jottings. 'Better make that a hundred thousand, then. Good round sum. I warned you that things had gone up. Experience, you see.' Once more he wagged a knowing finger. 'No substitute for experience.'

Ken was beginning to wonder. And the odd nature of this musical still troubled him. He couldn't run through City doors babbling about bog-mists and orgies in the Vatican. He needed an angle here. A bankable asset. A name to conjure with, one with marquee-value. Suddenly he had one.

'FUCK ME DEAD!' he bellowed, slapping his naked thigh so hard that Toby threw his budget in the air and felt for his heart. 'POLANSKI!'

'Do be careful, my dear fellow,' said Toby faintly. 'You nearly had me over then.'

'Sorry, old pal.'

'And what's Polanski got to do with it?'

'What's Polanski got to do with it?' Ken stared at Toby in amazement. 'Smarten up, old pal! We say he's going to direct it, that's what he's got to do with it!'

'By jove!' Toby was impressed. This young man was learning fast. 'An audacious move, but not unheard of. I recall that Irving Lazar once. . . .'

'I'll say it's audacious!' Ken was on his feet now, striding up and down, eyes blazing with excitement. With Polanski in his saddle-bag he could ride through some highly respectable doors in search of finance. It was still a bankable name, Polanski. Yes sir. It was time now to play his other card. He'd mention sheilas and see whether his pal's eyes lit up as they had at the mention of finance. 'Now, old pal. The casting.'

'The casting?'

'Ex-*actly*! It occurs to me that what we need – what we really fucking need – is someone we can hype. Yes sir. Undiscovered superstars are the name of the game today.' The highly confidential nature of the information he was about to impart caused Ken to squint cunningly at Toby and drop his voice to a low whisper. 'Now. I happen to know that Roman has a slight weakness for the sheilas. Plenty of mad sheilas in this show of yours, are there, old pal? Fucking can-can girls and so forth?' Toby, who had got to his feet to join the excited pacing up and down, now received a nudge in the ribs that sent him sprawling.

'Simply teeming with them, my dear fellow, simply teeming with them.' So! He'd been right. It was an introduction to young ladies that this young man was after. 'That's half the point, do you see? In fact, for some time now . . . er, without the Chief realizing, you understand' – no harm in letting him think that he was on the look-out too – 'I've been keeping half an eye open for someone to play Satan's daughter herself.'

'You rascal! Without the Chief knowing, eh? I like it!' Good thing he'd mentioned sheilas. He'd been wrong. The poor old soul *was* still vulnerable to the sheilas. It would be plain sailing now.

'It's a key role, you understand. In many ways the crux of the play. She gives the Pope syphilis, you see.'

'Stone *me*!' This latest bombshell brought Ken's excited pacing to a halt. Now he had to run among his backers with the news that the leading lady of this musical about bog-mists and orgies in the Vatican was a low-life type who gave the Pope syphilis. 'She gives the Pope syphilis, does she, the mad sheila? A really low-life broad, is she, the devil's daughter?' He couldn't hype a moll like that.

Happily, Toby was able to put his mind at rest. 'On the contrary,' he said. 'That's the irony of it. She's irresistibly pure and innocent. That's why she's so lethal. She should be young, blonde and exquisitely lovely. A sort of "English unofficial rose".'

Ken was immensely cheered. 'An English unofficial rose, eh? I *like* it!' He could hype an English unofficial rose.

'You do?' Toby was surprised, but gratified. Perhaps this delightful young man was more cultured than his appearance suggested. Energetic *and* cultured. 'You relished the sly borrowing from Rupert Brooke?'

'Rupert Brooke, eh?' Ken was suddenly concerned. 'Here. He isn't out on the toe searching too, is he, old pal? We don't want a cock-up here.'

Once again Toby was able to reassure him. 'No no. You'll have the field entirely to yourself.'

'Right. I'll start searching right away. No time like the present. Young, blonde, English rose. I'll hop straight into the King's Road and gather a selection now. Plenty of au pairs in the King's Road at this time of day.' Ken moved briskly towards the front door. 'Hooroo for the moment, old pal.'

'Er—just a word of advice,' called Toby. He in no way wished to dampen the ardour of his new associate, but a gentle hand on the tiller from time to time couldn't come amiss. 'I think she should be a member of Equity if possible.'

'Right. Got it. Member of Equity if possible. Catch you soon, old pal. On second thoughts, I think I'll use the fire-escape. Don't want to bump the chief coming back, do I? By this evening, old pal, you and I will have discovered a brand new *international* fucking superstar! See you in the winner's enclosure!' He prepared to exit through the kitchen.

'Should you take your trousers, do you think?'

'Trousers. Right.'

Ken picked up his trousers and, with a cheery wave, departed via the kitchen.

For the last forty-five minutes, Dolores and Steady Eddie had, unbeknown to them, been going about their business – some of it lawful – with a police escort provided by Detective Sergeant Pyle. They'd been sighted leaving Nell Gwynn House by Detective Constables Blagden and Perks, who, on reporting by radio to Pyle that Dolores and Eddie were moving off in a taxi, had been told to follow them. This, Perks and Blagden had done: first monitoring their visit to Mad Harry (well known to D/S Pyle as a dealer) and then tailing them to Dolores's flat in Westbourne Grove, where a slight hiccup in the operation had occurred. Dolores had been paying off the taxi, when Eddie, still dressed, as reported to a disgusted Pyle, in the gym-slip and white socks Jane Birkin had worn in *Passion Flower Hotel*, had become suspicious of the car in which Smiley and Harris sat and, hastily followed by Dolores, had climbed back into the taxi, which had then driven off. On seeking further instructions, Smiley and Harris had been told by Pyle to stay where they were, in case Dolores and Eddie came back to the flat, while Blagden and Perks had been told to tail the taxi. Dolores and Eddie were now returning, still with a police escort, to Nell Gwynn House – or such was Pyle's hunch. He himself was about to leave Chelsea Police Station for Nell Gwynn House, where he intended to take up an unobtrusive position in the lobby, in case Perks and Blagden lost touch with the taxi. It seemed to Pyle a battleship to a rubber-duck that Dolores and Eddie, alerted somehow to the fact that their place was being watched, would attempt to hole up temporarily with Dawn. This turn of events, though unexpected, was now recognized by Pyle as a handy development for him. If his hunch was right, and Dolores and Eddie did indeed move in with Dawn, he'd have the lot of them bang to rights. Disregarding any infringement of the Obscene Displays Act of which Eddie might be guilty, Pyle now knew, thanks to the stop-off at Mad Harry's, that Dolores was carrying illegal substances – unless she'd been selling to him, which was hardly on the cards. If she and Eddie did indeed move in with Dawn this evening, Pyle would apply for a warrant in the morning to search the flat for drugs tomorrow night. It was a million that at some stage of the evening there'd be a punter on the premises, in which case he'd have Dawn for running a brothel; and if there wasn't, at least he'd have her for the drugs. Pyle felt highly pleased with himself as he set off for Nell Gwynn House. He looked forward to seeing Dawn's face when her door came down the following night. She was well overdue.

5.00 p.m. Nell Gwynn House.

Toby, who, since Ken's departure, had been snoozing on the sofa, woke suddenly with a start and pulled a gold half-hunter from his waist-coat pocket. Confound it, he was missing the cricket. He stumbled over to the television set to be greeted, when he switched it on, by an apologetic link person informing him that rain had, for the moment, interrupted play at Lord's.

'Before showing you a prize-winning cartoon from Czechoslovakia,' said the link-person, 'I just have time to remind you that on *Nationwide* tonight, Jane Baker's guests in the special law and order debate will be the Commissioner of the Metropolitan Police, Sir Angus McDuff . . .'

'Fine man,' said Toby.

'. . . Dame Letitia Merryweather . . .'

'Good God! I thought she was dead.'

'. . . who, apart from being one of our most distinguished and best-loved actresses – a truly legendary star of stage and screen – is also President of the Britain is Great Society, a strictly non-political organization which opposes the infiltration of our ancient institutions by left-wing activists. They were to have been joined by Mr Nigel Mount-Hugh MP, one of the most vocal of the Prime Minister's supporters, but we have just heard that he is indisposed. His place will be taken by Mr Alan Clark MP. We will, of course, take you back to Lord's if the weather improves. And now the prize-winning. . . .'

'Bollocks,' said Toby. He switched off disgustedly and trundled back to the sofa, nodding off as the front door opened and Dawn came in. She was about to announce her arrival with a cheerful 'I'm home everyone!' when she noticed him sleeping on the sofa. She approached him on tiptoe and kissed him lightly on the forehead, being careful not to wake him. What a sight he was, bless his heart. Unshaven, buttons missing – she'd sew them on later – wearing odd shoes, his tie, frayed at the knot, half-way round his neck. She wondered what had happened to the hundred pounds she'd given him that morning with which to apply some improvements to his wardrobe. She hoped the interview had gone well with Gabbitas and Thing. She would so like him to be a teacher. A service to the community and that. He seemed to be dreaming, mumbling to himself, so she bent down, trying to catch his words. Something about getting it right this time, going for the big one. He was in a bit of a dream-world, bless him, asleep or awake. Sometimes she wondered whether he even noticed what she did for a living. He never showed much interest. When he woke up he probably wouldn't even ask her where she'd been. She preferred it like that, of course. Most men got a buzz out of living with tarts. All her previous boyfriends had been pimps or perverts, getting off on what she did, asking for details when she got home, not seeming to understand that the atrocious things she'd just done had made no impression on her at all. Toby was different, thank God. He understood that it wasn't *her* fucking these awful men, that she was acting, that her real self was quite uninvolved in those sad charades. He probably grasped this because he'd been of the theatre too. And at least he enjoyed the occasional funny bits. She didn't mind telling him about them. When he woke up, she'd be tempted to describe her tussle with the Wanker, but she must restrain herself. She didn't want to spoil the moment tomorrow night when he came dancing through the door as the Sugar Plum Fairy with a rabbit on his head. She hoped he'd be up to it, mind. What a state the poor man had been in when she'd left! Lying on the bed in shock, moaning that he'd let his leader down. She'd had to ring the BBC on his behalf, cancelling an appearance on *Nationwide* that evening. She hoped he'd have recovered by the following night; she did want to give Toby a laugh. She suddenly noticed the rates demand lying on the floor. She picked it up and began to read Toby's jottings in the margin. 'Set – £20,000. Costumes – £10,000. . . .' Oh God, he'd been planning his come-back. She gave a little groan of horror, waking Toby.

'Hullo, my dear,' he said. 'What's up?'

'Nothing.' She hastily hid the rates demand, not wanting the evening, for which she'd had such expectations, to get off on a note of acrimony and mutual accusations. Unless she trod lightly on his theatrical dreams he'd flare up frighteningly or, worse, sulk for weeks. And she still had hopes of getting her fantasy off the ground. Even the Wanker's disgusting performance hadn't managed to destroy that. She'd had a bath and now felt as fresh as a daisy, ready to play the part properly for Toby. 'Sorry,' she said, sitting down next to him on the sofa and trying to look like Jane Baker, crossing her legs demurely and looking sweet and that. 'Didn't mean to wake you.' She wanted to ask him how his interview had gone, but she knew she mustn't quiz. He couldn't stand being quizzed. Anyway, Jane Baker never asked provocative questions. She recrossed her legs, revealing a bit of thigh – most unlike Jane, but never mind – and smiled shyly at the floor. She was beginning to enjoy herself. 'What sort of day did you have?' she asked sweetly, using her Jane Baker voice, projecting herself somewhat, as though they might be on camera.

'Not bad at all, my dear, not bad at all.' He stretched and came awake. 'Care for a drink?'

'Golly yes. I could certainly use one.'

'Get me one at the same time, there's a dear.'

'Well!' she said. 'That *is* nice!' But she hauled herself up and fetched them both a drink. Then she stood in front of him in her Jane Baker pose, clutching her imaginary clip-board, smiling sweetly, eyes cast demurely down. She must look adorable, she thought.

'Christ, you look tired,' said Toby.

'Oh – er – not really.' Dawn was disconcerted. She attempted a vivacious smile. 'I've been out seeing someone, haven't I?'

'Good God! Dressed like that? You look like a secretary. Someone isn't choosey!'

Oh well, that was the end of that. Full of disappointments, life. Dawn sagged, her fantasy in ruins. Suddenly she did feel tired. 'My MP,' she said. 'Dolphin Square.'

'Oh yes. Dolores mentioned something about it.'

Dawn walked across the room and took a picture off the wall, revealing a small safe. 'Might as well put the money away while I'm up,' she said.

Toby chuckled derisively. 'Ah! The safe!'

'I know you think it's an unnecessary precaution, my sweet, but you can't be too careful these days.' Dawn put the money away and then withdrew a little black book into which she entered a figure. She then returned this to the safe and closed the door. 'Did I ever tell you why I had it installed?'

'I don't think you did, my dear.'

'Well,' said Dawn, sitting down again. 'One day Pretty Marie's entertaining this flash young man, isn't she? Not a punter type at all, if you know what I mean. After they'd got busy he gave her three hundred pounds in crisp twenty-pound notes. "Wow!" said Pretty Marie. "You're doing all right. What's your dodge, then?" Nosey, but that's Pretty Marie, isn't it? "I had a bit of luck," said the flash young man. "I used to work in a garage. One day a rich old geezer drives up in a Rolls-Royce. We got talking and the rich geezer gives me the secret of his success. 'My boy,' he said. 'I worked hard, saved hard, and put my money into property.' Lesson I never forgot." "You went into property?" said Pretty Marie. "No, I nicked his Rolls," said the flash young man.'

'A delightful anecdote, my dear!'

'Wait. When Pretty Marie got back from the bathroom, the flash young man had gone, plus the three hundred pounds plus her handbag. I had the safe put in the next day.'

'Probably the right decision,' admitted Toby.

'And there's my little black book, of course.'

'Ah yes. The little black book. But are you sure that's so wise, my dear? I mean, should there be a bust – Dolores mentioned something earlier about a Mr Piles – there wouldn't be much doubt, if they found the little black book, about what you do, would there? Your business, of course. Not for me to interfere.'

'You're missing the point, aren't you, my sweet?' said Dawn. 'If old Bill turned me over I'd *want* them to read the little black book. I mean, it's all in there, just as you say. Names, dates, special requirements. Half the establishment's in that book. Old Bill's bottle would go if he ever read my little black book. Take Jean Horn. Old Bill busts her. What happens? Fined a hundred pounds. And why? Friends in high places. Been working for the Foreign Office for years. At it again the same night. First booking, the magistrate that fined her.'

'*No*? Really?'

'Well, speculating, aren't I, my sweet? And take Janie Jones. Fixes up a few pop stars and what does she get? Seven years and told she's an evil woman into the bargain. Hadn't bothered to ingratiate herself with the right people, had she? Oh no, I'm not stupid, me. If I get done I want them to know *exactly* who my friends are. All in there, isn't it? In the little black book.'

Toby was impressed. 'I have to admit it makes sense, my dear. I take my hat off to you. Careful planning. I like to see that.'

'To say nothing,' continued Dawn, 'of types running around loose like that cowboy who was here earlier.'

'When was that, my dear? I've seen no cowboys.'

'Australian. All talk and no trousers. Pornography in the home. Ran through the front door and tried to get busy with Dolores. The soppy cow didn't seem to mind. Almost had to throw a bucket of water over them.'

'Good gracious. How distressing for you, my dear. I saw nothing of that nature.' Toby judged it best not to tell Dawn about his meeting with Ken – and of their blossoming business relationship – until he was more certain of her mood. How strange it was, he thought, and sad too, that one had to keep secret from the person one lived with just those areas of one's life that mattered most. It was never like this in one's dealings with men, of course. He and Ken, within minutes of meeting, had scarcely had a secret from each other; had been able to reveal their innermost dreams without the slightest fear of being squashed. You could never achieve this intimacy with women. It was the price you paid, he reflected gloomily, for not being a homosexualist. But then homosexualists, no doubt, being emotionally involved, had to deceive each other too in precisely those areas that mattered most. Never mind. Ken would return soon, and Dawn would see for herself what could be achieved with a little courage and imagination, what could be done at 'the dangerous edge of things'. She would be his ball and chain no longer. He wouldn't throw her out. It was, after all, her flat. She could come along for the ride. But she would have to abandon her stifling bourgeois values.

'How did your interview go?' asked Dawn, able to contain herself no longer.

Toby started guiltily. 'What inter . . . oh, of course. Miles away, my dear. Er – quite well, I think. They'll be letting me know.'

'You didn't buy yourself any new clothes, then?'

'Ah. I'll tell you what happened there. I was in Fortnums, do you see, *precisely* as instructed, when I spotted this bag in Gifts and Accessories. Before I knew what I was doing, I'd bought it for you.'

'For *me*?' Dawn gave a little cry of delight. He'd never bought her anything, even with her own money. The first year they'd been together, she had particularly, and for sentimental reasons, wanted him to give her a birthday present and, to this end, had insisted that he accompany her on a small shopping expedition, financed, of course, by her. But he'd complained so bitterly about being 'dragged around London on such a damn fool enterprise' that she'd abandoned the project after a while and had returned home fighting back the tears to which she'd eventually succombed. 'Can I see it?'

'Ah well, there is a slight snag,' Toby explained. 'No sooner had I bought it than I turned against it. Decided it was common.'

'Oh.' Dawn was crest-fallen.

'Gave it to the first person I thought would appreciate it. Over lunch I met this woman, Caroline I think her name was. . . .'

'Here,' said Dawn, sensing untidiness. There'd been no lunch on the schedule. 'What lunch?'

'Just *lunch*,' said Toby, guilt causing his voice to take on an irritated note. 'Perfectly normal milestone in the day. I am *allowed* lunch, am I?'

Dawn was frightened. 'Sorry, I didn't mean to. . . .'

Toby was working himself up into a rage. 'I'm almost certain I signed the *exeat* book before setting forth, with a full explanation of my movements.' This was preposterous. He was a man of forty-seven – though few would credit it to look at him – he was about to go into production with the revival of the season and he had to account for his luncheon arrangements! She probably couldn't help it. It was her function, as a woman, to squat over his life like a malevolent nanny. It was all right for her, of course. She could do what she liked. She'd been out enjoying herself, indulging her fantasies for the sake of some Tory backbencher – something she never did for him – and now that she'd got home all she wanted to do was snip his balls off. Why should she think that such behaviour was attractive? Any minute now she'd be offering to sew his buttons on. Couldn't women understand that if a man had wanted a mother he'd have stayed at home? Rage at all this childish pretence boiled over in his brain. 'As it happens,' he said nastily, 'I was having lunch at the Ivy with an angel from the old days. . . .'

'Oh dear.'

'Yes, isn't that terrible? And after lunch I came back here and met Ken. We. . . .'

'Ken? So you *did* meet him?'

'I'm afraid so, my dear. But you weren't here, do you see, to save me from myself, so the meeting was. . . .'

'*Please.*'

'. . . inevitable.'

'Sorry.'

'And so you should be.' Still, he felt better now the truth was out. He could afford to be magnanimous. That, he reflected, was one of his strongest qualities: an inability to bear a grudge for long. 'Actually, I thought he seemed quite a decent fellow.'

'*Decent*? And how did he get back in? I left Fred with *strict* instructions to keep an eye out for him.'

'Really? Well, you're perfectly entitled to keep anyone out of your flat who falls short, in your judgement, of your own high standards of probity and. . . .'

'*Our* flat,' Dawn insisted.

'Of course, of course.' *Their* flat, indeed! That was a laugh. *She* could have anyone she liked around – colleagues, punters, perverts, politicians – but a friend of *his*, someone who had *his* interests at heart, was deemed a threat at once and barred from entry. Never mind. She'd be looking very silly in a minute. Ken would return and she'd discover that her mean-minded feminine need to stunt and curb was powerless in the face of their combined masculine drive. He'd savour the moment, but he'd be large-spirited enough to let her share it – *if* she behaved herself. 'But Fred was quite blameless, I assure you. Ken gave him the slip and came up the fire-escape. He's of the theatre, you see.'

'Oh dear.' Dawn groaned as loudly as she dared.

'He knows Annie Ross and he's going to engage Polanski to direct the piece. Isn't that exciting?'

'Piece? What piece?' Anxiety had brought on a quizzing tone, but Dawn couldn't help herself.

'*Satan's Daughter*, of course. Going to get it right this time. Owe it to Thrush, do you see?'

'Oh dear. You've never been brooding on *that* again?'

'Not brooding, my dear. I just happened to mention it to Ken in passing, and I'm very glad I did. That's how I discovered he was of the live theatre too. Appearances can be deceptive. Had him down at first as an outdoor type. Turned out he knows everyone. And, as I say, he's going to engage Polanski as director.'

'*Polanski*? *He's* not very nice. Isn't he always out chasing little girls and that?'

Borne by his fantasy into a world where anything was possible, Toby wasn't listening. 'And what do you suppose he's doing now?'

'Out chasing little girls, I should think.'

'That's right!'

'I told you.'

'Told me what, my dear?'

'That he's not very nice.'

'Who?'

'Polanski, my sweet.'

'Not Polanski. *Ken.* What do you suppose *Ken's* doing now?'

'Burglarizing Harrods, I imagine.'

'Ha! Ha! Very good, my dear. No, I told you. He's of the live theatre.'

'Oh well. In that case I imagine he's taking tea with Bernard Delfont.'

'Damn. Wish you hadn't reminded me. I said bollocks to him earlier. On the phone.'

'*Did* you, my sweet?' Dawn was momentarily cheered. The more people in the theatre Toby said bollocks to the better, in her opinion. 'That wasn't very nice. So what's he doing now?'

'Who, my dear?'

'Golly, my sweet. The Australian. The cowboy.'

''Oh, *Ken.* Bags of go, that fellow, bags of go. What do you suppose he's doing now?'

'That's what I'm trying to find out, my sweet.'

'He's out there – casting!'

Dawn was horrified. *Casting?* This was even more serious than she'd feared. Casting, if she remembered rightly from her days of doing bits and pieces as a dancer, came at quite an advanced stage of production. '*Casting?* Casting what?'

'I told you!' cried Toby impatiently. '*Satan's Daughter.* He's out in the King's Road now, specifically looking for someone to play Syphilis. Isn't that exciting?'

Phew, that was all right, thought Dawn. They were crackers, the pair of them. Nothing too terrible could come of this. Ken was just getting his rocks off, running around Chelsea giving the girls a fright. Better that he should be doing it in the King's Road than in her flat. She must choose her words with care, however. She didn't want to bring on another of Toby's tantrums.

'It *is* exciting, my sweet. It's just. . . .'

'Bags of go, that young man, bags of go.' Toby lay back and closed his eyes, knocked for six, it seemed, just by the thought of so much go. His exhaustion made Dawn more confident, causing her to over-play her hand.

'Bags of bullshit, more like. I mean, can you be certain. . . .'

'*Certain?*' bellowed Toby, sitting up in rage at this new attempt to dash his hopes. 'No, of course I can't be certain. *Certain?* What a dreary, petrified word. Do we have to be *certain* about everything? Can't we ever take a risk? Don't you want me to do *anything?* Am I merely to be your *thing?* Your tethered goat? Your creature?'

Sometimes she might have laughed, but hurt and anger vied titanically now for a monopoly on Dawn's emotions. Had anger won she might have screamed: 'You fucking heap, how dare you! If I wanted a creature don't you think I could do better than you? Of *course* I want you to do something. *Anything.* I've fucked half the Monday Club up the arse so that you can eat, you disgraceful lout.' But hurt prevailed and so she said: 'God, that's unfair. Of *course* I want you to do things. It's just that I don't want you to be disappointed. I *know* how much you want to be back in production. But with *him?* Ken? Come on, my sweet. He's a cowboy. You must be able to see *that.*'

'Nonsense, my dear!' said Toby, with a vilely superior smile that Dawn would have found most insulting had she been capable of feeling more insulted than she already did, and had she not been able to recognize it anyway as the death-rattle of his confidence. 'I'm an excellent judge of character, always have been, and I tell you that that young man's got what it takes. A bit rough at the edges, perhaps, but all the drive in the world. We could make a first-class team. With his energy and my . . . and my. . . .' He slumped again, suddenly exhausted.

Dawn could have left it there. She knew she had nothing more to worry about. Ken, obviously, had come back looking for Dolores, found she wasn't there and, after some insane fantasy talk with Toby, had gone off to make a fool of himself elsewhere. They certainly wouldn't be seeing him again. But she didn't want Toby to be disappointed, to build up his hopes on such an obvious time-waster. She couldn't bear the thought of him sitting there *expecting* Ken to come back, feeling the foolishness of gradual disillusion. She had to scotch that.

'He's a hustler, my sweet,' she said. 'And not a very good one. He was just looking for Dolores. Can't you see that? He won't be back.'

Toby was suddenly deflated, the thin, fugitive nature of his hopes quite unable to withstand Dawn's breezy common sense. 'Oh well,' he said dejectedly. 'If you say so.' He looked so forlorn, so utterly routed, his feet, incompatibly shod, a few inches off the floor, that Dawn could have bitten her tongue off. Seeing him like this, she was inclined to run into the street in search of Ken herself, to a drag him back for Toby's sake. She began to hope fervently that she might be wrong, that he might come back. She could handle him, after all, run rings round him. If he hurt Toby she'd kill him, simple as that.

Toby stirred and opened his eyes. 'Perhaps I'll watch the cricket,' he muttered sulkily. 'That should be safe enough. No danger of too much excitement there.'

Dawn hurried to turn the television on, her mind racing. These sulks could last for weeks. He'd put her in Coventry. Refuse to speak. Take to his bed for days at a time.

Jim Laker's calming Yorkshire brogue suddenly filled the room. 'The pitch playing much more easily now after the rain. It's going to be a long haul for England now unless they can break this partnership. Botham starts his run-up from the nursery end. . . .'

'Fat git,' said Toby. 'I think I'll go to bed. No danger of too much excitement there either.'

He struggled to his feet and was half-way to the bedroom when there was a ring at the front door.

'My goodness!' cried Dawn with a brave attempt at gaiety. 'I wonder who that can be?'

'A friend of yours, no doubt,' said Toby nastily. '*My* friends aren't made to feel very welcome here.' Hoping to cause embarrassment, he went over to the front door and shouted venomously, 'Yes? Who is it?'

'Only me, captain,' said a cheery voice from the passage. 'Your old pal Ken reporting back. Yes sir.'

Dawn nearly fainted with relief and Toby, his ill-humour instantly forgotten, beamed triumphantly and cried, 'My word, that was quick! I told you he was on the ball. Now, please try to be agreeable, my dear. For *my* sake.'

'Of course, of course.' By God she'd be agreeable. Just so long as Ken was here on Toby's behalf and not in an effort to climb back into her or Dolores, she'd dazzle him with her agreeability. When Toby opened the door to reveal Ken chortling with triumph – as well he might since he had a head-lock on the prettiest little girl Dawn had ever set eyes on – she could have hugged him. He, on the other hand, suffered a momentary loss of steam on seeing her.

'Oh oh, the chief's back,' he said, and he might have backed off down the passage with his prisoner had not Dawn – with a cry of 'Darling! How marvellous to see you again!' – drawn him into the room.

'Hullo darling,' he said uncertainly, eyeing Dawn as one might a Doberman, presently in a mood to romp, but with a record for GBH. 'Er – You're looking more gorgeous than ever.'

'Excitement of seeing you!' said Dawn with a dazzling smile.

Ken now released the head-lock he had on his companion and, with a little prod in the back, put her on display.

'Well, old pal,' he said to Toby, 'what do you think? Not bad, eh? Miss Stephanie – smarten up! I want you to meet my friend Miss Dawn and my very good friend and production associate, Mr Tobe.'

146

'My goodness, aren't you *pretty*?' said Dawn, smiling warmly.

And indeed Miss Stephanie was, perfect in an unreal way, like a picture by a sentimental Sunday artist to be seen hanging on the railings in the Bayswater Road. Blonde, with a flawless complexion and huge blue eyes – dressed in a little white skirt and a blouse with buttercups on it – she stared demurely at the floor. Dawn knew people who'd pay thousands of pounds to get their mottled old hands on something as pure as this. Once she'd have had her at it by dinner-time. Still might, come to that. No – what a disgraceful thought. This could be Toby's leading lady.

'Pretty?' cried Ken, stepping forward like a marketeer about to show off the best points of his champion pig. 'I'll say she's pretty!' He pulled up her skirt, revealing her white, sweetly virginal knickers. 'Cop those legs!' He undid the top buttons of her blouse. 'Cop those fucking. . . .'

'Absolutely delightful,' said Dawn hastily, judging it was time to intervene. 'Look – won't you sit down?' She guided Miss Stephanie to the sofa. 'Sorry about the cricket. It's just one of those test game things.' She went over to the television set and turned the sound down.

'At Lord's,' said Toby.

'At Lord's, eh? Might hop down there later and catch the last few overs. Grab a beer afterwards with Dennis and Thommo.'

'Won't you have something now?' asked Dawn.

'I could certainly do with something, darling. It's as close as an Abo's armpit out. Perhaps an icy-cold from the fridge?'

Dawn turned to Miss Stephanie. 'What about you, my dear?'

Miss Stephanie looked to Ken for guidance.

'Between ourselves,' he announced confidentially to the room, 'she's a bit shy. Not too smart socially yet. But fucking smart in other respects. Yes, sir.' He bent down and once again pulled Miss Stephanie's crisp little skirt up to the waist. 'Cop those thighs. . . .'

'Yes yes,' said Dawn. 'Absolutely enchanting. Perhaps something cold too?'

Miss Stephanie nodded shyly.

'Where *did* you find her?' asked Toby, as Dawn went to the kitchen to fetch the drinks. He beamed reassuringly at Miss Stephanie, suggesting that she was in safe, experienced hands now, however unorthodox her escort here. Ken, he sought to convey, was merely his fetch-and-carry man and he, shortly, would be taking over. He threw in a conspiratorial wink, down-grading Ken and implying that she could expect a more sensitive approach from him.

'Snatched her out of Bodys in the King's Road,' said Ken. 'A lot of variety stretched out on the sunbeds there. Bollock nude. Laid out like fishes on a slab. Do a lot of my casting in there. Know what you're getting. Some molls these days – take them home, get their gear off – oh dear, oh dear. Not too sweet.'

'Good gracious! Surely you were in the girls only section? Weren't you rather conspicuous?'

'Not in the least, old pal, not in the least. Stripped off and sprang through the door in my ballet-pumps. "Right!" I shouted. "Smarten up! Equity members on your feet!" Quite a few jumped up, I tell you. Had a quick look round. Got a half-nelson on Miss Stephanie here. Clouted a masseuse who tried to intervene and exited very fucking smartly. In and out in thirty seconds. Now. What do you think? She's only just left RADA. Rival orntreepreneurs haven't had time to – er – snap her up yet, if you catch my meaning, old pal. She's brand new, this one.'

'She's certainly lovely. You don't have an agent yet, my dear?'

Miss Stephanie spoke at last, a demure whisper, eyes cast down. 'I'm seeing Ros Chatto tomorrow actually.'

'An excellent choice!' Toby beamed approvingly. Then, judging it was time he established his credentials here, he added, 'Done a lot of business with her.' Let's hope she's forgotten, thought Dawn, returning with the drinks. 'Mention my name,' said Toby self-importantly, tapping Miss Stephanie on her sweet little knee.

'That's right, darling,' said Ken. 'You mention his name. Do yourself a bit of good. The fact is my pal Tobe's the fucking king! Yes sir!'

Toby's beam grew wider and he blew his chest out, involuntary movements of the muscles that rather told against the attempt he now made at self-deprecation. 'Come now,' he said. 'I wouldn't put it quite as high as that.' What a delightful fellow Ken was, though. So eager to push others to the centre of the stage, to reveal them in the best possible light. What generosity of spirit! What loyalty on such a short acquaintance! With Ken at hand to speak up on his behalf he could be decently modest himself. 'I don't deny I've produced some interesting shows, but. . . .'

'Yes sir, he's the man!' shouted Ken, banging his fist angrily on the coffee-table in case anyone in the room might be disposed to dispute the matter. Dawn flinched, fearful for her furniture, but she said nothing. 'Who do you suppose discovered Robert Stack? And Dorothy Malone? And Rory fucking Calhoun?'

Toby began to look concerned.

'Your pal Tobe?' asked Dawn sweetly.

'Right! My pal Tobe, that's who. Yes sir. The fact is, very few people – *very few people indeed* – are conversant with the fact that my pal Tobe's the fucking king!' Toby's concern grew deeper. Something was not quite right here. 'You play your cards right, darling,' Ken advised, wagging an urgent finger under Miss Stephanie's sweet little upturned nose, 'and you could be the one to put him back on top!' He sat back in triumph and then, bouncing upright with a furious expression in his eyes, addressed himself to a shattered Toby. 'Yes sir, you're going to be back there at the top of the heap. And meanwhile, old pal, I want you to know – I want you to fucking *know* – that I won't let anyone presume to shit-bag you!'

'What!'

'No sir. Maybe you're not too sweet now. Maybe your arse is falling out of the back of your trousers. . . .' Toby, appalled, got up to inspect his rear. 'So what?' bellowed Ken. '*So fucking what!* Don't let *anyone* presume that you're not coming back. No sir, my pal Tobe's on the rise again and that's pre*cisely* what I tell them.'

'Now look here, I really must pro. . . .'

'Listen,' continued Ken, not entirely certain yet, it seemed, that his pal stood high enough in Miss Stephanie's esteem – she'd never agree to star in his musical if she thought he was a low-life type – 'I hopped up West last night and took in the last act of the new musical at the Wyndhams. Wanted to see how the Stephenson broad was shaping up.'

'One of yours?' cued Dawn helpfully.

'Pre*cisely*! Discovered her carrying a torch in a Sydney fleapit. "Listen, darling," I said, "with tits like yours you could be a star." Since then she's never made a move without consulting me. Anyway, first person I see – I'm back at the Wyndhams now, you understand – is old Sir Allboys striding up and down as though he owned the place. I gave him plenty! "You were fucking lucky to kick a goal, Sir Allboys," I said. "If it hadn't been for my pal Tobe you'd be on the shit-heap. Yes sir!" '

'Good God,' said Toby.

'Right! I gave him a heavy sledging. "*Who* are you!" he said. "You don't know me, mate," I said. "But that's your fucking loss. Yes sir. In the old days I could have been a big help to you." I gave him plenty.' Ken now forgot about the supposed incident with Sir Allboys, being suddenly undone, it seemed, by Miss Stephanie's amazing charms. 'Jes-*us*!' he cried. 'Isn't she a darling, though? Isn't she a perfect fucking darling?'

'She's absolutely lovely,' said Dawn, sensing what was about to come (Ken was now eyeing his ingénue a shade more greedily than a ravenous fox might eye a pullet), 'but I don't think this is quite the time or place. Later, perhaps. . . .'

'And talented!' he cried. 'What do you suppose she was doing this time last week? You tell them, darling.'

Miss Stephanie spoke – a demure, eyes-cast-down whisper. 'I was in Paris with mummy and. . . .'

'That's right!' shouted Ken. 'Knocking them dead in Paris, that's what she was doing. I tell you, old pal, this girl can do the lot! She's fucking mustard, this girl. You name it, she can do it. She can sing, dance, act, suck cocks. Rupert fucking *Brookes* wants to meet this girl! Talk about an unofuckingficial rose! Now be honest, old pal. Look at that face. Look at that body. Look at those legs, will you? Listen. I was on the dog to Polanski this morning and what do you suppose? He'd just been reading – no, wait for it! – he'd just been reading *Satan's Daughter*! How about that? And he loved it! Yes sir, he fucking loved it! "Ken, old pal," he said, "this one I *have* to direct." And he wants us – he wants *us*, mind – to discover a girl to play the title role!'

'That's very gratifying,' said Toby. He had a feeling that things were getting out of hand, and his earlier collision with the lamp-post was making it difficult for him to judge whether he was in the world of fact or fantasy. He was pretty certain that he'd only met Ken an hour or so before (in which case he couldn't understand how Ken had discussed *Satan's Daughter* with Polanski the night before), but he was no longer sure of anything.

'*Gratifying*?' yelled Ken, staring at him goggle-eyed. 'I'll say it's gratifying. Highly fucking gratifying! Now, old pal. Who'd be perfect in the title role? Who has the pure, innocent, fucking virginal demure quality you specified as. . . .'

It was time that he asserted himself here, Toby decided. Time to bring the full weight of his experience to the situation. 'Ah well now,' he said, 'let's discuss this. It's a central role, a pivotal. . . .'

'Right!' bellowed Ken, driving straight through him. 'Miss Stephanie here!' He grabbed her by the shoulders and, hauling her upright, waltzed her round the sofa in a little celebratory dance. 'Darling,' he cried, 'I tell you, you're going to be a fucking *star*! Yes sir!'

'It's a challenging idea, I admit,' said Toby, also rising to his feet. 'She's inexperienced, of course, but that, paradoxically, can often work to a production's advantage. And physically, of course, she's ideal.' He was enjoying himself now, back in production, waddling in a self-important circuit, his toes turned out, his right hand prodding the air from time to time to emphasize a point. 'She'd bring the required freshness to the role, the bloom of innocence, that suggestion of early morning dew. She has, as you rightly say, a remarkable purity, a virginal quality, an untouched. . . .' He had turned round to discover that Ken and Miss Stephanie were nowhere to be seen. 'That's odd. Where did they go?'

Dawn nodded towards the sofa, behind which, for decorum's sake, Ken had knocked Miss Stephanie to the floor, where he was now attending to her noisily.

'Good heavens!'

'Keep talking, old pal,' Ken urged him from behind the sofa. 'Je*sus*!'

Dawn got up and went over to turn the sound of the television up, hoping to drown the urgent, rhythmic grunts and groans of Ken's endeavours.

'I haven't got the record books beside me, Richie,' observed Jim Laker, 'but this must be the big Australian's best score this summer. He only needs three more to have knocked up a thousand in July.'

'I wish he wasn't knocking them up in my sitting-room, Jim,' said Dawn.

'Not a pretty performer to watch,' said Jim. 'Nothing particularly stylish about his movements. But his methods are certainly effective. Balls flying in all directions. I don't think I've seen anything quite as remarkable as this all season. Have you, Richie?'

'I don't think I have, Jim.'

'Neither have I, Jim,' said Dawn.

A bellow of fury from behind the sofa suggested a successful climax to Ken's present business with his ingénue. He got to his feet, seeming to pull his trousers, Miss Stephanie's knickers and Miss Stephanie up in the same deft movement, and addressed himself confidentially to Toby.

'Want to be second cab off the rank, old pal?'

'Not at the moment, I think. Very good of you to suggest it, of course.'

'Are you sure, old pal? A word in your ear. I think she likes you.'

'No really. But thank you for the thought.'

152

'Any time,' said Ken. 'Think nothing of it. Right, if you'll pardon me for just a minute. I'll hop into the brasco for a quick rinse round the old eight-day.' He turned to Miss Stephanie, still the picture of innocence, hands clasped demurely like a schoolgirl, staring shyly at her feet. 'Do you want to go for the heavy spray, darling?' Miss Stephanie nodded. 'Right. Come on, then.'

Ken led her to the bathroom, leaving Dawn and Toby stranded on the banks of an embarrassed silence.

'Er – I hardly know what to say,' said Dawn at last. She knew exactly what to say, in fact, but was determined to maintain her conciliatory posture.

Toby coughed nervously. 'You have to admit he's effective.'

'He's that all right.'

'Direct,' said Toby, gaining confidence. 'Spontaneous. Sheer intention manifesting itself in action. A hot simplicity of purpose. Letting his essence off the leash. I like to see that.'

'Well – you're a man, aren't you, my sweet? Speaking for myself, I'd as soon he didn't manifest all over my carpet. It cost me two thousand pounds, did that carpet. Nothing against your pal, of course,' she added hastily.

'Not exactly the methods I'd use,' admitted Toby. 'But I saw nothing to dissuade me from my earlier conviction: that we'd make a first-class team.'

'You didn't?' Dawn tried to keep the astonishment from her voice.

'I didn't. I'll provide the vision, Ken the – er – directness. I the know-how, Ken the drive. I the higher strategy, Ken the moment-to-moment tactics.' Toby was striding back and forth again, beating at the air, as though to drive out doubts. 'I the subtlety, Ken the – er – '

'Just so long as you can control him, my sweet.'

'What! I've been controlling types like Ken for half my life. I know what I'm doing.' Toby suddenly sat down, missing the sofa by a foot or more and thus being forced to squat casually on the floor.

'Careful, my sweet.'

'I know *precisely* how to use him,' insisted Toby, deftly redefining his squat into a languid impresario's lounge. 'He will merely execute my will, make good my purpose. Raise the capital and so forth. The mundane aspects of the job. The artistic side of things will be entirely my department. He will merely realize my vision, rather as the dum-dum bullet realizes the vision of the sniper. Not the most brilliant analogy, perhaps, but in the circumstances not entirely discreditable.'

'If you say so, my sweet,' said Dawn meekly. 'You know more about these things than I do.'

'For instance,' said Toby, trying to rise importantly to his feet, but failing in this endeavour since his casual lounge had caused a constriction of the buttocks, locking his legs together. 'Damn. I seem to have a touch of cramp. Give us a hand, will you, my dear?'

'Of course, my sweet.' She lifted him gently and sat him on the sofa.

'Thank you, my dear. Now. Where was I?'

'You'd just had one of those analogies of yours.'

'Of course. Ah yes, I have it. All that – er – directness just now caused me to have an illumination.'

'I thought it might have done. Oh golly – sorry.'

Toby scowled at her. 'And so you should be. This isn't a *Carry On* film, you know.'

'Here. I was in one of them.'

'I'm not in the least surprised. Now. Do you want to hear about my illumination?'

'Of course I do.'

'I suddenly realized that – charming and innocent though that young lady is – we've been approaching this casting business – so often the key to a play's success – from a below the title point of view.'

'We have? Golly.'

'We have. Now why – last time round – was *Satan's Daughter* not the stupendous success it deserved to be? Why, in a word, was it a catastrophe?'

'Stage too small?'

'Yes. But there was another reason.'

Dawn almost panicked. If she got this wrong, he'd start shouting at her again. Golly, she ought to be able to remember. She'd heard this often enough. 'Wrong mimes?'

'Precisely!' cried Toby. 'Well done, my dear.' Dawn gasped with relief. 'It needed a star,' continued Toby. 'But not just any star. It needed a *mega*-star. A star who transcends and transforms the very material he or she is performing. It isn't an easy play. It's a play with a complex, uncomfortable message. A message not easily assimilated by an audience in Thatcher's Britain, running counter, as it does, to their deplorable moral and religious beliefs. A message they'll reject unless it's presented to them, as it were, subliminally.'

'Wow. How do we do that, my sweet?'

'I'll tell you, my dear. By casting as the Virgin Mary an *artiste* so totally identified with a different kind of theatre – an *artiste* of such unquestionable seemliness, an *artiste* so unalterably representative, on stage and off, of the old, traditional values. . . .'

'Here,' said Dawn, her attention suddenly wandering into areas of more immediate relevance. 'I wonder what they're doing in the bathroom? I hope your pal isn't manifesting himself on my bathmat. It's new, that bathmat.'

'Please, my dear.'

'Sorry, my sweet.'

'Where was I?'

'Golly – er. . . .'

'I have it. An *artiste* so unalterably representative, on stage and off, of the old, traditional values, that, with her first entrance, a disassociation of understanding will set in – a receptive confusion, as when a scrambling device has been attached to a transmitter – causing the audience to assimilate the play's message at some unconscious level before their anaesthetized prejudices can muster to reject it. What do you say to that, my dear?'

Dawn hadn't the slightest idea what to say to that, so she played safe. 'You are clever, my sweet,' she said.

'Thank you, my dear. It will be the first artistic transplant ever to be performed. It will become known as the Toby Danvers Effect.'

'My word! Who do you have in mind? This seemly *artiste* of such undoubted what you said?'

'Are you ready for it? It's a staggeringly audacious concept.'

'I'm sitting down.'

'Well. Just now on TV, before you got home, I saw a trailer for this evening's *Nationwide*. And there she was!'

'Who, my sweet?'

'Of course I didn't see it at once. It was too audacious a concept even for me. But a seed must have been sewn, because just now when Ken and that delightful young lady were – well, you know – it clicked. Fell whole into my brain.' Toby tapped his forehead, suggesting that there lay behind it a receiving instrument of quite exceptional sensitivity and power.

'*Who* for fuck's sake? Sorry.'

'Dame Letitia Merryweather! As the Virgin Mary! How do you like that?'

'Are you serious?' Dawn didn't want to be the object of a leg-pull. She knew of Dame Letitia only as a frail relic from those dreadful forties war films, sometimes to be seen on telly on a Sunday afternoon, but now visible in public for the most part only on flag-days, dressed as an honorary high-up in the WRAF.

'Of course I'm serious. What do you say?'

'Well.' Dawn searched uncertainly for the right word. She didn't want to be shouted at again. 'She is very *respectable*, I suppose.'

'Of course she is. She's a tradition, part of our heritage – like Black Rod or the Queen Mother – and people who sneer at her sneer at their peril. And they do sneer. Heaven help me, I've sneered myself. She can't act, they say. She couldn't ever sing. So what? To my purpose such considerations are neither here nor there. When she steps on to a stage she becomes the representative of everything that's unchanging in our island story. Good God, the *Sunday Express* has serialized her story eleven times.'

'Don't exaggerate, my sweet.'

'And small wonder,' cried Toby, deaf to such literal-minded objections. 'She has an aura – on stage and off – of such dazzling goodness that many people take her to be a saint.'

'It's a tremendous concept,' said Dawn uncertainly. Until she was entirely sure that Toby's good mood was here to stay she would greet the suggestion that she jump out of the window as a sound idea.

'Thank you, my dear. Who better to play the Virgin Mary? I mean there must be countless people who think she *is* the Virgin Mary. I'll be criticized, of course. Oh yes. Reviled, even. The theatrical establishment, their bland, paltry intellects quite unable to grasp the sheer audacity of my concept, will get out their rusty knives. "Irresponsible!" they'll squeak. "Uncommitted!" ' Toby struggled indignantly to his feet, swatting the air as though to disperse a swarm of buzzing theatrical pansies. ' "The action of a dilettante!" Lindsay Anderson himself will lead the shrill chorus of abuse.'

'Careful, my sweet.' An especially angry swat had seemed likely to spin Toby off his feet.

'But come the first night,' he cried, steadying himself against the sofa, 'and I'll be gloriously vindicated. With Dame Letitia's first dazzling entrance the Toby Danvers Effect will take over, so dislocating the audience's perception that they'll purr their approval as though at a revival of *Glamorous Night*. And the very people who sneered loudest will be compelled to creep backstage and, bereft of words, shake my hand in silent acknowledgement of my pre-eminence.'

'Of course they will, my swee. . . .'

Toby held up an arm. 'A moment, my dear. P. P. Thrush himself will sob in gratitude and I'll go down in history as one of the greatest impresarios of all time.' He collapsed with ecstatic exhaustion as Ken and Miss Stephanie emerged at last from the bathroom.

'Here, darling,' said Ken, addressing himself confidentially to Dawn, 'I really reckon that bidet of yours. I went for the heavy spray round the eight-day and under the warwicks. I've come up brand new.'

'Do you mind?' said Dawn indignantly. 'My Toby's just had an illumination.'

'Is that right? You cracked it, old pal?' Ken peered at Toby, who was lying back with his eyes closed. 'Here. Is he all right?'

Toby opened his eyes. 'Listen,' he said. 'Dame Letitia Merryweather! What do you say to that?'

'What do I say to that?' Ken looked around him for enlightenment, but none was forthcoming so he chanced his arm. 'What do I say to that? I say *fucking fantastic!*'

Toby turned to Dawn. 'You see?' he said. Surely she would now appreciate this fellow's solid worth, his boundless enthusiasm, the speed of his reactions compared to the sluggishness of hers. 'As the Virgin Mary,' he explained.

'As the Virgin Mary, eh? I *like* it! Do I hop out and gather the old tart now?' Ken was already half-way to the front door.

'No, no, I think not,' said Toby hastily. 'Not someone of Dame Letitia's stature. Normally the direct approach – of which, if I may say so, you've proved yourself a master – but in this case, the proper channels, I think, the proper channels.'

'If you say so, old pal, if you say so. You're the captain. And what might they be?'

'Her agent.'

'Right. Her agent.' Ken went immediately to the phone and lifted the receiver. 'And who might that be? I'll give him an earful.'

'Ah, well now,' said Toby. 'Not so fast here. It will be someone at London International, I imagine. Laurence De Vere Cole, no doubt. But I don't think. . . .'

'Right,' said Ken. 'What's Big Laurie's number, then?'

'Oh – er – I don't think I have it on me.' Toby tapped himself about the upper-trunk, as though the number might materialize. 'No, I don't seem to have it about my person. Look, I think I'd better handle this myself. We've got to get the approach exactly right. We're talking about Dame Letitia Merryweather here, and Laurence De Vere Cole isn't exactly some back-street operator to be rung out of the blue and told that this is his lucky day.' Nor was he. A gentleman agent of the old school, and far grander even than his clients (themselves the leading players in the land), he intimidated the most hog-confident producers with his elegance of manner, good taste and old-world rectitude.

'And why not, old pal? Now, what's this De Cole fellow's number? Stop jerking off here. We've got to get the show on the road.'

'He's right, you know,' said Dawn, of a mind now to give Ken enough rope to hang himself. 'The number will be in the book. I'll look it up.' She found the appropriate directory and then called out the number. Toby was glaring at her, utterly aghast, but how could he be angry? She was only trying to get the show on the road, wasn't she?

Toby made one last attempt to re-establish his authority. 'Look,' he said, consulting his half-hunter, 'it's after five-thirty. De Vere Cole will have left the office by now. First thing in the morning I'll. . . .'

Ken was unimpressed. 'Stop pissing about, old pal,' he said. 'Right. Here we go.' He dialled the number, while Toby slumped in horror on the sofa. Dawn, meanwhile, tried to suppress a smug, pussy-cat smile that tugged at the corners of her mouth. Ken, she reckoned, was about to self-destruct.

'London International? Pardoe International here. Ken Pardoe. Give me De Cole, will you, sweetheart?'

'De *Vere* Cole,' hissed Dawn. She didn't want Ken to be cut off before he'd buried himself.

'Thanks, darling. Hullo? Is that you, De Cole? Pardoe here. Ken Pardoe Worldwide. Call me Ken. That's right. Lobbed last night from the Coast. L and A, yes sir. Now, straight down to cases, Laurie. I'm a busy man and I dare say you are too. I don't suppose you're sitting there jerking off. . . .'

Toby groaned and covered his eyes.

'. . . Not the way to make a dollar, right? Now, the question is, are you still fronting up for old Dame Merryfeather? You are? You old rascal! Well, Laurie, this could be your lucky day.

Yes sir. Listen. I'm here at Tobe – er, fuck me dead, hang on a minute, will you, Laurie?'

Without bothering to cover the receiver, Ken addressed himself urgently to Toby.

'What's your name, old pal?'

Shock had deprived Toby of the power of speech. 'Danvers,' said Dawn brightly. 'Toby Danvers.' Toby was glaring at her so reproachfully that she had to look away. 'Only trying to get the show on the road,' she added nervously.

'You still there, Laurie? As I was saying, I'm here at Tobe Danvers's flat discussing the revival of *Satan's Daughter*. What's that, Laurie? Didn't pay who? Bouncing what? I don't know anything about that, Laurie. Ancient history, Laurie. I'm talking *now*, Laurie. I'm talking about *today*. Smarten up, Laurie. Now, what do you say to Polanski? Yes, that's exactly what I said. Roman fucking Polanski. How do you like that? Roman's going legit at last, Laurie. He's had it up to his bollocks with film people. He's figured them as a crowd of bullshit artists. And do you know what, Laurie? I tend to agree with him. Right. Anyway, the SP is that he's decided to direct *Satan's Daughter* as his deeboo in the live theatre. What? I bet you are! So. Is the old tart available? I'm talking about old Dame Merryfeather, that's who. Smarten up, Laurie. Part of a fucking life-time. Ur-huh, ur-huh, ur-huh. Trevor Nunn. Royal Bullshit Company. Highly fucking presteegious, Laurie, I grant you that, but you're talking maybe's, Laurie. I'm talking *now*. I'm talking contracts, Laurie. I'm talking *money*.'

Ken, without covering the receiver, addressed himself excitedly to the room.

'I think he's leaning my way.'

'Stick in there,' said Dawn. 'You're doing great.'

Toby moaned.

'We're moving fast here, Laurie,' said Ken, 'so smarten up or you'll be left in the starting-stalls. Casting's going ahead and already we've got Syphilis. How do you like that? Yes sir, that's what I said. What's that, Laurie? A young Julie Andrews, that's how. A brand new undiscovered superstar. Miss

Stephanie. What? Hang on a minute, Laurie. I'll find out.'

Ken spoke to Miss Stephanie. 'Come here a minute, darling. What's your name?'

'McDuff,' said Miss Stephanie in her demure little whisper.

'McDuff, Laurie. Stephanie McDuff. I tell you, Laurie, if you could see this girl's tits! Play your cards right, Laurie, and I could tip you into this one. Still, mustn't digress. Now, for obvious reasons I can't go into deep detail on the phone. I've got the script here and I'm stopping over for just forty-eight hours. What we'd like, what we'd really like, would be for old Dame Merryfeather to drop everything and hop over here to pick up the script and to partake of a spot of tucker with us. What do you say to that?'

Ken addressed the room. 'I think I've gathered the old tart.'

Dawn was too flabbergasted to comment.

'What about tomorrow night?' said Ken, back on the phone to De Vere Cole. 'Great. Great. Shall we say eight o'clock? No, Laurie, *tucker*. Ha! Ha! I *like* it! I'll tell them that one back in L and A. You know something, I'll say, that Big Laurie may look like a cunt but he likes a laugh. Yes, sir. Hooroo for now, Laurie.'

Ken hung up. 'There. The mad old sheila's coming over tomorrow night.'

Toby examined his finger-nails. 'One way of doing it,' I suppose. 'Personally, I'd have taken a rather more. . . .'

'Right,' said Ken. 'If I understand the situation correctly, this is a top-drawer type coming round here tomorrow night. A really elegant old broad, so she must think we're on the up and up.'

'Of course,' said Toby. His initial amazement had now worn off and he was beginning to convince himself that most of the credit for Ken's achievement was due to him. Ken, after all, was his discovery. Well, Dawn's discovery, perhaps, but he had seen the fellow's raw potential – something she had signally failed to do. It had been an audacious, though, in the circumstances, entirely justified decision of his to let Ken do the spade-work with Laurence De Vere Cole (the element of surprise had certainly put De Vere Cole off his guard), but now it was time for him to assume full control. This dinner-party, on which, he now saw, his whole future in the business rested, was something that only he could master-mind. 'Leave this to me,' he said, standing up in order to dominate the situation. 'I want you all to. . . .'

'So,' continued Ken, literally brushing Toby aside, knocking him backwards into the sofa, where he flayed around for a while, his little legs unable to get a purchase on the floor, ' 'scuse I for mentioning this, old pal, but I don't want any funny business, you read me?' He winked and made a suggestive gesture that would have started a riot in a Port Said brothel.

'Now look here. . . .'

'I don't want anyone here lowering the fucking tone,' insisted Ken. 'Now don't get me wrong, but some of the types I've seen running in and out of here – well, not too sweet, old pal, not too sweet at all. Take the razor-blade that was here earlier. . . .'

'Do you mind?' said Dawn indignantly. 'I take it you're referring to my friend Dolores?'

'Thank you, darling. That's the one. Your pal, Big Dolores. Well, we don't want her running through the door with her bongo-drums, do we? Nothing against your pal, of course. It's just that I've got a really grand old tart coming over here tomorrow night and I've got to think of my reputation.'

'*Your* reputation?' said Dawn. 'Good God!' She would have gone further, but she'd lost some confidence in the last five minutes, had experienced an uneasy sensation of the ground moving beneath her feet, making her unsure of everything. Ken, against all sane odds, had delivered Dame Letitia. What else might he not achieve? Perhaps, for a while, she'd better go along with this.

'That's right,' said Ken, 'and I don't want her ambushed in the hall by a big spade lady with a ring through her nose. I want the atmosphere just right in here. No spooks. No cowboys. No mugs. No horse's hooves. No dope. And above all, no monkey-business. I don't want anyone here unconversant with the fucking ettikay of these evenings. I don't want anyone letting themselves down by mixing punch in the bidet or putting on a Perry Como record. This is a top-drawer moll I've got coming over here tomorrow night. Yes, sir.'

'Now look here,' protested Toby, still fighting – and failing – to get upright, his little legs lashing around in mid-air, trying to get some plantage on the floor. 'I have done a certain amount of this sort of thing, you know. . . .'

Ken wasn't listening. 'Old pal,' he cried, 'I can see it up in lights already! Ken Pardoe Promotions Worldwide in association with – in fucking association with, mind you! – Toby Danvers Productions presents old Dame Merryfeather in *Satan's Daughter*! Yes, sir! Here we come! This is the big one!'

He let out a whoop of triumph and knocked Miss Stephanie to the floor, where he attended to her quickly. 'Right,' he said, getting to his feet. 'I'll be hopping along now. Catch you all tomorrow night. And remember what I said. G'day to you all.'

'Here!' cried Dawn, as Ken disappeared through the front door. 'You've left your ingénue behind. Oh well.' She turned to Toby. 'I say! Isn't this exciting? Dame Letitia Merryweather to dinner! Wait till my mum hears about this. Dame Letitia's her favourite *artiste*!'

'Don't go to pieces, my dear,' said Toby, quite missing the point, mistaking Dawn's genuine excitement for the onset of first-night nerves. 'Perfectly normal social occasion. Here. Give a chap a hand, will you? Thank you, my dear.' Dawn had helped Toby to his feet. 'Just take your lead from me,' he said, narrowly missing the coffee-table as he waddled uncertainly back and forth. 'Been in this situation countless times. I know how to handle these *artistes*.'

'Of course you do, my sweet.' She could cope. She'd take the day off tomorrow, plan the occasion properly for Toby's sake. Perhaps she'd do her duck in orange. And she'd better buy some decent wine. Wow! Dame Letitia Merryweather to dinner! This *was* exciting!

'Gently but firmly,' Toby said. 'Like children, the lot of them. Leave it all to me.'

'Of course, my sweet.' What should she wear? She must look lady-like. Golly – if Dame Letitia of all people suspected for a moment that she was dining in a . . . Christ! The thought was too dreadful to be entertained. Ken the cowboy had been right about that at least. God, if anything unseemly happened! She shuddered. The prospect was not to be contemplated. No, nothing would go wrong. She'd take special precautions.

'I speak Dame Letitia's language, do you see?' said Toby. 'I respect the tradition that she represents. Her world is a world I understand, and in some ways, I often think, it's a better world than the one we live in now. As Old Tom Eliot used to say: "Of course we know more than them; but they are what we know." Something like that. I shall be able to match her anecdote for anecdote.'

'Naturally, my sweet.'

'Anecdote for anecdote! Did I ever tell you about the time I took luncheon at the Ivy with Binkie, Henry Sherek, Harold Hobson, Robert Morley and Coral Browne?'

'Yes, my sweet.'

'Fabulous anecdote. I'll never forget it. Binkie was in drag. No, Henry was drunk – that's it – no, Coral arrived a little late and said – I'll never forget this – Coral was a celebrated wit, you understand, still is for all I know – Coral said . . . bugger me, I've forgotten! Never mind. I'll have remembered by tomorrow night.'

'You'll be all right, my sweet.'

'Just be yourself, my dear,' said Toby, collapsing on the sofa and falling asleep seconds before there was an agitated ring at the front door.

'Bloody hell!' said Dawn, opening it to Steady Eddie, still in Jane Birkin's gym-slip and white socks, and Dolores, who had a serious wobble on. 'What's up now?'

'It's old Bill, isn't it?' gasped Dolores. 'They're on to us! Got home to find them staking out the flat.'

'Get away!'

'*Straight*. Two blokes in a white Cortina.'

'Two blokes? Could have been anyone.'

'*No*. Eddie recognized one of them. D/C Harris. Bust him a couple of years ago. We're only under surveillance, that's all! Can we crash here for a couple of nights?'

'Of course you can,' said Dawn. 'Mind you, I think you're over-reacting. I mean, how do you know they were watching *your* place? Still – if you'd feel safer here. Where's your gear?'

'Oh, I've got that,' said Dolores, taking a piece of pot, wrapped in silver paper, from her bag. 'Scored from Mad Harry on the way home, didn't we?'

'No, you daft loon. Not your smoking gear. Your *wearing* gear. Your clothes and that.'

'Couldn't get them out with old Bill watching, could we? Be all right for a couple of days. Eddie can wear something of yours.'

'Yeah. Wow.'

'Better than being in the sodding nick.'

'Nick nothing!' said Dawn. 'Oh, by the way,' she added casually, 'we're giving a small dinner-party tomorrow night. Hope you won't mind. Just a few friends over. Oh – and Dame Letitia Merryweather.'

'Dame Merryweather? She's a new one on me,' said Dolores. 'She been at it long, has she?'

'Get off! She's a lady.'

'Should do well, then. You heard of her, Eddie?'

'Yeah. Wow.' Eddie broke into song, a pleasant drawing-room baritone. 'We'll gather lilacs in the spring again, and walk together down an English. . . .'

'Christ!' said Dolores, spinning in alarm. 'What's that?'

'One of her songs, isn't it?'

'No wonder she took up hustling,' said Dolores.

'She didn't take up hustling, you big dollop. She's going to be in Toby's revival, isn't she? As the Virgin Mary.'

'Hey, that's wild. Sounds like a good gig, this dinner-party. I'm looking forward to it. Aren't you, Eddie? *Eddie!*'

For once Eddie had left his position in front of the mirror and was busily engaged on the floor with Miss Stephanie.

'Here,' said Dolores. 'Who's she?'

'Toby's ingénue.'

'Oh. Wow. She's cute, isn't she?'

'Join the queue.'

'Might at that,' said Dolores. 'Will she be here tomorrow night?'

'Suppose so. We seem to have inherited her.'

'She is decorative. Quite a buzz, in fact. She'd look good over there by the curtains.'

'Tell you what,' said Dawn. 'She can be the maid. That'll impress Dame Letitia.'

'Right! And Eddie can be the butler. That'll knock her out! And I'll do the cooking. I'll do my soul food. That'll swing her your way. I'll touch it up a little.' Dolores pointed to her gear and made a crumbling gesture. 'Blow her mind, know what I mean?'

'I don't think so, darling,' said Dawn. 'Last person sampled your soul food was later found naked, if I'm not mistaken, dancing round the Cenotaph. A kindly meant offer, I'm sure, but I think I'll do my duck in orange. And then we'll have fritters.'

'More than likely,' said Dolores.

Later that night in bed, while Toby muttered in his sleep beside her (rehearsing anecdotes, no doubt, with which to dazzle Dame Letitia over dinner), Dawn prayed earnestly that the evening would go without a hitch. She'd learnt her lesson. If Toby wanted to be back in production, then back in production he'd be. Perhaps the Australian cowboy *could* make it happen. Perhaps others would be swept along by his fantasist's belief that asserting a thing to be the case was the same as its being the case. Perhaps everything was a fantasy. What was it Toby had once said about the Queen only being the Queen by virtue of her playing that role, by general agreement, in the collective fantasy? Weird, that. She'd always thought of the Queen as the Queen, end of story, with sort of Queen-like qualities, not simply as someone playing a part. If she wasn't really a Queen, what else might not be the case? Perhaps she,

Dawn, wasn't really a tart. Here – that was right. *She* knew she wasn't a tart – not inside, where it mattered. And this flat wasn't really a brothel; it merely assumed the properties of a brothel in the fantasies of certain people. To Dame Letitia, visiting it with different expectations, it would be the tasteful home of an important producer and his girlfriend. Everything would be all right tomorrow night if she, Dawn, could believe in the fantasy as strongly as Toby and Ken. Christ, she must. She didn't want to be up-ending members of the Monday Club for the rest of her life.

Thursday. 12.15 p.m. The Water Rat, Chelsea.

In a corner of the Water Rat, the World's End pub where the police and villains can carry out their business with discretion – distinguishable, to the layman, from each other only by the fact that the villains are the ones that are too short to have become policemen – Ronnie Snipe waited impatiently for his meet with D/C Smiley. When Smiley at last showed up, Snipe came briskly to the point.

'Well? Got my twenty grand yet?'

'Give us a chance, Ron,' said Smiley, ordering himself a large gin and tonic. 'Haven't had a fucking moment, have I? That basket-case Pyle has had us following a black tart and her ponce all over London, hasn't he?'

'Oh yes?' said Snipe, who had been so busy in the last twenty-four hours that he hadn't yet made good his four and a half years of enforced celibacy. 'Any form?'

'Which one?' asked Smiley.

'The tart, of course,' snarled Snipe.

'Oh, the *tart*. Thought you might have picked up some unsavoury habits in the nick.' Smiley saw no harm in reminding Snipe which one of them was the convicted villain. 'Yeah, she's quite tasty, as it happens. For a jungle-bunny.'

'Tip me in,' said Snipe shortly. 'So – why can't you get the money now?'

'Leave off. Back on sodding tart surveillance in ten minutes, aren't I? Nell Gwynn House. Look. I'll go to the bank first thing in the morning. Meet you here at twelve, right?'

'Okay,' said Snipe. 'But don't let me down. Any info on that other matter?'

'What other matter?' Smiley knew he was talking about Toby Danvers, the dodgy theatrical who'd done him up, but he didn't intend to give Snipe a run at him just yet; not until he'd sussed the set-up inside Dawn's flat – something he hadn't been able to do yet, thanks to Pyle squatting in the hall himself, like a sodding potted plant. And now it looked as if he wouldn't get a chance. With the spook and the shirt-lifter inside Dawn's flat, it was certain that Pyle would be going for a bust tonight. He certainly didn't want Snipey running through Dawn's door with his knuckle-dusters at the same time as Pyle. Look bad all round. He wished now that he hadn't mentioned Nell Gwynn House. Snipey looked so keen to get his end away, he might stake the place out, hoping to bag the spade. He didn't intend to hand the dodgy theatrical over to Snipey until tomorrow, after the bust tonight. He'd let Snipe exact a terrible revenge, and then have him pulled. With his record, if he did enough damage to Danvers – and he looked sick enough to kill him – he'd draw fifteen years. They'd done well together over the years, but now it was time to have the mad-eyed little psychopath banged up for good, leaving the business to be split fifty-fifty between him and Honest John.

'Whereabouts of Danvers,' said Snipe. 'Toby Danvers.' Saying the name caused his bleak little eyes to shine momentarily with a glint of animal savagery. 'I know he's in London. Saw him up West yesterday, didn't I? Took a swing at the fat sod, but he escaped in a fucking taxi.'

'Is that right?' said Smiley, thinking again that he wouldn't be in this Toby's boots. 'Yeah, well I might have a lead on him at that. Nothing solid yet. Should be able to let you know something tomorrow.'

'Let's hope so,' said Snipe.

'So Coral turned to Ivor and said: "Don't be a goose, darling! If I'd married you I'd be a hundred and twenty-six!" '

'Delightful!'

'Quite priceless, Dame Letitia!'

'Priceless!'

'Quite delightful!'

The dinner-party so far was a triumph, the sparkling atmosphere and *bonhomie* due, in no small part, to Dawn, who, that morning, had spent seven hundred and sixty-three pounds, to the nearest pound, on wines, having ruled that the vintages looted by Toby from the German Food Centre in Knightsbridge were hardly distinguished enough for a guest of Dame Letitia's stature; and to Dolores as well, who, disregarding Dawn's instructions, had, when her back had been turned, laced the duck in orange with enough cannabis resin to take the balls off a fighting bull. Nor had Toby failed in his duties at the head of the table. Resplendent in a burgundy smoking-jacket, reminiscent, as to cut and style, of something Sherlock Holmes might have climbed into after dinner, and at his most loquaciously expansive, he had, as promised, matched Dame Letitia anecdote for anecdote, topping her, even, from time to time (a tendency that would have much displeased that steely old lady had she not been feeling so curiously relaxed), and she, thanks to the wine and the cannabis resin and the warm shower of flattery and reminiscence under which she'd been bathed by Toby, had, after an apprehensive start, blossomed like a crocus. Miss Stephanie sat demurely at the end of the table, silent but smiling radiantly, Eddie hovered as the butler, and Dolores, judging that by staying in the kitchen she could smoke herself legless without lowering the tone, had insisted on staying hidden as the cook. Ken, for reasons yet to be discovered, had not turned up; his failure in this respect in no way a matter of regret to Toby, who had taken advantage of his absence to dominate the stage. Having allowed Dame Letitia to dwell briefly in the spotlight with her boring anecdote about Ivor, he now shouldered her tactfully into the wings.

'A charming anecdote, Dame Letitia,' he said, 'quite charming. Coral was a fabled wit, of course. I recall a superb remark she once made to Kenneth Williams – a master of the theatrical riposte himself, of course.'

'Oh, a master. An absolute *master*.'

'Coral was telling Kenneth over lunch – I forget where – about a forthcoming production of *Julius Caesar*, in which she was to appear as Caesar's wife. "Nothing in it for me, I suppose?" asked Kenneth, who, amazingly, was temporarily out of work. "I don't know," said Coral. "Let's have a look," and she leafed through the script, which she happened to have with her. "Ah, here's something!" she cried. "A camp just outside Rome. Perfect for you, darling." '

'What a marvellous remark!'

'Superb!'

'Magnificent!'

'Priceless,' said Steady Eddie, refilling Dame Letitia's glass from a bottle of *Château Yquem*.

Encouraged by the success of his latest anecdote, Toby was about to follow it with Coral's witticism at the Ivy – the point of which he'd just remembered – when he realized in time that its punch-line (an intimate operation on a distinguished actress had resulted, Coral had informed the Ivy, in the discovery of nothing more serious than Olive Harding's gardening-glove) was a trifle risqué, perhaps, for the present occasion. His temporary pause, while he gathered his resources, gave Dame Letitia a chance to return to the world of Ivor.

'Of course,' she said, with a wistful look in her enormous, still beautiful eyes, 'it was always such *fun* at Ivor's. Laughter and music from morning till night. I sometimes wonder if young people today, with all their noise and protest, haven't forgotten how to have *fun*.'

'Another world, Dame Letitia, another world.'

'And gorne for good, alas,' said Dawn. 'Some more coffee, Dame Letitia?'

'Thank you, my dear, I'd love some.'

'Edward, some more coffee for Dame Letitia, please. A fresh pot, perhaps?'

'You've got it, man,' said Steady Eddie, retiring to the kitchen.

'My *dear*, that young man's a positive *treasure*,' said Dame Letitia, who still had an eye for attractive young men and had taken a very obvious liking to Eddie: a preference that had been noted with displeasure by the cook, peering from time to time through the kitchen-hatch. If she was going to lose her Eddie it wasn't going to be this horny old tart. 'Where *did* you find him? You keep an eye on him or I'll be *luring* him away! I can get nothing but foreign girls who break everything in sight. I had this exquisite little figurine, you know. . . .'

'You still *do* have, Dame Letitia,' said Dawn, with a consoling pat on Dame Letitia's spidery old hand, 'you still *do*.'

'*No*, my dear, alas I don't. Last week my Portuguese girl *swept* it to the floor. Smashed it to smithereens. And it had been in my family for almost three hundred years.'

'Oh well,' said Dawn. 'Just so long as it wasn't new. Look on the bright side!'

'Oh delightful! Yes, the silly little goose was probably dreaming about her love-life. They seem to be over here for the sole purpose, I sometimes think, of entertaining a different young man each night.'

'Oh, don't tell me!' cried Dawn. 'I used to employ girls, but their boyfriends became such a problem. Of course, to keep staff at all these days one has to make allowances that would have been unimaginable once.' This remark was aimed at Steady Eddie, who, having returned from the kitchen with a pot of fresh coffee, had decided to suspend his buttling duties for the moment and join the guests, placing himself at the end of the table next to Miss Stephanie, the increasing radiance of whose smile was not unconnected with the positioning of his left hand, hidden from view between her thighs. Eddie got up at once, his abrupt withdrawal causing Miss Stephanie's radiance to dim, as though something had suddenly become unplugged.

'One certainly does,' agreed Dame Letitia wistfully. 'Times change, times change. But where was I?' She had noticed that Toby was cranking himself up, with little preparatory grunting noises, to discharge another anecdote and she wasn't disposed to relinquish the floor for the moment.

'At Ivor's,' said Steady Eddie, once more hovering dutifully in the background.

'*Thank* you, my dear,' she said, favouring Eddie with one of her most glittering smiles, a smile that one night at the Café Royal had captured the heart of the Prince of Wales – or so the rumour went. 'Dear Ivor, the very soul of thoughtfulness. For his friends nothing was too much trouble. I remember one summer in Capri – a few of us were staying at Ivor's villa. Binnie and Sonnie – brother and sister, but they fought like cat and dog for all that, you know – and Noël and Graham and. . . .'

'Willie and Sirie?'

'Don't mention Sirie, man,' warned Steady Eddie.

'Er – we never did, we never did,' said Toby quickly. 'Thank you Edward. That will be all for the moment.' He jerked his head in the direction of the kitchen, but Eddie remained beaming on the spot.

'No no,' said Dame Letitia. 'Binnie and Sonnie and Frank and Boo – this was *after* Sonnie and Boo, you understand, but there was still a certain atmosphere, as I recall. And a strange thing – Binnie always took Boo's side against Sonnie. Well, I think she thought Jessie wasn't quite our sort of person. Oh dear! What a *dreadful* old snob I must sound to you young people.'

'Not at all,' said Steady Eddie. 'Rock on, darling.'

Toby glared at him and jerked his head more violently, but to no avail. He lit a cigar to calm his nerves, and then found himself echoing Eddie's point. 'Not at all, not at all,' he agreed. 'It's one of life's central dilemmas, I always think. How to be

172

true to one's standards and at the same time make allowances for those less fortunate than ourselves, for people who haven't, perhaps, had the advantages.' He glared at Steady Eddie, who beamed back at him, causing Toby to ask Dawn in an aside whether, perhaps, Eddie had had more of the duck in orange than the rest of them.

'Wouldn't be surprised,' said Dawn, in a discreet whisper. 'But don't worry. It's going well.'

'Indeed, indeed. Anyway,' he said more loudly, 'I recall saying to Binkie once. . . .'

'Yes, yes,' said Dame Letitia quickly. She had no intention of being silenced yet. 'Anyway, years later when they were in *One Two Three* together at the dear old Duke of York's. . . .'

'Jessie and Boo?'

'No no, my dear. . . .'

'Not Frank and Ivor, surely?'

'No no. . . .'

'She means Binnie and Sonnie, man,' said Steady Eddie.

'*Thank* you, my dear. What a *charming* young man. You're so lucky.' For a moment Dame Letitia seemed quite distracted, recalling the days and nights, perhaps, when charming young men like this had crowded her dressing-room rather than her dreams, sipping champagne and vying chivalrously for her favours. 'Oh dear. Where was I?'

'With Binnie and Sonnie at the Duke of York's,' said Steady Eddie.

'Of course! Well, they hardly spoke at all. When Sonnie became ill and Bobby had to take over in the show at a moment's notice, I believe Binnie was quite relieved even though it meant a *mountain* of new work for her. And Bobby was never the easiest person to work with, you know.'

'Don't tell me!' cried Toby. 'A clever little monkey, but – well, let's leave it at that.'

'How wise, my dear, how wise. There's quite enough unkindness in the world today, so let's not add to it. Oh dear! I *can't* imagine what's the matter with me.' She looked hopefully towards Steady Eddie, who didn't fail her.

'At Ivor's villa, darling, in Capri.'

'Of course. Thank you, my dear. Well, Cole came down from Paris for a few days and his visit happened to coincide with his thirty-fifth birthday. Dear sweet Ivor *wracked* his brains trying to think of something really original to give him. I mean, what *did* one give to a person like Cole who literally had everything already? Eventually, of course, Ivor came up with the answer.'

'Trust Ivor!'

'A pair of solid gold braces!'

'Brilliant!'

'Superb!'

Eddie, immensely impressed by the ingenuity of Ivor's gift, and wishing to be at closer quarters to pick up any other sartorial hints that might be coming, joined the party once again, placing himself, as before, and much to her relief, next to Miss Stephanie.

'I remember the presentation as though it was yesterday,' continued Dame Letitia. 'We all gathered after breakfast in the morning-room, where Ivor made a graceful, witty little speech and then handed Cole his present. Cole unwrapped the parcel, smiled with delight and then made an even wittier speech of thanks. I only wish I could remember it.'

'One for the anthologies, I imagine,' said Toby.

'Indeed. Then Cole took off his jacket, *threw* the solid gold braces he was already wearing into the waste-paper basket and replaced them with Ivor's!'

'Magnificent!'

'Sheer theatre!'

'Style, do you see? That was the abundant quality in those days. Style. With Ivor, Cole, Elsa, Noël . . . well, it was in everything they did. It was there in their lives, their work, their friendships, above all in their music. So different to that dreadful noise young people make today. The music of the jungle, I always call it.'

'Oh don't!' cried Toby. 'Pop music. We know where that leads.'

'We certainly do. Er – where, my dear?'

'May I be explicit?'

Dawn looked alarmed, but Dame Letitia assured Toby that he mustn't feel obliged to hold back on her account, adding archly that young people had known how to have a good time in her day too, you know. She took another sip of *Château Yquem*. She must be careful; she felt quite tipsy. But she couldn't remember when she had last enjoyed herself so much. She felt so at *ease* with these charming young people, so extraordinarily relaxed. She was experiencing a warm, almost dreamlike sensation of well-being, quite unlike anything she'd known before. That nice young man, the butler, was beaming at her from the end of the table. She was certain it was most unusual for the butler to sit down with the guests, but for some reason his having done so made her want to giggle. She felt quite strangely reckless. Perhaps there'd be dancing after dinner. She'd sing to them, perhaps.

'Drugs and nudity,' said Toby.

'My goodness!' cried Dame Letitia. She hadn't expected anything like that, but the dear young man was absolutely right, of course. 'I do so agree, my dear. Filth and squalor everywhere. And as for the theatre, I must confess I'm shoulder to shoulder with that Willie Whitehouse woman. I was saying to Sir Angus – the Police Commissioner, you understand, a close personal friend of mine – I was saying to him only yesterday evening – we were on television together, I wonder if you saw it. . . .'

'No I didn't,' said Toby rudely. He'd had quite enough of Dame Letitia's rambling reminiscences and wished to steer the conversation towards a more interesting subject: namely himself and his contribution to the theatre. This, after all, was primarily a business occasion and he was eager to lure Dame Letitia into his trap before Ken could show up and, with one blundering excess, scare her off. 'But one thing I can say,' he said. 'For twenty years I've fought filth and depravity in the theatre with every fibre of my being. And, I like to think, with some success.'

'*Wham Bam Thank You Mam*,' said Steady Eddie helpfully,

175

while Miss Stephanie's smile, coincidentally, grew more radiant still.

'Thank you, Edward,' said Toby icily. 'We're not keeping you from your duties in the pantry, I trust?'

'I'm cool, man,' Eddie assured him.

Dame Letitia, for some strange reason – certainly inexplicable to herself – was suddenly convulsed by peels of merry laughter, obliging her to take a tiny lace handkerchief from her bag and dab her eyes.

'Oh dear,' she said. 'I cannot imagine what's the matter with me. Please forgive me. It's just that I'm having *such* a good time.'

'Right on, darling,' said Steady Eddie.

'Actually,' said Toby, 'I would have mentioned *Over The Edge*.'

'Ah, yes,' said Dame Letitia, bravely pulling herself together, 'Laurie told me that that was one of yours. Those four clever young vets.' The notion of four vets upon a London stage struck Dame Letitia as so richly comical, for some reason, that she was gripped by convulsions once again, from which she rescued herself with a sharp self-admonishment along the lines of 'be*have* yourself Letitia!'

Toby corrected her severely. 'Dental students, actually. Yes, an amusing trifle. Odd thing was no one else could see its potential. I could. Saw it at once. Mere boys, they were. Just out of medical school. Quite unpolished. But I saw something in their little show that no one else could. Needed a strong hand at the helm, of course. My privilege to provide it. The theatrical establishment scoffed, needless to say. "You can't put four dentists on to a West End stage with no sets and no dancing gals and call it a revue," they cried. I admit I wavered. Was I about to make my first mistake? Something told me to press forward. A natural showman's instinct, I like to think. And of course I was entirely vindicated. Still running actually. The cheques keep rolling in. Got one today, as it happens. Where did that one come from my dear?'

Dawn, caught by surprise, could only gape. Any conjunction

of cheques and Toby was, to her, so bizarre, as to freeze the mind.

'That's right,' continued Toby, 'Moosejaw.'

'*Moose*jaw?' Dame Letitia seemed on the point of further convulsions.

'Canadian tour,' Toby explained.

'Oh dear,' said Dame Letitia, pulling herself together. 'How very lowering for the cast. In my day we never had to go to Canada.'

'Dedicated *artistes*,' said Steady Eddie.

'And how refreshing to hear it,' said Dame Letitia. 'Dedication, alas, is hardly the quality one expects to find among today's young players. All *they* want to do, it seems, is squabble over money and *tear* their clothes off. Nudity, violence and the language of the gutter – that's all the theatre has to offer nowadays.'

'How true!' cried Toby. 'Do you know what I always say? I always say that old Bill Shakespeare didn't have to resort to four-letter words to get his point across. That's what I always say. What, after all, is the most erotic play in the English language? I'll tell you. *Anthony and Cleopatra*. Yet you can search it high and low without finding a four-letter word.'

'Ex*actly*,' agreed Dame Letitia fervently. 'Do you know what one of my greatest pleasures used to be?'

'Let me guess. To take your grandchildren to a matinée?'

'Good heavens! How *did* you know?'

'And now it's no longer possible? Nothing suitable? Don't tell me! Nothing to be found except obscene language and young women *thrusting* their bosoms in your face?'

'*Precisely*!' cried Dame Letitia excitedly. This young man could read her mind. And to think she'd been apprehensive about coming here this evening! 'That's not what I go to the theatre for. To have young ladies *thrust* their bosoms in my face.'

'Nor I,' said Toby. 'Might I – without straying into impertinence, I trust – try and hazard a guess as to why you *do* go to the theatre?'

'Oh *try*, please try!'

'To be entertained?'

This was uncanny. How had he known? The words had been on the tip of her tongue. 'My dear,' she trilled, 'it's as though you can read my mind!'

'There's no mystery,' said Toby modestly. 'I like to think – without presuming too much, I hope – that you and I are kindred spirits, united in our loathing of gross behaviour. Do you know who I blame for the present parlous state of theatre? I blame the managements. Standards must come from the top. The generation before mine – I'm talking now about the great impresarios: Cocky, Firth Shepherd, Tom Arnold, old Sir Bronson Albery – set an example in their shows and in their private lives which we, who followed them, sought to emulate.'

'Exactly, my dear,' said Dame Letitia. 'But who sets the standards now? Take that young man who's all the go at the moment. Michael White.'

Toby groaned and raised his eyes in horror to the ceiling. 'Oh please! A lightweight! A frivol! At best a giver of amusing parties, at worst a suburban pornographer.'

'How *thrilling* to hear you say so.' This young man had been right. They *were* kindred spirits, of this she was now certain. 'Do you know he sent a script to my dear friend Boo Laye the other day that simply defied description? Poor dear Boo was quite shaken, but she had the presence of mind, thank goodness, to put it to the flames before her Philippino boy could read it. It's hard enough to keep servants these days without *thrusting* pornography under their. . . .' Dame Letitia suddenly broke off, embarrassed, it seemed, at having discussed staff problems with the butler sitting at the table. '*Please* forgive me, my dear.' She smiled winningly at Eddie.

'That's cool, darling,' said Eddie. 'Wasn't it Auden, after all, who said: "No unearned income can buy us back the gait and gestures to manage a baroque staircase, or the art of believing footmen don't hear human speech?" No offence taken, darling, I assure you.'

Dame Letitia was dazzled. Not only did he have the aspect of an angel, the butler, but a mind richly stocked with the classics from our literature. Well, not quite the classics, necessarily, Mr Auden hadn't been exactly . . . what? Never mind. She turned to Dawn. 'What an amazing young man, my dear! You keep an eye on him or you'll be looking for another butler! I shall be carrying him off into the night!'

Dolores, who'd been listening from the kitchen, had heard enough (the dinner had already cost her a pair of gold braces, unless she was very much mistaken). She now swayed uncertainly across the room and, glaring at Dame Letitia, sat herself menacingly close to Eddie, her proximity, however, in no way inhibiting his rhythmic rummaging between Miss Stephanie's thighs.

Toby, having made a mental note not to avail himself of Eddie's services at any future theatrical occasions at which he himself intended to shine, now returned to the attack. 'It defeats my understanding,' he proclaimed, 'why anyone should want to present a so-called entertainment glamorizing copulation. Do you know that Ken Tynan came to me originally with the idea for *Oh! Calcutta*? Well, Tynan had a few brains – there's no denying that – but he was obsessed, poor man, with matters – excuse me, Dame Letitia – below the belt. I wanted nothing to do with the beastly thing, and I told him so. I could see the *commercial* potential, of course.' He let out a single, derisive snort of laughter, as though at the very notion of his being swayed by such crass considerations, and, aiming at the ashtray, tapped his cigar out into Dame Letitia's coffee-cup. 'I'm not blind,' he said. 'But never have I passed up millions with a lighter heart. Introduced him to White. Two peas in a pod.'

'You should congratulate yourself, my dear.'

'For refusing to compromise my standards?' The very idea caused Toby to throw up his hands in horror. 'With respect, Dame Letitia, when that becomes a matter for self-congratulation I shall call it a day. Is there something wrong with your coffee?'

'Well, yes, it is a little – er. . . .'

'Edward! The coffee's disgusting! Another pot, if you please.'

'Yes, sir! With you in a second.' Moments later, Miss Stephanie cried out once, threw her head back with a little gasp, shuddered briefly and then went limp, a look of strange contentment on her face. 'Right!' said Eddie, getting to his feet. 'Fresh coffee coming up.'

'Which brings me,' Toby said, 'to the point of what has been, to me at any rate, an unforgettable occasion.'

'And to me *too*,' Dame Letitia fervently assured him.

'*Satan's Daughter*.'

'Of course, of course.' Dame Letitia felt that she was floating a few feet off the ground – it really was a most peculiar sensation, but by no means a disagreeable one – but she mustered herself gamely and gave Toby as much of her concentration as she still had at her disposal.

'Of one thing I am very sure,' said Toby. 'In the sort of climate about which we've been talking, with lust and permissiveness off the leash, nothing could be more timely, more necessary, than P. P. Thrush's cleansing vision.'

'Indeed, indeed,' said Dame Letitia, squinting as she tried to follow him. 'An *interesting* play, from all I hear.'

'Interesting indeed. But if I can say this without sounding pretentious, I see it as more than a play. I see it as a crusade.'

'A crusade! My dear, you're quite a romantic!'

'Dame Letitia, if it is the mark of a romantic to believe that the times cry out for an impassioned assault on prurience, corruption and moral relativism – then I plead guilty to the charge. But I make no apology for that.'

'Nor should you, my dear.'

'But I have to say this: a production of *Satan's Daughter* without you as its moral mainspring, Dame Letitia – well, it's frankly inconceivable. Only you among contemporary players – thank you, Edward, just put the pot down there – has the spirituality – I can put it no other way – to ensure that this very important play – so wantonly compromised in its last production – becomes what it so richly deserves to be: a religious as well as a theatrical experience.'

'You tell her,' said Eddie, sitting down again, but this time on Miss Stephanie's other side, since Dolores had now moved into the chair formerly occupied by him, with no apparent diminution, as a result, in the radiance of Miss Stephanie's smile.

Toby ignored him. He leant forward and, taking one of Dame Letitia's frail little hands in his, gazed into her eyes. 'Dame Letitia?'

'Yes?'

'Will you – can you – shoulder the burden?'

'Oh my dear,' she croaked. She was afraid she was going to faint with ecstasy. 'Am I worthy?'

'Only you can judge. I think so.'

Dame Letitia pulled herself together. For the last half-hour at least she'd known that nothing and no one, no agents, natural calamities, acts of God, would prevent her from appearing in this play – she'd do it for nothing if that meant she could dine from time to time with these enchanting young people – but old instincts now stirred, passing messages to her reeling mind to the effect that she shouldn't appear too eager. 'I'd have to read the script,' she said.

'But naturally.'

'And I'd have to be satisfied that the production would be in perfect taste.'

Toby's purple jowls quivered like jellies, caught in a raging war between hurt and indignation. 'Dame Letitia!' he shouted. 'In the last twenty years I have produced some fifty theatrical entertainments. Not all of them made money.' He paused momentarily, ready to smother any sarcasms from the butler's end of the table, but none was forthcoming, so he continued. 'Some dozen or so were presented for other reasons. Finer reasons, I like to think. But. . . .'

'*Farts And Arses*,' said the butler.

'Thank you, Edward. The title, of course, was *Arts and Farces*, but we're grateful to you for all that. As I was saying, a charge of tastelessness could not have been levelled at *any* of my productions.'

Dame Letitia had never felt so chastened. 'Oh my dear,' she cried. 'I meant no offence, I do assure you. To have met you both' – she smiled glowingly at Dawn – 'to have been entertained in your delightful home and to have met your enchanting young friends' – she directed her most radiant smile towards Steady Eddie and in return got a look from Dolores that would have frozen her to her seat had she still been able to see a foot beyond her nose – 'is to be *entirely* reassured on that score. I simply cannot conceive of any one of you being associated with anything in the slightest bit distasteful.'

'How very sweet of you to say so,' said Dawn.

'That goes for me too,' said Eddie.

'I'll read the script,' said Dame Letitia, 'and – no! I'll do it anyway! I confess that to play the Virgin Mother has always been an ambition of mine, and since I now have *total* faith in your judgement, why shilly-shally? Yes! I'll do it! There. You have my word on it.' Dame Letitia sat back with the gracious, yet modest, half-smile of the Queen Mother conferring an honour.

Dawn gave a little cry of happiness. Toby had pulled it off, and without any help from that Australian bandit. Thank God *he* hadn't turned up to dunk his moustache in the soup and otherwise take the edge off Toby's triumph. Nothing could go wrong now. She got up and kissed Dame Letitia on the cheek, and then she kissed Toby, who swatted himself free of her attentions as he might an over-persistent fly. This was no time for girlish excitability, he judged; he'd only been doing his job, and Dame Letitia had made a wise decision: a point that he now brought gravely to her attention.

'Dame Letitia,' he said. 'You have just made one of the most important decisions of your career, and one that you won't regret. On that you have *my* word.' Dame Letitia's solemn undertaking, he managed to suggest, had been returned with interest. 'Edward! Another bottle of *Château Yquem*, I think!'

'Yes sir!' said Eddie, getting to his feet. 'One bottle of *Château Yquem* coming up.' As he was walking to the kitchen, the telephone rang.

'Dolores, would you be so kind?' said Dawn.

The cook, who had risen from the table with the butler and had been tailing him to the kitchen where she'd intended to raise, quite forcibly, a couple of points with him concerning his table manners, went dutifully instead to take the phone. As she did so, there was a ring at the front-door.

'My goodness!' said Dawn. 'Whoever can that be?'

'It will be Ken,' said Toby. He was delighted that Ken had at last arrived to share this moment of triumph. He could afford to be generous. Some of the credit, after all, was due to him. He, Toby, had landed Dame Letitia, but Ken had baited the hook. 'A junior executive of mine,' he explained to Dame Letitia. 'A bit of a rough diamond, but you'll take to him, I'll guarantee it. I'm breaking him in, as it were, for a mutual friend.' Toby lowered his voice confidentially and spoke from behind his hand. 'Kerry Packer, actually.' Toby couldn't have produced a name better qualified to meet with her approval. Dame Letitia was an ardent admirer of Mr Packer, for his healthy right-wing views and his support for family values. 'Benefit of my experience. If he proves satisfactory I've assured Kerry that I'll keep him on.'

'Oh Ken, of *course*,' said Dawn, with, to her surprise, a small feeling of relief. She was usually the last to jump when the door-bell went. As she got up from the table, she tried to pin down and identify a little tug of concern that had been nagging at the back of her mind for the last few seconds. 'I'll get it.'

'Yeah?' said Dolores on the phone. 'Yeah? Is that right? That's great. Catch you later, then. Bye.'

'Who was that?' asked Dawn, passing Dolores on her way to the front door.

'Only the Wanker,' said Dolores, compelled, since she was on her way to sort matters out with Eddie in the kitchen, to convey this information to the room in her most carrying voice. 'He's on his way.'

Dawn stopped dead in her tracks. *That* had been the worry buzzing in her mind, fucking Mount-Hugh. She'd forgotten all about him, not given him a thought in the excitement of the last twenty-four hours. Christ, Toby would kill her. And rightly. Just when he'd dazzled Dame Letitia with his integrity and rectitude, a freak, thanks to her, would dance through the door as the Sugar Plum Fairy. It was a punishment, of course. Her past burying Toby's future. They didn't let you get away with it, and she'd been mad to suppose it could be otherwise. 'Er – Mr Wankle,' she explained, trying to take some of the edge off Dolores's raucous announcement. 'Tory MP, Thatcherite,' she added, judging that the coming dance might be received more broad-mindedly if performed by a monetarist. With her mind racing, trying to think of a solution to this problem, she opened the front door to a more immediate one.

'God almighty!' she cried. 'It's Pillock!'

'Yes, I know,' said Pillock. 'Feeling spare, thought I'd drop in on the off-chance. Up in town with Vanessa, but mislaid her at the RAC. Not the first time it's happened. Having a drink in the bar, turned round to discover she'd beetled orf. Hullo. What have we here?'

'We're having a dinner-party,' Dawn explained. She tried to push Pillock back into the corridor, but he brushed past her and was already bearing down on Miss Stephanie, who seemed to have caught his eye.

'Er – Dame Letitia,' said Dawn, grabbing Pillock and steering him in her direction, 'may I introduce Geoffrey Pillock? Ex-2 Para, banged his head at the Upland Goose, now with British Intelligence.' His qualifications, she felt, would go some way towards explaining such buffoonish behaviour as would inevitably take place.

'Ssssh. Security. My masters at MI5. Walls have – what?'

'Geoffrey, this is Dame Letitia Merryweather.'

'Well done,' said Pillock, adding, in an aside to Dawn, 'bit past it, isn't she?' and struggling in her grip to get at Miss Stephanie.

'How do you do, Mr Pillock?' said Dame Letitia, delighted by the arrival of yet another charming-looking man. Really, they had the nicest friends, this young couple. Kerry Packer, an MP, on his way over from the House, and now this fine-looking young man who was a member of the security forces. It was hardly to be wondered at that she'd felt so at ease here. These were her sort of people. 'British Intelligence, you say? How *fascinating*!'

'Sssshh.'

'Of course.'

'And this is Toby,' said Dawn, somewhat nervously. Toby had been glaring nastily at Pillock, and at her too. She pulled a helpless face, suggesting that this potentially catastrophic interruption had been of her devising, and, with little jerking movements of the head, tried to indicate that she'd shoot him out just as soon as was decently possible. She felt quite sick with fright.

'Good show,' said Pillock, sitting down next to Toby, but leaping up with a yell when he received a vicious kick on the ankle.

'Roger' he said, hopping around in pain. 'You're ahead of me in the queue. My fault. Should have known. Sticky moment. Better push orf.'

'Oh dear,' said Dame Letitia. 'Surely you don't have to go so soon, Mr Pillock?'

'Yes he does,' said Toby nastily.

'I say,' said Pillock, who'd been staring at Toby with a puzzled frown. 'Don't I know you?'

'Certainly not,' said Toby. 'How dare you?'

'Weren't we at Shrewsbury together?'

'No we weren't.'

'Surely we were! Danvers, isn't it?'

'No it isn't,' said Toby furiously.

'Come orf it, old boy! Jackson's, 50–55. You were in Mallett's. Well I never. Long time no see!' Pillock, after the manner of his kind on meeting an old acquaintance, suddenly thumped Toby hard in the chest, bringing Toby snarling to his feet, fists raised, crouched to swing an upper-cut.

'Watch it!' he bellowed.

The truth now dawned on Pillock, causing him to close one eye in a knowing wink and shrewdly nod his head. 'Got the picture,' he said. 'Slow on the uptake. Here under an assumed name. Very wise.'

'An *assumed name*? I live here, you fucking idiot!' raged Toby, letting go the upper-cut, which would have taken Pillock's nose off had its delivery not coincided with a decision by Pillock to step down the table towards Miss Stephanie. In the event, its momentum merely swung Toby off his feet and into Dame Letitia's chair, where he would have flattened her, had she not been removed from it seconds earlier by Steady Eddie, who, returning from the kitchen with the *Château Yquem*, had, to distract her attention from what he'd quickly summed up as an untidy situation, hauled her to her feet with the request that she instruct him in the Charleston.

'He's a friend of the cook's,' Dawn explained, stepping in and dragging Pillock away from Miss Stephanie. 'Dolores!'

'Is he really?' said Pillock. 'Good show.'

'Not him, you fucking idiot,' hissed Dawn. '*You.*'

'Roger,' said Pillock. 'I'm a friend of the cook's. Should have known. Sorry.'

'Get this clown into the bedroom before he nauses everything up,' said Dawn to Dolores, who had followed Eddie out of the kitchen. 'And for Christ's sake keep it *quiet.*'

Dolores steered a grateful Pillock ('Don't mind if I play through then? Damn decent of you!') across the room and managed to get him inside the bedroom, from where, for the next few minutes he was catapulted from time to time as though connected by elastic to the dining-room table, still seeking information as to Toby's background and on each occasion wearing one article less of clothing.

'What an *interesting* young man,' said Dame Letitia, released by Steady Eddie and back at the table, a little out of breath but ecstatically happy. 'British Intelligence, you say?'

'Sssh. Security.'

'Of course. A fine young man. He reminds me of my dear late husband. . . .'

'Remember Salter?' bellowed Pillock, this time without his jacket.

'NO! Odd fellow. He seems to think he knows me.' Toby turned to Dawn. 'A friend of the cook's you say?'

'Yes, my sweet. She met him on her day off. I expect he's trying to establish – oh dear, what do they call it? – a special relationship with the third world.'

'*That* will be it,' cried Dame Letitia, more than satisfied with this explanation of all that had occurred and, thanks to the euphoria-inducing substances she'd taken, scarcely noting it as odd that the cook should be receiving in the master-bedroom.

'Remember Pringle-Fisher?' shouted Pillock, this time without his trousers.

'NO! Well, whatever he's up to, I really must apologize,' said Toby. 'Cook shouldn't have people round when we're entertaining, my dear.'

'Not her fault exactly, my sweet,' said Dawn miserably, wondering how she'd explain the arrival, any minute now, of Mount-Hugh with a rabbit on his head. 'He dropped in unexpectedly.'

'Please don't worry on my account,' said Dame Letitia. 'He looked like a perfectly splendid young man to me. My dear late husband was in Military Intelligence during the war, you know. For that reason, I have always held the security forces in the very highest regard.'

'I think we all do, Dame Letitia.'

'It is in peacetime, particularly, I think, that we should honour our servicemen in the fight for freedom. During the war one did one's duty unquestioningly, of course, but in these soft times such devotion to an ideal is all too rare, alas.'

'Going to the Grafftey-Smiths this weekend?' enquired Pillock, stark naked now except for his boots.

'NO! And now, while we're waiting for my assistant to turn up, why don't I get you a copy of the script? We don't want you leaving without it, do we?'

'Well, that would be nice,' said Dame Letitia. 'I certainly look forward to reading it, but nothing, of course, will alter my decision to appear as the Virgin Mother. You couldn't stop me now if you wanted to! Everything that's happened here tonight has persuaded me that I must put myself *entirely* in your hands.'

'And you will not be disappointed,' said Toby, trundling off to search for the script among his belongings in a corner of the room.

'What a *charming* young man, my dear,' said Dame Letitia, turning to Dawn. 'He seems to be – now don't be offended – almost of the old school. And do you know something? I came here this evening with certain qualms.'

'You did? My word. Why?' She wished she was dead.

'The generation gap, I suppose. Most young people today – well, one hardly speaks the same language. But you two – now don't be offended by my saying this. . . .'

'I'm sure I won't be.'

'You seem in many ways to be throwbacks to a more gracious era. Your home, your friends . . . oh I'm just a silly old goose!'

'Oh goodness!' cried Dawn, raising her voice in an attempt to smother a loud sequence of grunts, groans and protesting bedsprings emanating from the bedroom. 'I think that's the nicest compliment I've ever had.'

'I *mean* it, my dear. A more gracious era.'

'Here we are,' said Toby, returning with the script. 'I can hardly wait for your reaction. 'I'm confident you'll agree that the part of the Virgin Mary might have been written with you in mind.'

'My dear, I'll read it tomorrow, I promise.'

'As for the other leading roles – well, your casting suggestions will be invaluable.'

'But I wouldn't *dream* of interfering!'

'As God I see Michael Hord. . . .'

'Oh *dear*. Nothing against Michael, of course, a divine man and a lovely actor, but he *has* appeared in some rather odd things recently, don't you think? What was that Joseph something?'

'Andrews,' bellowed Toby, trying to drown out the gasps and groans that were now coming more loudly from the bedroom, since Dolores had added to their volume with her own hoarse cries and yelps of simulated ecstasy. 'An amusing romp.

Written by a friend of mine, as it happens. Scoot. Alan Scoot.'

'Disgracefully crude, I thought,' said Dame Letitia.

'More of an acquaintance, wouldn't you say, my dear?' shrieked Dawn.

'Who?' screamed Toby.

'Scoot,' screeched Dawn.

'Never heard of him,' Toby thundered.

'Poor Michael was prevailed upon to appear in one scene without his clothes,' said Dame Letitia, her eyes widening with horror at the depravity of it. ' "Oh dear," I thought, "what *do* you think you look like?" It's so sad, I think, when one of our leading players feels obliged to keep up with the latest trends. Whether it's for the money or from a desire to shock, I really don't know. But, as to who plays opposite me, well, my dear, that's *entirely* your decision, of course.'

'A joint decision, Dame Letitia, a joint decision, I hope.'

'Do you remember Ingrams?' asked Pillock, dressed now in Dolores's underwear. 'Slave to self-abuse.' The shrieks and groans of simulated ecstasy continued, mysteriously, to fill the room.

'NO!'

'Oh.' As Pillock withdrew, perplexedly shaking his head, the phone and the doorbell rang at the same time.

'Oh my God!' cried Dawn.

'Don't go to pieces, my dear,' said Toby. 'It'll be Ken. Let him in, will you? Edward – perhaps you could take the phone?'

Dawn walked with thumping heart towards the door, resolved, if it was Mount-Hugh, to keep walking, along the corridor and into the night, never, perhaps, to be seen again. She opened the door and Ken ran past her in a rush, bent slightly at the knees and holding his cock.

'Sorry darling,' he cried, heading across the room. 'Fucking Fosters. Brasco. Quick.'

'That was Mr Wankle,' said Eddie, putting down the phone. 'He can't make it after all. Held up at the House.'

'What a *shame*. An all-night sitting?' asked Dame Letitia, as Ken sprinted past her.

'No,' he said. 'Just a quick slash. Keep your legs crossed, darling, I'll be out in a jiffy.'

'Ha! Ha! I told you he was a bit of a rough diamond. Heart of gold, however.'

'I'm sure he has,' said Dame Letitia, looking rather faint. 'Er – will he have anything to do with the artistic side of things?'

'Good heavens no!' said Toby. 'That will be *entirely* my department, I assure you. His function is really very trivial. He's scarcely more than the office-boy. Rather a colourful way of expressing himself at times, but he means no harm. I'll have a word with him about it.'

'Oh don't worry about that on my account,' said Dame Letitia. 'My goodness, I've worked in films, you know. In the old days at Gainsborough under Korda – well, by the end of the day the air was *blue* with bad language. One of the mistakes you young people make is to assume that we old-timers have never heard a rude word! No, no, I'd be *very* surprised if your young friend came up with anything I hadn't heard before.' She patted Toby reassuringly on the hand.

'That's more like it,' said Ken, adjusting his fly as he came out of the bathroom. 'Missed the tucker, did I? Never mind. Make do with a glass of *Pol Roger*. Mouth's as dry as a nun's nas. . . .'

'Let me introduce you properly,' said Dawn quickly. She'd recovered all her confidence now that she knew the Wanker wasn't coming – at least Ken wasn't her responsibility. 'Dame Letitia, this is Toby's assistant, Mr Pardoe. Ken Pardoe. Ken – Dame Letitia Merryweather.'

'Call me Ken,' said Ken, bowing chivalrously over Dame Letitia's extended hand. 'Pardon my breath, it was eggs for tea. Hullo! hullo! hullo! Someone's pulling my prick here! I simply do not believe that this beautiful young lady can possibly be *the* Dame Merryfeather. Come on, darling! Tell us who you really are. Sophia Loren? Brigitte Bardotte? Own up. The joke's over.'

'My dear,' said Dame Letitia, looking far from displeased by these compliments and making no attempt to recover her hand from Ken's devoted grasp, 'this young man's quite a charmer, isn't he?'

'Well, whoever you are,' said Ken, 'you're still a heart-breaker, darling! You've still got a mischeevious twinkle in your eye!' He suddenly dropped Dame Letitia's hand, and took Dawn to one side. 'A word in your ear, darling. What's the horse's hoof doing here? It isn't a cock-up, is it?'

'Not *yet*,' said Dawn furiously. 'Toby's doing very well so I'd thank you not to fu. . . .'

'Leave this to me,' said Ken returning to the table. 'I'll sort this out.'

'Tell me, my dear,' said Dame Letitia, 'I gather Kerry Pa. . . .'

'With you in a minute, darling,' said Ken. 'First I've got some highly important business to discuss with my pal Tobe here. You'll be wondering, old pal, why I lobbed a little late. I'll tell you. On the way here I happened to drop in at the RAC where I had the good fortune to meet this rich old auntie. Money coming out of her arse. Contact from the past. Vanessa Pillock of the Annoir millions. And where do you suppose she wants to put some of her loot? Into a fucking musical, that's where!'

'Very gratifying, I'm sure, but I don't. . . .'

'Right! So naturally I told her about *Satan's Daughter* and old Dame Merryfeather here. And what do you suppose? It only transpires that Dame Merryfeather is her favourite *artiste*!' Ken turned to Dame Letitia. 'How do you like that, darling? She saw you in *The Dancing Years* before the war.'

'*During* the war, my dear.'

'That's right! During the fucking war!' Ken broke into song. ' "We'll gather lilacs in the spring again. We'll walk together. . . ." They don't write songs like that any more, no sir!' He turned to Dawn. 'Here darling,' he said. 'Don't we have anything appropriate to put on the record-player at this moment?'

'Toby has *Noël Coward At Las Vegas*, I believe.'

'Dear Noël,' said Dame Letitia faintly.

'Perfect!' cried Ken. Dawn went over to the record-player and very soon Noël was thinly assuring the room that there were 'bad times just around the corner'. 'Take it away, Noël. Now, old pal, when I told Mrs Pillock that old Dame Merryfeather here was starring in your musical, well, the mad old sheila nearly dropped the lot.' Judging that it was now time to rectify any falsely modest picture that his pal Tobe might have painted of himself and his contribution to the theatre, Ken now set about the urgent business of putting the record straight. 'I take it, darling,' he said, 'that the old scoundrel's being telling you about his big one?'

'He has. . . .'

'On the uppers now, of course, on his uppers,' Ken assured her, 'as you can see. Backside falling out of his trousers. Writs flying through the letter-box. Daren't answer the door. Coming for the furniture any day now. Flat to the boards. Up to his bollocks in trouble.'

Toby, his eyes bulging with rage, at last found his voice. 'Now look here. Dame. . . .'

'Lost the lot!' cried Ken cheerfully. 'Written off by everyone. But not by me. No sir, not by me. I saw something in the old scoundrel no one else could. Took it upon myself to mark his card. "Look here," I said. "You're six lengths behind the field. The jockey's fallen off a couple of times, but you're still in the race. You've done it once – *Over The Edge* – and you'll do it again. So – straighten up, wipe the mud off your boots and get in there," I told him.' Dame Letitia looked as if she'd swallowed her dentures, Dawn, without success, made little squawking attempts to stop the flow, and Toby sat pole-axed in his chair, feeling for his heart. 'But words are cheap,' Ken assured the table. 'I didn't leave it at that. No sir. I fixed his come-back. Wasn't easy, I can tell you. Couple of black marks against him. On the bad-egg list. But I managed it. His last chance. *Satan's Daughter*. And I persuaded Polanski to climb aboard. He wasn't keen, I can tell you. "Is it art, Ken?" he said. "Art?" I said. "Art who? Smarten up, Roman. This one's commercial. It's got the lot, this one. God. The devil. Popes.

Orgies. Old Queen Mary. Naked sheilas lobbing from nowhere and biting one another in the box. The mugs will be knocking the doors down to see this one, Roman." "Okay," he said. "I'll do it. As a favour to you, Ken. And as a tax dodge." I tell you, darling, with a classy old tart like you in the lead it can't miss. Can't fucking *miss*! Pass the *Pol Roger*.'

Ken sat back beaming, satisfied that he had now made good any damage done to his pal's project due to his unfortunate absence earlier in the evening. Then he saw Pillock coming out of the bedroom wearing nothing but Dolores's knickers.

'Stone *me*! What's this?'

'I say. If you are going to the Grafftey-Smiths this weekend perhaps you could. . . . Good God! It's Pardoe! I say. Shouldn't I be getting a dividend soon from Pardoe Mining Pty?'

As Ken floundered for an answer, as Dame Letitia stared at Pillock in amazement, as Dawn tried to get her mind off thoughts of suicide by telling herself that nothing else could now go wrong and as Toby wondered who to take a swing at first – Pillock, Dawn, Ken, Dame Letitia or the fucking butler? – D/S Pyle knocked the front door down and ran into the room with Smiley, Perks, Harris and Blagden.

'Fuck me dead! It's a bust!' cried Ken.

'Right!' shouted Pyle, 'No one move!' And no one, since paralysis held them in their chairs, did, except Pillock who put his hands up, this gesture of surrender causing Dolores's knickers, which were a size too large for him, to fall around his ankles. 'I have reason to suppose that these premises are being used for immoral puposes.'

Dawn found her voice. 'Oooooh! *That's* not a very nice thing to say! Whatever next! There's nothing immoral going on here, I do assure you. It's a theatrical dinner-party, this.'

'Ah's fucking you so good!' screamed Dolores, alone in the bedroom and therefore, it might have seemed, carrying simulated ecstasy to unnecessary lengths. 'You've *never* been fucked this good before. No, sir!'

Dawn got up and closed the bedroom door.

'Right, that's it!' said Pyle triumphantly. 'I've heard enough.

This is a brothel.'

'A *brothel*, young man?' Dame Letitia rose indignantly to her feet. 'Have you taken leave of your senses? I have a business relationship with these young people. I'm to be in their next production.'

'Oh yes, madam?' said Pyle unpleasantly. 'Well, you should be ashamed of yourself.'

'How *dare* you, Inspector!' cried Dame Letitia. 'Wait till the Commissioner hears about this. Sir Angus happens to be a personal friend of mine.'

'That's what they all say.'

Toby, still holding his heart, rose unsteadily to his feet in defence of his leading lady. 'This, my dear Superintendent, is Dame Letitia Merryweather.'

'Oh yes, John?' said Pyle. 'And I'm Lord Lawrence of Arabia. Take down her particulars, Smiley. I reckon she's behind this. Smiley! Cut that out, Smiley!'

'Right, skip,' said Smiley, who had fallen instantly for the charms of Miss Stephanie and, having backed her against the wall, was interrogating her around the inner-thigh. He abandoned Miss Stephanie with reluctance (the questioning being taken over, almost immediately, by D/C Perks) and seized Dame Letitia by the arm. 'Okay, darling,' he said, 'be a good girl . . . cor, fuck me!' A tremendous blow from Dame Letitia's handbag had caught him in the mouth.

'That's it!' cried Pyle. 'Assaulting a police officer! Perks! Harris! Cut that out, Perks! Get her outside.'

Dame Letitia, squealing angrily and swinging her handbag, was carried into the corridor while Ken ran after her with the script. 'Here. Don't forget the script, darling! And thanks for dropping by. We'll let you know.' He turned to Toby. 'Mad old auntie. Fancy leaving without the script.'

'Right,' barked Pyle, nodding towards Pillock. 'Who's she?'

'Pillock, Chief Superintendent.'

'Watch it!'

'No no, Commander. That's his name. Geoffrey Pillock. He went to Shrewsbury.'

'I can see that.'

'He might invest in my new show. He's on the short list.'

'He certainly is,' said Pyle contemptuously. 'Right, Pillocks. You can relax now. No one's going to shoot you.'

Pillock lowered his hands and pulled his knickers up.

'Hullo hullo,' said Pyle, suddenly noticing a piece of pot, not used in the duck and orange and left by Dolores on the table. 'And what do we have here, I wonder?'

Ken stepped forward and picked up the piece of pot. 'This, Assistant Commissioner,' he said, 'as a smashed Abo could see, is a piece of cooking chocolate.' He handed it to Pillock. 'Eat that, Pillock.'

'Here!' screamed Pyle, as Pillock swallowed the pot. 'That's destroying the evidence, that is! And who might you be?'

'Roman Polanski,' said Ken.

'Better and better. You're long overdue. Outside!'

'Leave this to me, old pal,' said Ken, giving Toby a huge wink as he was frog-marched into the passage to join the other prisoner.

'Golly,' said Dawn.

Friday. 11.30 a.m. Nell Gwynn House.

'What are you going to do, then?' asked Dolores, for the tenth time that morning.

Dawn, after a sleepless night, during which plans for a slow and painful death for Pyle had dominated her thoughts to the exclusion of more practical solutions, had come to one conclusion: there was precious little she could do. The situation, as she saw it, was at least clear-cut. She was finished as a business-girl (this scarcely bothered her) and Toby, thanks to her, had received a shock from which it seemed unlikely he'd recover. After he'd tried on three occasions the night before to throw himself out of the window, she had, with Eddie's help, given him a sleeping-draught that would have concussed an ox.

But that had been a short-term measure. There seemed every reason to suppose that, on waking this morning, he would try to repeat the exercise, having, and excusably, in her opinion, first killed her. Fear of what he might do to himself in her absence had so far stopped her from visiting Mount-Hugh: the only person she could think of who might be able to help. Other little flutters of activity, undertaken more from a desire to be doing something than from any real hope that anything could come of them, had led to nothing. Most dispiriting of all had been a telephone conversation with her man in the Rubber-heels Squad, eliciting the information that Pyle was uncorruptible, a protégé of the Police Commissioner's and about to move, as an Acting-Chief-Inspector, to an important job at Scotland Yard.

'Might see the Wanker, mightn't I? Once Toby's up.'

'Think he can help?'

'Doubt it.'

'Oh God,' wailed Dolores, staring miserably at a cup of coffee that Eddie, dressed in a negligée of Dawn's, had just brought in. 'We've had it, right?'

'Right.'

'Here. Do you get the papers, then?'

'Yeah. Over there. Why?'

'Want to read my stars, don't I?' said Dolores.

'I've read mine,' said Dawn. 'I've got to watch out for a disagreeable surprise. As if I hadn't had one.'

Dolores found the appropriate page in the *Daily Mail*. 'That's odd,' she said. 'It says I'm in for a disagreeable surprise too. Silly, these stars.'

'What are you, then?'

Dolores looked up in suprise. 'Here. you know what I am. I'm a fucking business-girl, me.'

'*No*, you great dollop. . . .'

'Christ, you're right,' groaned Dolores, putting down the paper. 'I'm an *ex*-fucking business-girl, aren't I?'

'I meant what *star-sign* are you?'

'Oh. Virgo.'

'Well, there you are. So am I. That explains it. They're not so daft, you see. I mean, the person doing them can't have known that, can he? Yet he says the same for both of us. Uncanny, really.'

'Yeah. Wow.' Dolores's eyes rolled in wonder. 'Here,' she said, turning over the paper and reading the front-page headlines. 'You read the paper, then?'

'Yeah. I told you. The important bits. My stars. The problem of being a woman and that. The City page. I'm long in ICI, as if I didn't have troubles enough.'

'That's cool, then.' Dolores put the paper down and sipped her coffee.

'Why do you ask?'

'Just wondered.'

'Wondered what?'

'What you made of the story on the front page.'

'What story?'

'The one about you.'

Dawn shrieked with alarm and, snatching the paper from Dolores, read the headlines. ' "Dame Letitia Merryweather and Roman Polanski held in Chelsea Vice Swoop". Fucking hell! We're only in the sodding papers!'

'I told you.'

Dawn shot to her feet, clutching her head. 'Right! That's it, isn't it?'

'What are you going to do?'

'I'm going to see my lawyer, aren't I? Pratley and Smith.' Like all those who perceive themselves as operating slightly outside the rules, Dawn had a tremendous faith in lawyers. 'I'm going to take legal proceedings, me.'

'Yeah? Against who?'

Dawn looked at her scornfully. Really, the naïvety of these black chicks. If she knew against who, she'd be a lawyer, wouldn't she? '*I* don't know against who. My lawyers will tell me that. That's what they're there for, isn't it?' She went to the phone and, speaking, almost imperceptibly, on the right side of hysteria, made the necessary arrangements. That done, she looked doubtfully at Dolores. 'Right,' she said. 'Nothing for it but to leave you in charge. If Toby wakes up, don't on any account let him see the paper. That's vital. Got it?'

'Got it.'

'In his condition the shock could finish him.'

'Wow.'

'Tell him that I've just popped out do some shopping. Say I'll be back soon.'

'Back soon. Got it.'

'You'd better answer the phone if it rings, but just take messages. For God's sake don't accept any bookings. We're probably being watched.' That must be so, thought Dawn. Pyle didn't have a case against her at the moment – unless he could persuade Dolores or Pillock to give evidence against her, which seemed unlikely – and she assumed that the evil little rat was out there now, planning to strike again. He must be particularly vexed, she thought, that he hadn't been able, thanks to Ken's resourcefulness in getting Pillock to swallow the pot, even to make a drugs charge stick. In the circumstances he'd be back, and sooner rather than later.

'Wow!' said Dolores. 'Watched!'

'Got all that, then?'

'Sure. You leave everything to me.'

'Okay. Catch you later.'

Dawn left, far from happy at leaving Dolores in charge and trying to convince herself that this appointment with her lawyer really couldn't wait, that she wasn't just scarpering in panic, fearful of the consequences of being around when Toby woke. Seconds later, Pillock appeared from behind the sofa, and, still dressed in Dolores's knickers, lurched groggily after Dawn into the corridor, closing the front door behind him.

'Wow,' said Eddie. 'He all right, do you think?'

'Don't know. Swallowed all my gear, didn't he? Good stuff, that was. Have to get some more. I could do with a smoke.'

'Yeah.'

'Why don't you ring Mad Harry? Tell him to come here, though. We're being watched.'

'Yeah. That makes sense. Right.'

While Eddie placed his order on the phone, Toby suddenly emerged from the bedroom in an ancient dressing-gown and, eyes staring wildly like a National Theatre player's in a mad scene, duck-walked theatrically towards the sofa. He lowered himself gently and, with a long sigh, lay back and closed his eyes. At last he spoke. 'Oh dear, oh dear. My lovely shattered dream. How sad, how very sad.'

Dolores and Eddie stared at him in horror, scarcely daring to breath. He looked appalling. His hands trembled, his voice was clogged with induced sleep and his eyes were filmed over like stagnant puddles.

Suddenly he sat up and, with one hand raised dramatically like an old-hat actor-manager's silencing the gallery, he said, 'It would have made history, do you see? Dame Letitia as the Virgin Mary. What a concept! Who but I could have dreamed that vision into being?'

Dolores sought nervously to reassure him. 'No one, man,' she said.

'For as long as stage-managers still called the half, for as long as footlights came on in playhouses throughout the world – I'd have been remembered. But now? Whenever and wherever two or three or four true men of the theatre meet to talk of concepts and production values, I shall be hung by the heels, albeit metaphorically, and spat upon.'

'Wow,' said Dolores.

'And why? Because of the random, unthinking action of . . . of . . . of a pol-*ice*man! Ohhhhhh!' He slumped in the sofa and closed his eyes. The phone rang. 'Say that I'm dead.'

'Yeah. Right,' said Dolores. She went to the phone. 'Hullo? Who? I'm afraid not. He's dead, man. That's right. Just now. Over he went. Dead as a rat. I'll say it's tragic! Right. Keep cheerful!' She hung up and gave the news to Toby. 'It was that Laurence De Vere agent fellow for you.' Toby groaned. 'Took it badly. Said it was tragic.'

'And so it is. Where's Dawn?'

'Pratley and Smith,' said Dolores, quite forgetting her instructions to the effect that Dawn was shopping.

'Estate agents? Sensible as always. Put the flat on the market and clear out while we can. A small island in the Mediterranean, perhaps. A room looking over the harbour. Wake up to the sound of fishing boats returning with the morning catch. Not such a bad life, perhaps. Peaceful. Calm. No harassment. Might open my museum. "Ah, *buenos dias*, Pedro! Do come in, my dear. Let me show you round. This is James Agate's walking-stick, and these, if you can believe it, are the actual teeth Kenneth Williams wore to the first night of *The Pirates Of Penzance*. That will be five hundred pesetas. *Gracias*." Not a bad life at all. Never say die, do you see? Never too late to make a fresh start. Examples abound. Who was that stockbroker who chucked up everything in middle age to travel round Africa on a bicycle? Got eaten by a giraffe in Basutoland. Ah well. I'd better get my effects together.'

Toby clambered to his feet and tottered slowly to his corner of the room, where, mumbling to himself about the old days, he began the sad task of stacking his theatrical remains in little piles.

'Cracked,' said Dolores.

'Yeah,' said Steady Eddie. 'Poor old sod.'

There was a ring at the front door. Dolores, reckoning there was nothing more to lose, opened it without even looking through the spy-hole, to be confronted by a beaming Ken with Pillock in a head-lock.

'Brown Owl reporting back,' said Pillock.

'Found him wandering round the streets looking for a taxi,' said Ken. He released Pillock, who immediately disappeared behind the sofa. 'Morning darling! Morning Phyllis! Hey, that really suits you.'

'Ta,' said Eddie.

'Hullo hullo!' Ken had noticed Toby in his corner, dejectedly leafing through some ancient cuttings. 'What's up, old pal? Not feeling too bonhominous today?'

Toby gazed at him with the pain-wracked eyes of a maddened bull, seeking a quick despatch. 'Oh God,' he groaned. 'Give me strength.'

'That's more like it!' cried Ken enthusiastically, slapping him so hard on the back that he pitched head-first into his memorabilia, scattering the neatly-stacked little piles like chalets in an avalanche. 'That's more like it! Never give up. So you dropped a slight clanger last night. . . .'

Toby, on his back, his little legs beating the air, like an over-turned beetle fighting to get upright, croaked with indignation. 'What! *I* dropped a clanger?'

'That's right, old pal. But never mind. The point is, I managed to turn the situation to our advantage. Yes, sir. Did you read the papers? Well? Well? Not bad, eh? Front fucking page in every one!' Toby groaned and gave up struggling. He closed his eyes and lay still among his relics. 'Too good for you, is it, old pal? Too fucking exhilarating being back in production? Well well well. I never thought I'd see the day when a man of the theatre couldn't stand the excitement of being on the front page. Do you know how much you'd have to pay for that sort of exposure? Anyway, down to cases. Has Big Laurie phoned yet?'

'Never heard of him,' said Toby.

'Come on, old pal. Smarten up. The old tart's trainer. Laurence De Cole. Has he phoned? He must have read the papers.'

'Yes. He phoned.'

'And?'

'And? *And*?' Toby stared lividly up at him. 'I declined to speak to him, of course.'

'Declined to speak to him?' Ken was aghast. 'Oh dear, oh dear. You aren't *au fait* with the modern way of doing things, old pal. Thanks to us, that mad old sheila is better news this morning than she's been for years. Even *she* realizes that. Yes, sir. If you've been over the jumps as often as that mad old moll you get a pretty fair understanding of the form-book. She's not some frisky two-year-old out on her first gallop, you know. She's a wily old stayer, that one. I tell you, if I was her trainer I'd enter her for the Ascot Gold Cup. She'd *piss* in. Yes, sir.'

Toby stared up at him in wonder. 'She *liked* being arrested, did she?'

'Funny you should mention that, old pal. As it happens, she didn't take too kindly to that at first. But I soon straightened her out. Had a stiff talk with her. Took her to one side in the charge-room. "Smarten up, you mad old tart," I said. "And stop hollering. It's all a PR stunt. The police are working for *me*." I explained that I had to get out on bail to hype things here but that she must stay in the cooler for forty-eight hours prior to appearing before the beak on Monday morning. Imagine the column inches we'll get on that one, old pal! Dame Letitia Merryfeather on an immorality charge! She got the picture in the end. Now. I'd better give the SP to Big Laurie.'

'Here,' said Dolores. 'I spoke to him. When he phoned. Told him Toby was dead.'

Ken was stunned, open-mouthed with admiration. 'I *like* it!' he bellowed, slapping his knee so hard that Toby, who had just managed to struggle upright, fell flat on his face again into his memorabilia. 'Old pal, I take back what I said! Fantastic! Imagine the headlines I can get on that. "Orntreepreneur drops down dead on the eve of the big one"! On that I can get the front page again. I'll hype that just as soon as I've spoken to Big Laurie.'

Ken went to the phone and soon had De Vere Cole on the line. 'Hullo? Laurie, you old scoundrel! On top of it, this morning, are you Laurie? What's that? Yes. Very fucking tragic. Like that. Bang! Having his breakfast. Reading Irving Warble on last night's big one in *The Times* and SMACK! – head-first into the All-Bran. Dead as mutton. Heart. One of the last of the all-time great orntreepreneurs. Fixing the funeral now. The vets – Medler, Crook, Bummett and Moon – have agreed to carry the coffin. Nice gesture. Buried at sea. Last request. Naval man. Full honours. *Abide With Me* and swoosh – over the side. Now. Down to cases, Laurie. About Dame Merryfeather. You've read the papers? Great. Now . . . Laurie. Laurie. Laurie! Will you *listen* to me, Laurie. I was on the phone to Polanski last night. "We've got old Dame Merryfeather," I said. "Dame *Merryfeather*," he said. "*That* mad old broad! You couldn't get her arrested!" Well, Laurie, I did! Roman's delighted, of course. Rang this morning just as soon as he got the news. Wants to go into rehearsal as soon as possible. Who? He has, eh? Wants us to open at the Piccadilly, does he? Well, you tell Sir Allboys we didn't just fall off the turnip-truck, Laurie. Tell him to bludge some other sucker into his theatre. Well, I must leave you now, Laurie. Got to hype this story about poor old Tobe. I'll be in touch, Laurie. Hooroo for now.'

Ken disconnected himself and immediately dialled another number. While he was waiting for the call to be answered, there was a ring at the front door. 'Take that, will you, Phyllis?' He turned to Toby. 'About to alert the gossip columns to your untimely demise, old pal. Hickey and Dempsey. Hullo? *Daily* fucking *Mail*? Put me through to Niggle Dempsey, will you, sweetheart?'

As Ken prepared to launch his hype, Eddie opened the front door to the Commissioner of the Metropolitan Police, Sir Angus McDuff. Twenty stone of Scottish rectitude and social maladroitness, uniformed for the occasion and wired to the Yard for sound, McDuff stood at the threshold hat in hand, shifting nervously from foot to foot, and more than usually purple in the face since, by an enormous intake of breath, he had temporarily persuaded his stomach to join his barrel chest above the belt.

'Hi, man,' said Steady Eddie. 'What's going down?'

'Good morning, madam,' said McDuff, the expulsion of air causing his stomach to drop like a landslide to its normal position below the belt. 'I've pressing business to enact with a Miss Dawn Codrington. Would that be you, madam?'

'Who are you, man?'

'Auch, I'm the Commissioner.'

'Wrong floor, man. Downstairs. At the front with a brolly. Helping the tenants.'

Eddie pushed McDuff into the passage and closed the door.

'Hullo? Hullo?' Ken shouted, on the line to the *Daily Mail*. 'Niggle? Pardoe here. Ken Pardoe Worldwide Musicals. Call me Ken. Listen. Tobe Danvers has caught the ferry, Niggle.

Yes sir, he's kicked the bucket . . . hang on a minute, Niggle, the door-bell's gone again. Get that, will you, Phyllis?'

Eddie opened the front door to McDuff.

'Auch, this is important, madam. I'm here on important matters.'

'Stay loose.' Eddie, without letting McDuff into the flat, sought the advice of Ken. 'It's the Commissionaire, man. What shall I do?'

'Hang on a minute, Niggle,' said Ken. 'I've got the doorman here. Tell him to wait, will you, Phyllis? I'm trying to hype a story here. Sorry Niggle. Now. . . .'

Eddie turned to McDuff. 'You heard what he said, man. Hyping a story at the moment.'

'Auch aye. Of course, of course.'

'And be sure to spell it right,' urged Ken. '*Satan's Daughter*. That's right. Old Dame Merryfeather arrested and now Tobe Danvers drops down dead. How do you like that? Fan-*tastic*, isn't it? Here, Niggle, I think I fucked your wife once. Skinny sheila with hardly any ti. . . . Hullo? Hullo? Niggle? Strange fellow. Oh well. Now for the *Express*.'

McDuff, with a series of nervous coughs and clearings of the throat, tried to attract Ken's attention between calls. 'Er – auch – I'm here to. . . .'

'Just a minute, captain,' said Ken. He dialled another number. 'Hullo? *Daily* fucking *Express*? Put me through to Mr Hickey, will you, sweetheart?' He turned to McDuff, cradling the receiver while hanging on for Mr Hickey. 'Grab a seat, captain. With you in a minute.'

'Auch. Thank you.' McDuff moved uneasily into the room and sat down next to Toby, who had managed to haul himself off the floor and was now stretched out on the sofa, apparently asleep.

'Not *there*!' yelled Ken. 'He's dead!'

McDuff, in so far as a man of twenty stone, corseted in a uniform a size and a half too small, could be said to leap, leapt to his feet. 'My word! The poor wee laddie! Have the authorities been informed?'

'*Informed*?' cried Ken. 'It was the fucking authorities that did it, captain! My deceased pal Tobe there is the victim of a police raid. Yes, sir!'

'Aye, aye,' said McDuff, shaking his massive head from side to side in slow self-mortification. 'That's why. . . .'

'Well, not *dead* exactly,' Ken admitted. 'Just in shock.' McDuff gasped with relief, the sound of two scrums going into action, and looked to the ceiling as though offering up a prayer of thanks. 'The raid,' continued Ken. 'Dame Letitia Merryfeather arrested and then. . . .'

'Aye, a terrible mistake,' said McDuff, strangling his cap in anguish. 'I'm here to. . . .'

'I'll say it was a terrible mistake!' shouted Ken, still holding on for Mr Hickey. 'Look at the state he's in. Never be the same again. That was one of the all-time great orntreepreneurs, captain! And look at him now. A cabbage!'

Toby opened an angry eye at this, and, lifting his head an inch or two off the cushions, managed to speak. 'One thing you can do,' he said to McDuff, 'is fetch me my deed-box. Over there, under the Osbert Lancaster.' He waved a frail arm in a vague unhelpful circle, causing McDuff to swerve off in the wrong direction, like a flat-footed Ipswich centre-back cruelly dummied by a Continental winger. 'No no! Not the Carl Toms,' cried Toby disgustedly. 'The Osbert *Lancaster*. Good God, man!'

'Sorry. Sorry,' gasped McDuff, his sense of social inadequacy in no way eased by this appalling *gaffe*. 'The Lancaster, not the Toms. Here we are, laddie. Will there be anything else?'

'Perhaps you'd be so good as to fetch me that rug over there. I find I'm a trifle cold round the knees.'

'Aye, it's parky for the time of year.' McDuff fetched the rug and draped it gently over Toby's knees. 'There we are. Is that better, laddie?' His duties over for the moment, he now lowered himself heavily into a nervous squat, but before his backside touched the sofa, a cry of rage from Toby shot him upright like a man finding himself at stool in a bed of nettles.

'Watch where you're parking yourself, my good man! That's

Constance Cummings's hat you nearly sat on.'

'Auch, I'm a clumsy great thing!' cried McDuff in anguish. 'I'm sorry, laddie. Here.' He handed the hat to Toby. 'I don't think it's damaged.'

'Well, do be careful.'

'Aye, aye.'

'And turn that damn radio off,' shouted Ken. 'I'm on the dog to the papers, aren't I? Don't want them to think I'm phoning from a mini-cab office.'

McDuff's radio had begun to make little bleeping noises, alerting him to heaven knows what catastrophes, but with one agitated tweak he silenced it. 'Sorry. Sorry. Professional matters. Not important.' He hovered miserably for a while and then, after some preliminary 'auchs' and 'ayes', tried once more to explain the reason for his visit. 'Er – I'm here as a matter of urgency to see Miss Dawn Codrington. . . .'

'Not in, captain,' said Ken. 'But I'll be with you in a minute. Dolores, darling. Look after the Commissionaire, will you?'

'Do what? Oh, got you. Yeah? Care for a drink, man?' It didn't seem quite right, the doorman having a drink on duty, but Dolores couldn't think what else Ken might mean.

'Aye. Aye. That would be very welcome. A wee sherry, perhaps.'

'The Algerian, I think,' suggested Toby from the sofa.

Ken, tired of hanging on for Mr Hickey, suddenly banged the receiver down. 'Sorry about this, captain. Putting on a show.'

'Aye, that's why I'm here. . . .'

'With you in a minute,' said Ken. 'First I'd better ring Chelsea police. See what sort of shape the Dame's in. What's the number, I wonder. Dolores, be a darling. . . .'

'741 6212,' said McDuff.

Ken was impressed. 'My word! Carry them in your head, do you captain? Handy for the tenants, I suppose. Poodle burglarized – straight through to the local nick.' Before McDuff could explain, there was another ring at the front door. 'Take that, will you, captain? Bit short-handed here.'

'Aye. Aye. Delighted.'

McDuff marched importantly to the front door and opened it to a beaming Rastafarian, hand-jiving in the passage.

'Hi, man!' cried Mad Harry. 'Where's the fire? Ho! Ho! Is the man in?'

'What man, laddie?' asked McDuff, eyeing Mad Harry with a certain degree of disapproval.

'Steady Eddie, man! You tell him that Mad Harry's here with the stuff.'

'Just a moment, please.' McDuff, having made it clear to Mad Harry that he should wait at the door, addressed the room: 'Er – excuse me, but I have a Mr Mad Harry with the stuff. Would there be a Mr Steady Eddie present?'

Steady Eddie had, moments earlier, tracked Miss Stephanie into the bedroom, so Dolores dealt with the order in his absence. 'That's cool,' she said. 'It's Eddie's gear. Here, give him this, will you, darling?'

McDuff, acting as go-between, had the deal sewn up in no time. 'Here we are, laddie,' he said, handing over Dolores's money and receiving a small, neatly wrapped packet in return. 'Ah yes, this will be the gear.'

'Thanks, man,' said Mad Harry. 'Say hullo to Eddie, will you? Keep jogging.'

'And good day to you too, sir,' said McDuff. He closed the door and handed the gear over to Dolores.

'Thanks, darling.'

Ken, meanwhile, was far from pleased with the management at Chelsea Police Station. 'Not *in*?' he shouted. 'Well put me through to someone else. This is a matter of theatrical *urgency*.' He was about to give the room his opinion of the police in general and of Chelsea police in particular when there was a ring on Dawn's private line, the one she kept for incoming business calls. 'Take that, will you, captain?'

'Of course, of course,' said McDuff, delighted at the confidence now being placed in him. 'Hullo? Miss Dawn? I'm afraid she's out at the moment. In half an hour, sir? If you'll just hang on, I'll endeavour to find out.' McDuff covered the receiver and spoke to Dolores. 'It's a gentleman wishing to know whether Miss Dawn will be available to see his dance – postponed from last night – in half an hour?'

'Ask him where he's calling from, darling,' said Dolores, now busy rolling herself a joint.

'Where are you calling from, sir? Really? I'm from that way myself. Hang on, please. He's in Dolphin Square.'

'Must be the Wanker. Yeah, that's cool.'

'Yes, that will be cool, sir. See you in half an hour. We'll be looking forward to it. Excuse me, but would you be the Wanker, sir? What! And you, laddie! I'm the Commissioner of the Metropolitan Police, that's who I am!'

Dolores shrieked with laughter. 'You tell him, man!' He was a card, the doorman, quite a gas, in fact.

'So you keep a civil tongue in your head! I see. Well good-bye to you, Mr Rooney!' McDuff hung up, shaking his great head ruefully at the grossness to be come across these days. 'Auch, he's in a pawky temper. He said that if I was the Police Commissioner, he was Mickey Rooney!'

'Can't blame him, darling,' said Dolores, still honking with delight at the doorman's riposte.

'Funny wee fellow, though. Liked him as Andy Hardy, I recall.'

'Wanker, darling,' said Dolores shortly.

'Is that so? Well. Theatricals, you ken.' McDuff's simple, knobbly features gathered into a compassionate facial shrug, suggesting that allowances should be made for those of an artistic bent.

'Yeah. Wow. Care for a smoke, darling?' Dolores had decided the doorman was cool.

'Thank you, no.' McDuff held up a hand, as though fearful that she was about to thrust one on him. 'I managed to beat the craving two years ago. My good lady, that's Lady McDuff, you ken – well, I'm sorry to say that she still indulges. Forty a day.'

'Forty a *day*!' Dolores was impressed. 'Wow! She must be up *there*, man! Here. Where does she score, if you don't mind my asking?'

'Score?'

'Get the goods, darling?'

'Oh aye. The goods. At our local off-licence. Corner of Chelsea Embankment and Lupus Road. She's got an account there. Wee extravagance since we came south.'

Dolores was bolt-eyed. 'The local *off-licence*? Wow! Can you just walk in and – you know – like, pick up?' This doorman was *organized*.

'Auch, you need references.'

'That's cool.' Dolores nodded understandingly. 'Could I give your name?'

'Oh aye. Mention my name by all means.'

Dolores was about to ask for further particulars when a bellow of rage from Ken diverted her attention.

'They've sprung the old tart!' he shouted, banging the phone down angrily. 'How do you like that? Let her out this morning. My God! Roman was right! You *can't* get her arrested!'

The news, however, seemed to please the doorman. 'Auch, that's good,' he said, beaming with relief, 'that's very good.'

'*Good?*' yelled Ken furiously. '*Good?* It's a fucking outrage! First they arrest the mad old sheila when they shouldn't have done, and then they haven't the savvoy-fair to hold the old auntie while I hype the story.' Ken tugged angrily at his bandit moustache. 'The police these days! Beats me how they find their way to work.'

McDuff took this as his cue to say his piece. 'Auch, could I say a wee word at this point?'

'Right, captain. Sorry to have kept you waiting. What's your problem? Emergency meeting of the Tenants' Association? Big Dawn not paid her service charge? Let's have it. We've got a show to put on here.'

McDuff cleared his throat and came stiffly to attention in the centre of the room. 'Er – my name is Sir Angus McDuff and I'm the Commissioner of the Metropolitan Police. I'm here officially in that cap. . . .'

'He's the Police Commissioner!' chuckled Ken. 'I *like* it!' He was a time-waster, the doorman, but a character for all that.

'Wild!' cried Dolores, echoing Ken's sentiments precisely

She pulled deeply on her joint and hooted with enjoyment. 'Yeah *yeah!*'

'Oh dear, oh dear,' said Ken. 'Nice one, captain, but we're trying to hype a show here. If you'd come to the point. . . .'

'Of course, of course. I'm here pursuant. . . .'

'He's here pursu. . . .' But suddenly the penny dropped. Ken put an arm round McDuff's massive shoulders and, speaking urgently out of the side of his mouth, began to walk him round in tight, confidential circles. 'Assumed you were here incognito, Commissioner. Didn't want to blow your cover, you read me? Don't worry. Stay cool. Dolores! It's the *Police* Commissioner!' Dolores went instantly into shock, the symptoms involving paralysis of the limbs and the loss of her eyeballs into her skull. She stared into space, jaw sagging, frozen in mid-chuckle, the joint hanging from her mouth. 'What can we do for you, Commissioner?' asked Ken, still revolving him in little circles.

'I'm here,' said McDuff, 'Pursuant to last night's regrettable events. . . .'

'Ur-huh, ur-huh,' said Ken, the wise nodding of his head in no way suggesting the furious activity underneath the bonnet, where his brain was revving up like a turbo-charged Ferrari on the grid. 'Pursuant to last night's regrettable events.' They'd drawn a heavy visit here and no mistake. The man himself. The circles in which he spun McDuff grew wider as he steered him first towards the door and then the open window.

'. . . at the express wish of Dame Letitia Merryweather,' continued McDuff, his twenty stone easily walking the pair of them away from the window and back to the safety of the centre of the room, 'who happens to be an old dear friend of mine.'

'Old and dear friend of yours. Got you, Commissioner.'

'She asked me, as a personal favour to her, to come round here this morning and apologize for the shocking miscarriage of justice that took place last night.'

'Ur-huh, ur-huh, shocking miscarriage of justice that took place last night.' Ken, who, by a mighty effort, had managed to steer McDuff once more towards the open window, now wheeled him back to safety.

'That an actress of Dame Letitia's stature, an *artiste* who down the years has given so much pleasure to so many people. . . .'

'So much pleasure to so many people. . . .'

'. . . should have been abused in this way is deeply shocking.' McDuff shook his great head in wonder that such things could happen.

'*Deeply* shocking,' echoed Ken with furious urgency. 'And what about my pal Tobe here?' He planted McDuff beside the sofa. 'Look at the state *he's* in! *There's* a victim of police abusement if ever I saw one!' The advantages to be drawn here were beginning to fall like ripe plums into Ken's racing brain.

'Aye. Aye,' agreed McDuff, his huge jowls wobbling with concern. 'It's a terrible thing that happened here. Alas, the arresting officer on this unhappy occasion went off duty last night unaware of the havoc he'd caused. But just as soon as he reports in today he'll be brought to book. On that you have my personal guarantee. Aye, he'll be brought to book, and all due compensation will be paid.'

'Compensation?' Ken released McDuff, aghast, and took a pace backwards. 'Compen*sation*? 'Scuse I, Commissioner,' he said, shaking his head in pained disgust, 'but your men have shattered a dream here. What compensation can there be for this great man of the theatre other than to see his dream fulfilled?'

McDuff was chastened to his roots, his great head bowed in shame that such a paltry notion as mere financial recompense could have nested cuckoo-like therein. 'Auch,' he moaned, 'is it too late? Can nothing now be done?'

'It could well be too late, Commissioner,' said Ken scoldingly, 'it could *well* be too late. By releasing Dame Merryfeather, you've let the air out of my hype and now I've got to get it off the ground again. I owe it to my pal Tobe here to get the big one rolling. We *all* do,' he added, with a pointed look. He had no finished plan as yet, but he saw no harm in the Commissioner of the Metropolitan Police feeling the heavy undertow of personal involvement.

'Oh aye, we all do,' McDuff agreed. 'We owe the laddie that at least.'

'At the *very* least,' cried Ken, driving home his advantage with heavy emphasis. 'Yes, sir! It's all hands to the pumps now. With the Dame sprung, we've got to move like lightning here. We'll have to raise the capital while we're still on the front pages. Yes, sir.'

'Aye. Aye. That's canny business.' McDuff nodded approvingly.

'Now. What have we still got?' To tighten the bonds of personal involvement, Ken gathered McDuff into a shoulder-hug again and walked him up and down. 'We've got Dame Merryfeather and we've got ... by God!' Ken adroitly switched the direction of their walk so that the Commissioner wouldn't see Miss Stephanie, who, at that moment, had run out of the bedroom, naked and chirruping winningly, pursued by Steady Eddie. With a little cry of alarm, she ran back into the bedroom, still pursued by Eddie. 'And we've got the ingénue! Tits like ... legs like ... Jes-*us*!' Ken released McDuff so that he could sketch suggestive pictures in the air. 'Yes, sir! Aimed in the right direction, we could raise a lot of capital on the ingénue.'

The bleak remembered winds of the Commissioner's Scottish up-bringing momentarily swept clouds of dismay across the wide landscape of his face. 'Auch, surely that won't be necessary.'

Ken winked. 'The English way of doing things, Commissioner,' he said.

'Aye?' The Commissioner still looked troubled.

'Only kidding, Commissioner,' said Ken, noticing the look. 'Only kidding. Now. Back to cases. What's our next move? Money. That's what we need now. *Money*.'

'Aye?'

'That's right. The capital to get the dodge off the ground.'

'Aye. The working capital.'

'The working capital! I like it!' Ken hurried over to the sofa and shook Toby roughly by the shoulder. 'Wake up, old pal!

We're back in business here. How much did you say we needed? I'm talking capital here.'

'Capital?' Toby stared groggily around him. '*Capital*? Capital for what?'

'You see what you've done to him?' cried Ken, seizing the Commissioner by the neck and forcing him to contemplate his handiwork. 'Once if you'd said capital to this great man of the theatre he'd have been out of the starting-stalls like a fucking *grey*hound!' He released McDuff and, bending down, slapped Toby lightly on either cheek. 'What *for*, old pal? For *Satan's Daughter*, that's what for. Get a grip on yourself, old pal.'

'*Satan's Daughter*?' With a courageous effort, Toby raised his head an inch or two off the cushions. 'How superb that would have been! A *proud* production!'

'Yes, yes, old pal. It *will* be a proud production. We're going to get it right this time, aren't we Commissioner?'

'Oh aye, we are, laddie, we *are*,' said McDuff, stricken to the depths of his honest heart by Toby's state. 'If it's humanly possible we're going to get it right.'

'So, old pal, how much do we need? Where's your budget for the dodge?'

'Budget? Dodge? What dodge? I perpetrate no dodges. I father – I *once* fathered – theatrical miracles. What dodge?'

'*Satan's Daughter*, old pal.'

'How lovely that would have been, how very lovely.' Toby lay back exhausted, clutching his deed-box to him like a comforter, and closed his eyes.

'Yes, old pal,' said Ken urgently, climbing on to the sofa and lifting his head again. 'But how much? I need the budget. I must have the figures. For God's sake – the budget, old pal!'

'Budget? Who knows? Who cares? Not my department. Mere figures on a piece of paper. Let the clerks attend to such matters. Columns of heartless symbols scratched in musty ledgers. Fifty thousand? Sixty thousand? A *hundred* thousand? What difference does it make? Pound notes have no reality for me. I deal – I *dealt* – in theatrical reality. I dealt in lovely fictions.' He began to rummage distractedly in his deed-box.

'Ah, what have we here? A bill from Berman's. The costumes for *Fallen Angels*. Must pay that some time. Getting a bit behind here.'

'Cracked,' said Ken. 'Gone. Delirious.'

'Aye. It's tragic.'

'Can't be helped,' said Ken briskly, withdrawing his support so suddenly that Toby's head hit the cushions with a dislocating thump. 'Right. Let's assume that we need sixty thousand pounds. That's heavy bread.'

'Aye, heavy bread,' agreed McDuff.

'Where do we go for that sort of money?'

Before McDuff could speculate, Miss Stephanie, still with Eddie in attendance, but fully clothed on this occasion, came out of the bedroom and, with a little ecstatic cry, ran into her father's arms.

'Daddy!'

'Auch aye!' cried McDuff, beaming with pleasure and amazement. 'It's the wee lassie! What are you doing here, bairn?'

'I'm in the show, daddy! Isn't that super? It's my big break!'

'Aye! That's tremendous news!'

Ken, open-mouthed during this charming scene, now pulled himself together and took Dolores briefly aside to mark her card. 'Seems to be the ingénue's father,' he muttered out of the corner of his mouth. 'Embarrassing for him, finding her in a place like this. Don't blow it. Be discreet.'

'Yeah. Wow.'

'Don't worry, Commissioner. We're cool.'

'I'm playing Syphilis, daddy,' cried Miss Stephanie.

'*Syphilis*, bairn? Auch, what sort of part is that?'

'Satan's daughter, daddy. It's a modern immorality play, you see.'

'Morality,' said Toby weakly from the sofa. 'A modern *morality* play. A metaphor for our predica. . . .' He collapsed, exhausted.

'Auch, of course,' McDuff's features, which had gathered up in an expression of concern, now heaved briefly and resettled, like a geophysical phenomenon, into one of vast relief. 'A modern morality play.'

Ken, unconcerned by such niceties, was striding angrily up and down. 'Sixty grand, sixty grand. That's a lot of wind to raise. We need investors.'

'Aye,' agreed McDuff. 'We do. We do.'

'Daddy!'

'Yes, bairn?'

'Why don't *you*?'

'What, bairn?'

'Start the ball rolling? Invest?'

McDuff recoiled with shock, his face puckering as though he'd bitten on a lemon. '*Invest*? *Me*? Auch, not really a gambling man. Had a wee flutter once. The 2.30 at Ayr, as I recall. November 14th 1954. Ten shillings each way. Paid back 13/4d!'

'There you are!' cried Miss Stephanie. 'You're lucky, you see! Come on, daddy! For *me*.'

'Auch well, why not?' said McDuff bravely, biting harder on the lemon. 'For the wee bairn. And for the poor laddie there. Er – the minimum, perhaps.'

'You're on, captain!' shouted Ken, slapping McDuff across his massive shoulders. 'I'll put you down for one unit. A thousand pounds.' The Commissioner winced. 'Now. Only fifty-nine thousand still to go. Let's think. Heavy punters, that's what we need, heavy punters.'

'Aye, heavy punters,' boomed McDuff, his enthusiasm at boiling-point now that he had an investment to protect.

He and Ken were both striding up and down now, beating their foreheads, seeking inspiration.

'Heavy punters, heavy punters,' shouted Ken.

'Heavy punters, heavy punters,' boomed McDuff.

'You're in the right place, man,' observed Dolores.

'We are?' Ken had stopped his pacing.

'We are?' echoed the Commissioner.

'What do you mean?' asked Ken.

'Well,' said Dolores. 'You *know*.'

Ken didn't know, so Dolores was compelled, for discretion's sake, to convey her meaning with a suggestive pantomime, consisting, for the most part, of indecent thrustings from the pelvis.

'She means Dawn's punters, for goodness sake,' said Miss Stephanie impatiently.

'Darling, you've *cracked* it!' shouted Ken. 'Yes sir! Big Dawn's clients! Why didn't I think of that?'

'Clients?' said McDuff.

'Catering, daddy,' said Miss Stephanie quickly. 'Directors' lunches. That sort of thing.'

'Oh aye. Catering.' McDuff nodded with approval. 'There's always money in that. People have to eat.'

'Absolutely right!' cried Ken. 'Now. She must keep a list of her – er – customers somewhere, Big Dawn.' He gazed around the room, looking for a likely hiding-place.

'In the safe,' said Miss Stephanie. 'Behind the Osbert Lancaster.'

Ken strode across the room and removed the picture from the wall. 'Of course! The fucking safe!'

'Theatricals, daddy,' Miss Stephanie explained. 'It's the way they express themselves.'

'Auch aye. Theatricals.'

Ken was examining the safe. 'Never seen one like this before. Here, take a look, will you, Commissioner? Expert opinion?'

'Auch aye,' said McDuff, offering a quick appraisal. 'This is a simple one.'

'It is? Could you open it?'

'Aye, I could beat this one. Learned a thing or two as a young D/C in the Gorbals, you ken. Auch – but do you think we should?' McDuff stepped back, looking troubled, his investment, for the moment, imperilled by his principles.

'All in a good cause, Commissioner,' urged Ken.

'Just protecting your investment, daddy,' said Miss Stephanie shrewdly.

'Aye,' said McDuff miserably. 'But without the lass being here, it doesn't seem right.'

'She'd *want* us to open it,' urged Ken. 'For Toby's sake. For the sake of his concept. Wouldn't she, Dolores?'

'Yeah,' said Dolores doubtfully. 'Wow.'

McDuff was swaying in their direction. 'Auch, perhaps you're right. You know the lassie, after all.'

'And for Dame Letitia, captain.'

'Oh aye. For Dame Letitia.' McDuff was convinced. He stepped forward again and examined the safe. 'No. Let's see.' He put an ear against the lock and, with one deft twiddle of the fingers, the safe was open.

'Oh daddy! You're so clever!'

'Auch, it was nothing, lass.' But McDuff was beaming at his accomplishment.

Ken, meanwhile, had snatched up Dawn's little black book and was reading it with mounting astonishment. 'Stone *me*!' he cried. 'They're all in here. Names. Addresses. Telephone numbers. Special requirements. Some have peculiar appetites, I must say.'

'Aye, that figures,' said McDuff. 'Some will be particular about what they get. Especially those that have travelled on the Continent.'

'You can say that again Commissioner! Will you look at *this*!' Ken was about to pass McDuff a photograph, but then had second thoughts. 'No – perhaps not. She's certainly thorough, is Big Dawn.'

'Only way to run a business, laddie!'

'Will you listen to this, though. The Rt Hon Peter Wigglesworth PC, James Rocksavage MP, Major Freddie Buchanan-Swine, Lord Cunliffe-Pike, Nigel Mount-Hugh MP, Mr Peter Swainston, Admiral Christopher Marjoriebanks, Mr Justice Vanderpump, the Colquhoun of Colquhoun, Sir Peter Dinwiddy, Mr Richard Ingrams, Det Chief Sup . . . no, we'll leave him out, Major-General Sir Miles Fright, Mr Justice Littlehampton, Commander Pip Pipe RN, Vladimir Botvinnick, Sir Peter Coxcourt, the Rt Hon Lord Portaldown, General Sir Brian Hogg, the Grafftey-Smiths, Mr Geoffrey Pillock. . . .'

'On parade!' shouted Pillock, jumping up from his place behind the sofa.

'Stone *me*,' said Ken disgustedly, pushing him out of sight again. 'And that's only the first page.'

'Aye, it's an impressive list,' said McDuff admiringly. 'The lassie is certainly well connected. There must be a deal of money in this catering business, a *deal* of money. You should consider taking it up, bairn, should the theatricals turn out not to be everything you could wish.'

'Oh I have, daddy,' said Miss Stephanie, with her most radiant smile. 'Believe me, I already have.'

'That's a sensible wee bairn.'

'Stone *me*,' said Ken. 'This lot will be falling over themselves to ante up!'

'Oh aye,' agreed McDuff. 'They'll all have cause to be grateful to the lassie.'

'That's true, Commissioner, that's very true. Now. Where do we start?'

'If I could make a wee suggestion?'

'Feel free, Commissioner, feel free.'

'Sir Peter Dinwiddy happens to be a close personal friend of mine, a close personal friend. He should be the next Attorney-General. Very keen on the theatricals. Always takes a leading part in the Benchers' annual panto.'

'So I see, so I see.' Ken handed McDuff a photograph. 'Cop this.'

'Auch, I don't remember this one. Must have been playing the Wicked Fairy that year.'

'More than likely. I'll give him a ring now.'

'Aye, catch him in chambers.'

Ken went to the phone and dialled the number in the little black book. 'Hullo? Put me through to Sir Dinwiddy, will you, sweetheart? In conference, eh? Well, pull him out of it, darling. Tell him it's a matter of urgency. Pardoe's the name. Tell him I'm at Big Dawn's flat with the Police Commissioner.' Ken winked at McDuff. 'That should smarten him up.'

'Aye. That will get him to the phone.'

'Hullo? Is that you, Pete? Pardoe here. Ken Pardoe Promotions Worldwide. No, you don't know me, Pete, but you're intimate with a very good friend of mine. She – er – caters for you, you read me, Pete? Miss Dawn. That's right. I'm in her flat now and I've got the Police Commissioner with me. Hullo, hullo. You still there, Pete? Ah, good. Got your name from the black book, Pete. That's right. And Pete – I *love* the photograph! Wicked fairy, eh? You rascal! Now, here's the SP, Pete. We're promoting the big one here and we knew you wouldn't want to be left out. Yes, sir! We're going for *maximum* media exposure on this one, Pete, so it's very much in your interests to climb aboard. The newspapers have got the story already and . . . what's that, Pete? Yes, they've bought it in a big way, I'm glad to say, Pete. It'll be all over Dempsey and Hickey in the morning and by the evening we'll have it on television too. How about that, Pete? What's that? How much do we want? I'll tell you.' Ken addressed the room in triumph. 'I think he's keen!'

'Aye. You're doing well, laddie, you're doing well.'

'Sixty thousand pounds, Pete, that's what we want. Pete! Pete! You still there? Ah, I thought I'd lost you for a moment. But you'll have to be quick, Pete. Already we've got Syphilis. . . .'

Pillock sprang up from behind the sofa and ran in horror to the bathroom. 'My God!' he cried. 'I must warn the Grafftey-Smiths!'

'Yes, sir,' cried Ken. 'That's what I said. We've got Syphilis here and Dame Merryfeather's involved. We've just had confirmation from her agent. Hullo, hullo. You there, Pete? Funny. He seems to have rung off. How do you think I did?'

'Sounded fine to me, laddie.'

At that moment there was a ring at the front door. Since Ken and the Commissioner were already searching through the little black book for their next angel, Steady Eddie went to answer it. He opened the door, allowing Mount-Hugh to dance across the threshold, dressed only in his overcoat and a pair of ballet pumps. He had his coat unbuttoned and was about to let it fall provocatively to the floor when he saw McDuff. With a single, strangled cry of horror, he started to make a run for it, but McDuff had spotted him.

'Nigel!' he cried. 'Come in, man!' He advanced on Mount-Hugh and, beaming with pleasure at seeing his old friend so unexpectedly, marched him into the room. 'I heard you were poorly. Missed you on *Nationwide* last night. The wee lass, Jane Baker, was *especially* disappointed. It's good to see you up and about so soon. Here, let me take your coat.'

'No! No!' Mount-Hugh sprung himself loose and, holding his coat tightly round him, backed away in terror. 'What . . . what. . . .'

'Well, here's a coincidence,' chortled McDuff. 'We just came across your name in the lassie's little black book.' Mount-Hugh went grey and croaked like a frog. 'So you're a customer of hers. . . .'

'No! No! Wrong flat. Must go!'

'You can't leave yet, man! We're raising money from the lassie's book. We're going for *maximum* media exposure!' McDuff beamed with satisfaction, delighted at how quickly he was picking up the patter. 'It will be in Dempsey and Hickey in the morning and by the evening we'll have it on television! and *no* one escapes!' He winked. 'I'm in this myself, you ken.'

'What? I. . . .' Mount-Hugh, sheet-white and going at the knees, was caught by Miss Stephanie.

'Let me handle this, daddy,' she said, and she wheeled Mount-Hugh across the room for a word in his ear in private. What was said would remain their secret, but when they returned Mount-Hugh had his cheque-book out.

'How . . . how. . . .' His voice, a death-bed croak, was scarcely audible. 'How much are you demanding?'

'Auch, we're looking for sixty thousand, but. . . .'

Mount-Hugh gasped and went at the knees again, but Miss Stephanie had him under the arms. 'We'll accept ten thousand,' she said briskly. 'And perhaps you could make the cheque out to Toby Danvers Productions.' She softened the blow with her most radiant smile.

Mount-Hugh wrote out the cheque with a trembling hand

and then, with backward, reproachful glances at McDuff, scuttled from the flat. 'Auch, *he* didn't cough up with a very good grace,' said McDuff, shaking his head in disappointment. 'And it's we Scots who are supposed to be the canny ones! Still, the laddie's been poorly. And ten thousand's a handsome start, yes, a *handsome* start.'

'Still fifty thousand to go, captain,' Ken reminded him. 'Er – forty-nine, to be precise. 'Scuse I for mentioning this, but perhaps this would be a good time to take your gooses off you.'

'Gooses?'

'Cheque, captain. Goose's neck. Cheque.'

'Of course, of course.' McDuff wrote his cheque out and put it on the coffee-table next to Mount-Hugh's. 'There. My personal gooses.'

'Thank you, captain.' Ken was once again studying the names in the little black book. 'Now. We'd better get back on the dog.'

'Aye, that we had, that we had. Might I suggest we try Lord Portaldown next? Another personal friend of mine. You can mention my name.'

'Right. Lord Portaldown. Here we go.'

As Ken dialled the number in the little black book, there was another ring at the front door, which McDuff hurried off to answer. Outside stood the Manager of the German Food Centre.

'I'm the Manager of the German Food Centre,' said the Manager of the German Food Centre.

'Well we won't be needing you, laddie,' said McDuff, bowling him backwards into the passage with a sharp prod to the chest. 'We're in catering ourselves, you ken,' and he closed the door in his face. 'Auch, the cheek of it,' he said, coming back into the room. 'They set up business over here and. . . .' But he hadn't gone six steps into the room before there was another, more aggrieved ring at the front door bell. 'Auch!' cried McDuff, who had no great liking for Germans, 'I'll give this wee laddie something to remember!' He opened the front door and, reaching into the corridor with a massive arm, he gripped the Manager of the German Food Centre by the throat and lifted him into the flat, where he intended to straighten him out in the matter of trading door-to-door. The person he now had by the throat, however, was not the Manager of the German Food Centre. The Manager of The German Food Centre, unaccustomed, when collecting debts, to being suddenly belted by the Commissioner of the Metropolitan Police, had sensibly decided to write Mr Danvers's debt off to experience and was now half-way down to the exit in the lift. It was Toby's friend Scott-Dobbs, here, on Pillock's recommendation, for the first time, whom McDuff had by the throat, and, since nothing in Scott-Dobbs's life had led him to suppose that one day, when composing himself for entry to a brothel – straightening his tie and patting down his hair – he might be seized by the throat by the Commissioner of the Metropolitan Police and lifted inside, he now assumed he must be dreaming; either that, or still suffering from concussion forty-eight hours after Danvers had driven his head into the table-top at the Ivy.

McDuff, on the other hand, quickly recognizing his mistake, was mortified. 'Auch, I'm terribly sorry, laddie,' he said, releasing his grip on Scott-Dobbs's throat so suddenly that he dropped to the floor like an abandoned puppet in a legless heap. 'I thought you were someone else, do you ken?' He picked him up and, with great bear-swats, dusted him down, one of them catching him in the kidneys and doubling him up.

'Someone *else*?' croaked Scott-Dobbs. Who would want this sort of treatment? Why on earth had Pillock recommended the place? Perhaps he was in the wrong flat.

'Is it Miss Dawn you'd be wanting?' asked McDuff.

It must be the right flat. That was the name Pillock had given. 'Er – no!' gasped Scott-Dobbs, feeling for his kidneys. 'Must be off!'

'Auch, stay a wee while, laddie,' said McDuff, eager to make up for the rough handling Scott-Dobbs had received on arrival. 'The lass is out at the moment, but she'd want us to mind her clients in her absence. I take it you are a client?'

'Er . . . er . . . Pillock. . . .'

'And *you*, laddie!'

'No. No. Excuse me.' In his panic, Scott-Dobbs scarcely knew what he was saying. He wasn't dreaming, alas, he knew that now, but he must be having some kind of breakdown. For a dizzy-making moment there, he'd even imagined that he'd seen Danvers lying on the sofa draped in an *Over The Edge* poster! Dangerous things, knocks to the head. He'd better get home and ring his doctor. He tried to break away, but McDuff had him in a solicitous bear-hug.

'Look, laddie, why don't you tell one of the other lassies what your requirements are? There's no need to scamper off just because madam's not here. We've got to keep the business ticking over!'

Scott-Dobbs was goggled-eyed. 'Are you. . . .'

'Just helping with the organization, laddie. Now, this is Miss Dolores and. . . .'

'I think I'll. . . .'

'. . . this is my daughter, Stephanie!'

'My God!' Scott-Dobbs reeled at this bomb-shell, but McDuff caught him before he hit the floor.

'Aye!' he said proudly, 'she's a picture, the bairn!'

'Is she. . . ?'

'Just started! This is her big chance. So keep your fingers crossed! Now. When's it for?'

'*Tomorrow*,' said Scott-Dobbs hastily. Perhaps they'd let him go now.

'Tomorrow! That doesn't give us much time to organize anything elaborate. Will it be a big do? A band? Speeches? Are you expecting the Lord Mayor?' McDuff nudged Scott-Dobbs playfully in the ribs, cannoning him off the coffee-table into Ken, who, being engaged urgently on the phone, swatted him angrily aside.

'Er – it's just me,' squawked Scott-Dobbs. He must relax, stay calm, that was the thing. He'd read somewhere that one shouldn't fight a breakdown, least of all one as serious as this, its symptoms involving the belief that he was in a nightmare bawdy-house for masochists, peopled by grinning harpies, some black, some white, some dressed up as men, some as men dressed up as women (he'd just spotted Eddie, preening before the mirror), the whole presided over by the Commissioner of the Metropolitan Police. He'd agree to anything, do whatever he was told.

'Just you, eh? Auch you wee gourmet! You must be of a mind to stuff yourself! Dolores, would you be so good as to take down this wee fellow's requirements?'

'If you say so, man!'

As Dolores led a limp, unprotesting Scott-Dobbs towards the bedroom, Pillock came out of the bathroom.

'Scott-Dobbs!' he cried. 'For God's sake, old friend! We've all got syphilis! Too late,' he moaned, collapsing in despair behind the sofa as Dolores closed the bedroom door behind her.

Ken, meanwhile, had given the good news to the next six names in the little black book and, being temporarily off the phone, was able to assist McDuff in a personal matter.

'The wee laddies' room, captain? Oh, got you. The brasco.' He pointed to the bathroom. 'Straight ahead.'

While McDuff was in the bathroom, Sir Peter Dinwiddy, the next Attorney-General, arrived at the front door, scarlet with rage and carrying a bulky envelope.

'All right, you unscrupulous swine!' he bellowed at Ken, whose bandit moustache and ferocious eyes singled him out, in Dinwiddy's professional opinion, as the ring-leader in this conspiracy. 'I've brought the money, but it's all you'll get from me!'

'Who the hell are you?' said Ken.

'I'm Sir Peter Dinwiddy, sir, that's who I am and if you think you can bleed me dry you're very much mistaken! There's twenty thousand pounds in this envelope. . . .'

'Well, that's a start, Pete,' said Ken, who had taken the envelope and was beginning to count its contents.

'A *start*!' It seemed likely that Sir Peter was about to have a seizure. His hawk-like features, which had discomfited many a hostile witness in their time, had turned from scarlet to mauve, and flecks of foam were showing at the corners of his mouth.

'You abominable pig!' he roared. 'I told you. That's all you'll get from me. And if it wasn't for my dear wife's sake you wouldn't be getting that!'

'Very generous of you Pete,' said Ken. 'And I'm sure you won't regret it.'

'I regret it already, sir!' screamed Sir Peter. 'I never expected this of Dawn. Never! I've been coming here for the last eight years and. . . .' But he'd been stopped dead in his tracks by the sight of the Commissioner of Police coming out of the bathroom.

'Peter!' cried McDuff happily. 'What a pleasant surprise!'

'Angus! Good God! Don't tell me you're in this too?'

'Oh aye. I'm involved.'

'My God! How much?'

'Auch, they only got a thousand off me, but then I'm canny!' McDuff tapped the side of his nose and winked.

'You were lucky. This unspeakable cad just took me for twenty thousand.'

'Aye, but you're keener on the theatricals than me.' McDuff winked again, causing the blood to drain from Dinwiddy's face. 'Wicked fairy!'

Dinwiddy struggled to find his voice. 'Tell me,' he gasped. 'Is it true about syphilis?'

'Oh aye,' said McDuff cheerfully. 'We've got Syphilis, all right. I'm specially delighted about that. My daughter, as it happens. What do you say to that!'

'Your *daughter*? Not – not little Stephanie?'

'Aye! Isn't that grand? And she's only been in the business for a week or two. Stephanie, this is an old friend of mine. You've not met since you were a wee bairn. Sir Peter Dinwiddy.'

Miss Stephanie stepped forward, smiling radiantly, her hand extended, but Sir Peter screamed once and ran for the door, opening it at the precise moment that Ronnie Snipe, meaning to drive it in with a shoulder charge, began his run from the other side. Snipe's momentum carried him, bellowing revenge against Toby, clear across the room and head-first into

McDuff's well-sprung midriff, whence he ricocheted over the sofa, cracking his head against the coffee-table as he fell backwards to the floor. When he came round it was to discover the Commissioner of the Metropolitan Police kneeling on his chest, examining the contents of his shoe-box.

'What have we here, laddie?' McDuff was saying, 'what *have* we here?' What he had there was the money that Snipe had just collected from D/C Smiley: twenty thousand pounds in crisp new notes, neatly done up in little bundles with the bank's stamp on the wrappings and therefore, Snipe realized with disgust, easily traceable to Smiley's account. 'Were you thinking of making a wee investment in a musical, then, Jimmie?'

Snipe hadn't been thinking of that exactly, rather the opposite in fact, but even a hard man can make a commercially unsound decision when he's carrying twenty thousand pounds worth of hot money and he wakes to find the Commissioner of the Metropolitan Police kneeling on his chest, addressing him as 'Jimmie'.

'Something like that,' Snipe muttered. He'd certainly underestimated that fat berk Danvers, who, he now saw, was reclining on the sofa in his dressing-gown. With the Police Commissioner on the firm, no wonder he could take it easy. And who were all these other people in the room? Rubber-heels squad most likely. He judged that it was time to leave. 'Well,' he said, 'I won't be keeping you.'

'Auch, but first you must give us your name and address,' said McDuff, clambering to his feet and thus allowing Snipe to get at last to his. 'So that we can forward you an investor's agreement. There's profit-participation here, Jimmie.'

'That won't be necessary,' said Snipe, walking hastily towards the front door. He'd had profit-participation in a Danvers musical before.

'Auch laddie, but that's not canny business. . . .' But Snipe had gone – straight to London Airport and thence, he planned, to foreign parts. With the Police Commissioner running the rackets, London, he judged, was no place for the likes of him.

'Well, that *is* odd,' said McDuff. 'One doesn't like to take a laddie's money without knowing who he is.'

'Never look a gift-horse in the mouth, daddy,' advised Miss Stephanie shrewdly.

'Aye, that's true, bairn. But even so. . . .'

'And we're still nine thousand short, captain,' said Ken, who had been counting the capital accumulating nicely on what was left of the coffee-table.

'No we're not!' cried Dolores, running out of the bedroom, triumphantly waving a cheque above her head. 'Here. Ten thou. I said the price had gone up. He seemed to understand.'

Scott-Dobbs understood nothing. Sheet-white and feeling for his head, he followed Dolores out of the bedroom and, ignoring an invitation from McDuff to partake of a wee celebratory sherry, walked straight out of the flat, forgetting in his traumatized state to close the door behind him and thus allowing Dame Letitia to enter theatrically moments later, dressed in black from head to foot and carrying a wreath. 'My dears!' she cried, pausing dramatically at the threshold, 'I got here the moment I could. What a tragedy! That *charming* young man. Laurie just told me. A heart attack, was it? Cut off in his prime! And last night he seemed so well.' She walked heart-brokenly towards the sofa and laid her wreath on Toby's chest. 'A great man of the theatre,' she said. She stepped back a pace and, head bowed, observed a minute's silence. Then, in an urgent aside to Ken, she said, 'I trust this doesn't mean the show's off?'

Before Ken could reassure her on this point, Dawn suddenly arrived home after a far from satisfactory meeting with her lawyers. 'Here,' she cried, 'who's left the fucking front door. . . .' She'd noticed the bowed heads, the air of reverence, and then she saw Toby, stretched out on the sofa under Dame Letitia's wreath. She screamed and ran to his side. Toby sat up and rubbed his eyes, his sudden resurrection causing Dame Letitia to sink, fainting, to the floor.

'Auch,' cried McDuff. 'It will be the hot weather. Water!' He ran heavily to the bathroom.

'What's going *on* here?' Dawn demanded. The details of the scene were so bizarre, so richly unexpected in their impact, that at first she could make no sense of them. Then, focusing by instinct on essentials, she noticed that the door of her safe was open and, still more alarmingly, that Ken was holding her little black book. With a yell of rage, she ran at Ken and snatched the book from his hands just as Pyle, accompanied as before by Smiley, Perks, Harris and Blagden, took the front door off its hinges for the second time in twenty-four hours.

'Fuck me!' said Ken. 'We've drawn another visit!'

'Right!' shouted Pyle. 'No one move! You're all under arrest!'

Dame Letitia opened an eye and gave a little cry of astonishment at seeing Pyle again.

'Hullo, granny,' he said rudely. 'Sorry to see you're at it again so soon. Didn't learn your lesson last night, eh? Smiley, take her outside. Smiley! Cut that out!' Smiley, undone once again by the charms of Miss Stephanie, had wrestled her angrily to the floor. 'At ease, Pillocks!' Then, strutting jubilantly among his prisoners, Pyle seized the latest delivery of pot from Dolores, the working capital from Ken (who was trying to conceal it down his trousers) and, finally, the little black book from Dawn. 'Aha!' he cried triumphantly. 'What have we here? Been keeping records, have we, darling? Silly girl, silly girl. There should be enough in here to send you down for a tidy little stretch.'

But his triumph was short-lived. McDuff, running out of the bathroom with a bucket of water, tripped over Smiley and emptied the contents of the bucket over Pyle.

'PYLE!' he bellowed.

Pyle came drippingly to attention.

'What is the *meaning* of this?' thundered McDuff. 'Have you gone clean off your head, laddie? Have you any idea who these people are?'

'Yes sir, I. . . .'

'Silence, laddie! Wasn't your performance last night enough? Is this deliberate, *malicious* harassment on your part? Auch, words fail me, laddie. From the moment you left Hendon I had my eye on you. Marked you down as a laddie who'd reach the very top. And this is how you repay me! Harassing my friends!'

'Sir, I'd no idea. . . .'

'Hold your tongue!' roared McDuff. 'It's back on the beat in a tall hat for you, laddie! And hand me those.'

'But sir. . . .'

'At once, laddie! Do you hear me?'

A stricken Pyle passed the evidence and the working capital over to McDuff, who proceeded to distribute them among their rightful owners – the dope to Dolores and the little black book and the capital to Dawn.

'Sixty thousand pounds, madam,' said McDuff proudly, 'for the wee laddie's musical. Including my personal gooses.'

'Golly,' said Dawn. She walked over to Toby and put the bundle of cheques and notes into his hand.

'One way of doing it, I suppose,' he said. He closed his eyes and went to sleep, clutching the working capital.

'Right! Dismiss, Pyle!' bellowed McDuff. 'We've got a show to put on here!' He went over to the telephone and dialled a number. 'Hullo? Hullo? Get me Sir Allboys, will you, sweetheart? Hullo, Sir Allboys? It's the Commissioner of the Metropolitan Police speaking and we're promoting the big one here. You play your cards right, you rascal, and we might tip . . . what's that? Smarten up, laddie! It's the English way of doing things, you ken.'

HENRY ROOT'S WORLD OF KNOWLEDGE

From the man who brought you the immortal
LETTERS

Everything you thought you knew about everything
– the first and most comprehensive one-volume
encyclopaedia of British common sense ever to be
published, covering the *complete* A to Z from
Ablutions to God to Over-eating and Zoroaster:

★ Authoritative
★ Up-to-date
★ Readable
★ Clear and concise
★ Animals
★ Things
★ 9 Antelopes
★ 11,000 facts
★ 430 definitions
A world of knowledge in a nutshell

'A triumph for common sense'
Times Literary Supplement

Futura Publications
Non-Fiction
0 7088 2329 7

THE HENRY ROOT LETTERS

Henry Root

UNIVERSAL ACCLAIM FOR THE LITERARY
MASTERPIECE OF THE DECADE!

'One of the funniest books I have ever read'
Auberon Waugh *Private Eye*

'About as funny as pushing somebody fully clothed
into a swimming pool'
Lynda Lee-Potter *Daily Mail*

'A brave publishing venture'
Books and Bookmen

'The letters in themselves are of absolutely no
interest'
The Spectator

'Very funny' *Punch*

'A deplorable work . . . a disgrace to publishing'
London Review of Books

'If I found some of them difficult to read, it was only
because of tears of laughter'
Colin Welch *Daily Telegraph*

'Uninspiring' *Southend and District Standard*

'We probably won't see a funnier book published
this year'
Tony Davies *The Observer*

'Embarrassing' *Irish Times*

'It deserves to be bought by all who know a laugh
when they see one' Basil Boothroyd *The Times*

'A valid contribution, in my opinion, to the great
debate' Henry Root *Henry Root Wet Fish Ltd.*

Futura Publications
Humour
0 7088 1888 9

HOW TO BE A WALLY

Paul Manning

Learn about the wonders of Wallydom. Buy this book. Then buy a copy for a friend.

And you can both find out
HOW TO BE A WALLY
in the comfort of your own home!

Yes! With the help of easy, step-by-step diagrams, you can learn how to:

- ★ Stand outside DER showrooms in the rain watching "Game for a Laugh"
- ★ Feed prawn cocktail flavour crisps to the lions in safari parks
- ★ Get the best out of your Colonel Bogey car horn
- ★ Destroy a Spanish football stadium

plus much more besides!

HOW TO BE A WALLY
The complete, no-holds-barred guide to the wally lifestyle – at a price you can afford!

Futura Publications
Non-Fiction/Humour
0 7088 2440 4

YOU FAT SLOB

Anthony Palmer

If your F-Plan didn't go according to plan, and the Beverly Hills Diet made no impression on your mountains of flab –
GIVE UP THE FADS AND GET RID OF THE FAT
RELY ON YOURSELF

Anthony Palmer – 15½ years, 18½ stone – did, and now he's got a lot less of himself to rely on.

This is his diary; a hilarious and personal record of his determined efforts to become less like the Michelin Man and more like Clint Eastwood, by eating imaginary Jaffa Cakes, guzzling milk shakes (yes, really!) and braving the horrors of unisex aerobics. There is also a section of mouth-watering, but flab-fighting, menus and special diets.

Futura Publications
Non-Fiction
0 7088 2653 9

All Futura Books are available at your bookshop or
newsagent, or can be ordered from the following address:
Futura Books, Cash Sales Department,
P.O. Box 11, Falmouth, Cornwall.

Please send cheque or postal order (no currency), and
allow 55p for postage and packing for the first book
plus 22p for the second book and 14p for each additional
book ordered up to a maximum charge of £1.75 in U.K.

Customers in Eire and B.F.P.O. please allow 55p for
the first book, 22p for the second book plus 14p per
copy for the next 7 books, thereafter 8p per book.

Overseas customers please allow £1 for postage and
packing for the first book and 25p per copy for each
additional book.